LAST DRAGON

J.M. McDERMOTT

LAST DRAGON

Last Dragon

©2008 by J.M. McDermott

Cover art and design ©2008 Wizards of the Coast, Inc.

Published by Wizards of the Coast, Inc.

WIZARDS OF THE COAST DISCOVERIES and its logo are trademarks of
Wizards of the Coast, Inc., in the U.S.A. and other countries.

Printed in the U.S.A.

Cover Sculptures by Henry Higginbotham
Book design and Photography by Matt Adelsperger

First Printing: February 2008

9 8 7 6 5 4 3 2 1

ISBN: 978-0-7869-4857-4
620-21725740-001-EN

Library of Congress Cataloging-in-Publication Data:

McDermott, J. M., 1979-
Last dragon / J.M. McDermott.
p. cm.
ISBN 978-0-7869-4857-4 (trade pbk.)
I. Title.
PS3613.C38688L37 2008
813'.6--dc22
2007018085

U.S., CANADA,
ASIA, PACIFIC, & LATIN AMERICA
Wizards of the Coast, Inc.
P.O. Box 707
Renton, WA 98057-0707
+1-800-324-6496

EUROPEAN HEADQUARTERS
Hasbro UK Ltd
Caswell Way
Newport, Gwent NP9 0YH
GREAT BRITAIN
Save this address for your records.

Visit our web site at www.wizards.com

For my Grandmothers

My fingers are like spiders drifting over memories in my webbed brain. The husks of the dead gaze up at me, and my teeth sink in and I speak their ghosts. But it's all mixed up in my head. I can't separate lines from lines, or people from people. Everything is in this web, Esumi. Even you. Even me. Slowly the meat falls from the bones until only sunken cheeks and empty space between the filaments remind me that a person was there, in my head. The ghosts all fade the same way. They fade together. Your face fades into the face of my husband and the dying screams of my daughter. Esumi, your face is Seth's face, and the face of the golem.

Esumi, do you remember the night before you left? We threw a grand ball in your honor. A skald sang of the glorious deeds. My deeds, my husband's, and even yours were sung. And Adel's glorious song eclipsed us all. Three hundred cantos extolling her deeds were barely enough for the ones who didn't know her when she was alive. I knew her. You didn't. I don't know if she was really our savior, or simply the monster who fooled us all. Both, perhaps. I don't know. I never did. I think she was my friend, but even that's fuzzy. For all I know I was a weapon for her, no better than any mercenary. Or perhaps I was her friend, like a trusted weapon at her side, a trusted warrior. And, she is a hero worthy of song.

In these letters I wish to tell you of us and his empire, Alameda.

Our empire was forged in bloodshed. First was my family's murder, and my grandfather's execution. Then, there was Adel's husband, Tycho, by her own shattered hand. And then I killed one more wicked beast, and secured my throne in the deed. I didn't even know I had earned a throne at that moment.

I was just a girl. I was such a violent fool. You remember me after all of this was already over, Esumi. After you came home and we fought a war and took over the whole world for my foolish husband.

He tore us apart when our daughter was born, with your red hair.

Esumi, my love, come to me. I will take care of you, even from this bed. I will hold you close. I touch this vellum parchment and remember your rough skin. My stylus scratches into the page, and I remember my fingernails across your back.

My lips whisper softly what the ink tongues on the page.

I remember our daughter fading to a dream, and my dreams fading with her.

I remember Adel, and I remember a city. I remember my uncle who deserved to die, and his father who got what he deserved.

I remember so many things, Esumi. And I will give them all to you, for one glimpse of your true face again. Faces fade in this web, and my husband is tall and strong while you were fat and weak and then you are both together on the deck of a ship dazzling sailors with only a cloak and smoke. I yearn to see your face again, without all of the others tangled up in my web of death.

Come to me.

Proliux, of course.

I see it in my mind at sunset. Tall buildings have long shadows just before sunset. Shadows rise and fall on top of other buildings like the fallen and broken future of the structures when downtown would fade to ramshackle huts. When ramshackle huts would fall under their own weight and the weight of the poor inside.

There were so many poor.

I walked through these buildings before sunset. I found new places each night, but all the faces seemed too much the same for me. All of them brown, with high cheeks and slender eyes. None pale like mine, no matter how hard I looked. No round eyes. No words like songbirds. Only the purring and the clicking of Proliux. That language sounds like cats dying slowly. I thought in words like crickets and birds, and only the pigeons spoke to me their two long notes. *Coo Hoo Don't go. . . .*

And I walked in this city.

Walk three blocks; turn right. Walk two blocks; turn left. Walk three blocks; turn left. I mapped it out in my head. I had path-work grained into me by my sensei, in the Tsuin tundras and the pine forests. I rarely got lost. I always found new city blocks.

This night, this stretch of city, the cinnamon and yeast smells masked the normal stink of street. I was near a good bakery. My eyes lingered on the cinnamon sweetbread and the small teacakes. I hadn't eaten since the afternoon when the sausage-dealer sold me his most putrid creation yet.

I was not the only girl whose eyes lingered on the bread. A homeless girl, very young and all alone, stood on her tiptoes and reached up to the edge of the window. She peered over, barely tall enough to see the lowest sweet roll. She tried to stand taller. This only made her sway. She stumbled backwards into a pile of human refuse. The homeless girl uttered a foul curse. She sat on a filthy curb and slopped the refuse off of her bare foot with her hand. I slowed long enough to watch her do this, but when she cursed again, I looked away. I was the only person who cared to look.

Everyone else looked at me. My face is as white as death to these city folk. Their skin is dark as the cinnamon they eat all over their food. I can still taste bitter cinnamon on my tongue now, and remember their faces.

I kissed one of these dark men in a public house, and cinnamon poured from his whole body, bitter and slightly dusty. I can still see that strange man's amorous eyes, slanted over high cheekbones. His greasy black hair in my fingers.

I was drunk, and it was midwinter, and I was celebrating the weather. No snow. No snow there, at any time of the year. I couldn't believe it until the rains came and went and then the equinox and that was that. All the people dressed in red and danced in the public houses and I came, too.

The pigeons cooed knowingly all the next morning, and it didn't snow. The seagulls laughed at me from above, and pooped down on the other porters and me, pretending to be snow clouds. I laughed with them, because I was full of joy. I had found a land where Alastair-of-the-Wolf refused to lay down her white cloak of death.

I walked the streets only at sunset because I spent my days at the docks. The men and women of the seaside stared at me less, and I was as strong as most men. I was often mistaken for a man by these folk. I was a porter, among their strong men. The other porters avoided me, or chased me off with large numbers and empty threats. None would work with me. I did what I could alone. After work, I wandered the city until I grew tired. Then, I returned to the docks and slept until the first boats of morning rang their sea bells.

I shared an alley with two beggars and a large pack of tomcats. I slept with my back against the white plaster wall of a warehouse. A jagged metal rod was always ready in my lap.

The two old beggars picked through piles of garbage they had collected, giving what little edible things they had found to the cats. Then, the old men found a public house and drank as much as they could afford.

I woke up when they returned because they sang slurring songs. They slept and drifted in and out of sickness until morning. Some nights they touched each other, gently. I slept through it all as best I could.

Their noise and stench kept me from sleeping too deep. They left me alone.

My eyes closed; my face pointed at the fire. I sat up, and tried to
ignore the salt smell in the air, and the lurch beneath our floor. For
days after this boat, I would feel the ocean in my bones, pushing
and pulling. I hated the oceans. When I had any food I gave it to
the children of the boat, mewing at my legs like tomcats.

Uncle Seth touched my forehead. *Are you asleep?* he whispered.

Not yet, I said.

Are you feeling better?

No.

I hate the ocean, too, he said. *Last time I saw it, I nearly lost my leg.*

I know, I said.

I was bitten by Alastair-of-the-Wolf, he said.

I sighed.

He didn't listen to me. *My leg swelled up like a sausage. Baba cut me
at my knees and drained the yellow puss away. Another shaman, all the
way from Pascanus had come to the village, too. He had come to fight the
diseases there. Baba and I had only come to trade for herbs, and discovered
the village this way. She never got it. I nearly died. The shaman from Pascanus fed me all kinds of things. All of them tasted terrible. They thought I
was going to die. I thought I was, too. My leg hurt so much. A whole village
was infected with the same disease. People walked around with arms and
heads all swollen up. A woman had one breast the size of her whole body.
She wouldn't let Baba cut it open. She screamed and screamed all day long
until it exploded and she bled to death. I thought I was going to die. I smell
the air here, and I can remember it. Goddess, I hate the ocean.*

I opened my eyes, and I punched Uncle Seth's arm, hard. *Do you
always tell the same hideous stories over and over again,* I said, *or will you
eventually remember something new?*

He winced. He rubbed his arm. *I'm sorry,* he said. *I guess I do tell
the story a lot. Not much happened to me like that.* He poked the fire
with a black iron rod. A bruise began where I had struck him. His
bruise was the color of my sickness after I tried to eat anything.

We were on the deck of a ship. Other people sprawled out on the
deck, sleeping. We slept on the lowest deck around a wood fire burning in an iron bowl. We passengers stayed near the sides of the ship,

out of the sailors' way. When it stormed, we moved below deck until the bad weather passed. Below deck we huddled together, crammed in like seeds in a pod, and it stank horribly down there and it was so hot I couldn't see.

This night was clear enough. I had spent the day very ill. Uncle Seth told me to lie down, and he would take watch at least until I felt better. He told me that story three times in one week. I had heard it before, too many times. We had little to do on our long journey besides talking. We only had each other to talk to before we really learned the new language.

If you want my sympathy you won't have it, I said. *The first time you said it, I felt sympathetic. Now I'm just sick of hearing about it.*

I'm sorry, he said. *I just felt like talking, that's all. I just wanted to say something.*

A person at our fire rolled over and grumbled at us. We knew that he had told us to be quiet, though we didn't know precisely what he had said. We waited until the man's eyes drifted shut.

I spent my day throwing up, I whispered. *I don't want to hear about sickness. Tell me something else.*

Seth leaned in close. He whispered into my ear, *Right, I'll tell you a story about a shipwreck.*

A shipwreck? I snorted. *How comforting.*

A ship just like this one, he said. *I heard about it in that village. The other shaman told me. I don't remember his name. Close your eyes, Zhan. Lay back, and close your eyes.*

I found a remotely comfortable place on the foul-smelling wooden planks. The deck smelled like bird shit and old fish. I placed my hand beneath my head.

Uncle Seth's voice whispered over a vast abyss of darkness. I felt him breathing into my ear. I felt the heat of him, close to me. He whispered a story.

Fest Fasen stared at a spider web with glassy eyes. He stared at the web's ghostly shadow flickering in the torchlight. He tapped his fingers in time to Partridge's voice. He growled. He flashed his steel fangs. The spider was the monster, though. Fest was only a man.

The coin-sized monster held still while its shadow swam through stones. Its mandibles were only a slight twitching in the darkness across the trapped fly's wriggling back.

Seth told me about icebergs once, said Fest, too loudly, *and a shipwreck.*

Seth told me that story, I said. *He didn't tell it to me very much.*

He didn't like it, said Fest. He looked down from the spider. *That's why he didn't tell it much. How did it go, again?*

A ship came in to shore far from port to escape a strong storm out at sea. The ship struck an iceberg, and started to sink. Everyone on board jumped into the water to try to swim to the shore, even though it was far too far away to survive in the frigid water. One woman didn't scream, and didn't run away. She was a shaman.

She cried out and cried out to the men who swam away, *Why do you flee?*

The men screamed back, *The ship is sinking!*

The ship sinks into the same water you jump into, she shouted, *Why do you hurry so to your deaths? If we stay here, we can wait and eat a meal before we meet the Goddess!*

And the crew who were left nodded at her wisdom. They stayed, they started a fire, and as the ship slowly sank, they feasted on all the food they could find. The ship sank so slowly, that the men and the woman climbed up and up the deck, with all their food. The ship finally got so low that only the part caught on the iceberg remained. The sailors picked up their shaman, and carried her over to the very iceberg that sank the ship, with all of their food.

They sat on the iceberg, feasting into the night, singing and praying to Alastair. When morning came, the iceberg had run aground only half-a-day away from Le, where they had been journeying anyway.

And all the other sailors, who fled the boat?

Never heard from again. When this story is told to children, the ending is softened into a dream. The men who jumped into the water collected together into one mass to keep warm. They swam and swam, and eventually grew fins, and long noses that point always to shore. They jump out of the water, but they know that they have swum too long, and can never fully return to land. They are dolphins, saved by the mercy of the Goddess, but damned by their own fear of death never to return home.

A children's story. How lovely.

If it is true, the men drowned. Men don't turn into dolphins, merciful Goddess or no.

How do you know?

I know. That is all. Men don't turn into dolphins.
Do the children believe you?
Maybe.
Then maybe others know something different.
Perhaps.

Some nights, in my alley all alone, a shadow passed over me, and I jumped up with the metal rod in my hands, ready to fight.

These nights were longer than the rest. I couldn't sleep at all. I don't know if the feet running away in the night were real or a dream. I just couldn't face them with my eyes closed. I stared into the street, with the weapon in my hands.

Not even the tomcats bothered to watch over me after Seth was gone. The two drunk beggars snored. The cats moved in and out of the filth on the cobblestone.

I looked every evening for my Uncle Seth and also my grandfather in that last gigantic city where our grandfather had disappeared. My uncle and I had fallen apart in the human herd of ship docking.

I walked the streets because I was looking for both of them. I did not know what to look for, except our white skin, our round eyes, and maybe even red hair.

The brown faces stared at me.

All morning I moved boxes and luggage for coins when the other porters weren't looking at me. I ate terrible sausages and drank bitter wine in the mid-afternoon and it cost me everything I had earned. Mid-afternoon was too hot to do anything but wait for Alastair to pull her eye away from the earth.

When she turned away and cracked open her cool, winking eye, I was already far away, walking over bridges or through crowded marketplaces or somber yards of wicked temples. Strange idols packed in between the alleys and the buildings. The buildings were as close as hedges. Little light reached the street.

People in high windows shouted out, *KAIYEEYA!* and trash sloshed out from their windows. Refuse. Human shit. Dead rats. Crumpled scraps of cloth. It piled on the street, and drifted into gutters. A low fog of flies was constantly at the ankles. Pigeons and rats and small dogs lived down there. Small children lived there, too. Cats sat above these things, on the windowsills and broken crates of the alleys. Children sat there, too. So did adults. So did I.

Closer to the docks it wasn't so bad. More storehouses, fewer permanent residents, and a light drizzle every day to wash the worst of it away.

The farther inland I went, the worse it was. Too many people. My Goddess, that city stank.

I fought all the time on the streets. I punched men in the nose. I threw thieves into their own blades. I bloodied the eyes of porters who pushed me away. I punched and kicked and dodged every day. Only one fight sticks to this head.

A middle-aged girl with kinky, dark hair, and slanted Proliux eyes reached out a hand to me just after evening twilight. I was hurrying back to my alley, but she had caught me in the night and in the dying crowds. I probably looked more like a man in lingering light, because my filthy shirt hung loose and hid my curves in the shadows. Her fingers reached up my arms. I stopped.

She wore ribbons upon ribbons upon ribbons. All the colors of every flower rippled and glimmered a flash of skin when the breeze kissed her.

She ran a hand down my white face. I had a sunburn on my neck, and her finger was cool across it. I shivered. She whispered a mixture of Proliux and Rhianna to me. I only understood some of it. I had not heard Rhianna until the city gypsies spoke it, and I didn't know any of it. I still don't.

Would you like . . . cool water . . . A drink from the warmest . . .

I pulled away, and she grabbed me tighter and pulled me close. She cooed with the throaty rapture of a pigeon, *Don't go!*

She smelled like dust, sweat, and flowers. I pushed her off of me. I pushed her hard. She clattered on plaster. *Ooh.*

A man appeared behind me quick. He pressed a dagger into my throat. He snarled. He walked around my still body with the dagger nibbling at my skin. I could understand him because he spoke Proliuxian slowly. *You plague-witch. You damage my girl, I damage you.* He had eyes like black stones. His wide body puffed up to his one arm. His one arm pushed out to his dagger. Skin hung on top of those cruel intentions, flabby and loose. Every muscle in his body trembled.

I knew I could kill him because he was too tense.

He held a thin, jagged dagger as long as my forearm. He reached his other hand up to my skin and stroked my arm. He moved his hand to my chest. *Are you girl or boy?* he said. *I think you girl. Do you*

*got tits there, girl? Tits as white as your face? What color your little eyes,
I wonder?*

I smiled, and touched the hand that held the dagger. I moved
slowly. I moved with the eyes of a lover. My other hand went down
to his pants.

He smiled. *You goer ain'tchou. Yeah, I looked you and knew you goer.
Freaks are always goers. Take what they get.*

I moved before he could stop smiling. His wrist snapped like
chicken bones. I tugged and twisted to ruin it forever. I tossed him
against the same wall.

The man held his snapped wrist. I held his knife. I winked and
gave him my best, awkward Proliuxian, *You are goer. You are goer to
not here.*

He stood up with a curse in his heart. He kicked at me and punched
with his good hand. I dodged the kick. I stabbed him through his
fist with his own knife. His blood was deep purple, nearly red. He
jumped back. He yowled.

The street crowd had parted and watched patiently for our
exchange to end. In a city in my homeland beyond the mountains,
any man would stop this fight. With Seth missing, I was the only
one who could stop this fight. I said, *Hand heal, angry heal.* Pride—*I
know not your word, but it never heal. Kill yourself your own* pride, *and
live yourself long.*

He looked at his stabbed hand in wonder. I got him through the
palm, with his own knife. It trembled against his chest, and blood
trembled down his whole body. He backed away from me, with large,
white eyes, and pale skin. Bloodless skin. He moaned in horror. *I only
wanted scare to you,* he said. *I just wanted scare you, girl . . . My hand . . .*
And he staggered away, lumbering like a bear into the streets, mut-
tering in Rhiannan.

Behind me, the crowd returned to its quick-paced ways.

I kept the blood on my hands all evening when I wandered. Six blocks left, four right and I was almost in the alley for the night. I'd rinse my hand in the ocean, and slip into my resting place among the cats. I leaned into the water, and splashed the blood away. A woman's voice said softly, *You are a strange one, white girl, and dangerous.*

I turned to her voice. Other voices spoke, walking quickly through the darkness of this harbor. A man asked his companion if she had seen that. Someone asked someone else if the market was still open. Someone coughed with laughter at a joke I did not hear. None of these were for me. The woman's voice was for me.

A short woman with brown skin splotched by scars like linear freckles smirked at me. She had once burned her ear badly. It was a melted mess on the side of her face. Beneath all that—maybe before all that—was a stern woman, and a steady gaze. She had spoken directly to me.

She reminded me of my old sensei, when I was still an apprentice rider instead of an apprentice shaman.

You are strange for me, I said.

You'd best get off the street, she said. *Pimps usually have friends.*

I fear none, I said.

She shrugged. *So come with me to a pub, and I will buy you a drink, and you can tell me about yourself.*

I looked around at the street. My whole time here the only offers for company had been from curious men, or women who thought I was malformed, with spending money and desire.

I sell not, I said. *I buy not.*

I buy only your food and drink, she said. *I have never seen one as you, and I would like to know more about you.*

Her hand appeared in the air, held up in a gesture I had seen others do. Her hand was out palm-first, straight toward my face. Her forearm slipped from her loose, green dress. In her skin, etched in silver and black, a sword aimed at me.

My name is Adel, she said.

My sensei was old enough to be my grandmother. When sensei smiled, bison fled. When she snarled, cannibals dropped their spears and begged for mercy. At least, her apprentices fled and begged for mercy. I met her when I was just past twelve winters.

In my village, I looked down to my leg, and I ran in fear to my mother. I showed her the blood, and where I was bleeding. My mother sighed, and told me that it was about time.

Women die from the inside slowly, she said. *Women bleed and bleed. Girls don't. Girls live forever inside. When they die, they are born again right away. Women, though . . .*

And that night, I was sent off by my great-aunt. My mother had told her, and my great-aunt nodded and sighed. I was the second born, and I had finally bled.

Like all the second born who come of age against their will, I had to go. I was sent off to the grassland, three months travel north, and all alone. My great-aunt gave me a spear, a warm cloak, and a hug. And I was sent off north, to find a camp that moves with the bison herds.

When I finally reached the rider camp, I was led directly to sensei's leather tent. Sensei looked up at me and grunted. She waved my escort away. Then, she tore the cloak from my back and threw it in the fire. It burned.

She smiled.

I burst into tears.

And I was so lonely, Esumi. I cannot tell you the loneliness of cities.

I was so lonely.

I took the scarred woman's hand. Our clasped fingers swung down to our waists, and then we let go together. *My name is Zhan Immur,* I said. *I am north from far, far.*

Adel pointed down a street. *I know a good pub this way,* she said. *I don't understand. Are you from far north? Or are you very far north from something important?*

We strode side-by-side down the street. I was no longer walking alone.

Cold, very cold where from I am myself, I said. *I am from far. I am on boats to Proliux. Ride down waters to here with Seth. Seth gone. I am to Seth go.*

Adel shook her head. She scratched her skull. *This will be an interesting conversation, Zhan Immur. Cold, you say? So you are from the north?* She pointed with her hand toward the north star. It had only just emerged in the evening sky, a point of white upon the midnight blue.

I smiled. *Yes,* I said, pointing, *from north.*

Adel pointed west. She said, *I am a paladin from Rhianna, but I haven't been there since before the fall. What are your people? Are there many light-skinned folk like yourself?*

Yes. Many women with light skin. Many, I said. *I go for Seth. He has light skin, too. We go for . . . one more. Skin like mine.*

We reached the pub and stepped inside. The stench of city murmured beneath the stench of drink.

This woman was Adel. Esumi, You have heard of her, from all the skalds' songs and the rumors that have spread in the decades. I place no stock in most of them, but I know two rumors to be true. She was one of the greatest paladins once, before the fall, and love ruined her, twice.

I learned of those things one night, when we were crossing the cold mountains and she was still awake, staring into the milkweed fire. Seth, Fest, and Korinyes slept hard in the demon dreams, but I woke up from mine. I saw her staring into the intoxicating fire.

Grandfather's golem listened to us silently from his place beside the flame.

Always death, always Alastair-of-the-Wolf, said Adel, quietly, *laying her cloak down, sharpening her teeth in men's bellies, and gnawing on the human hearts.*

Always Alastair-of-the-Wolf, I said. I poked at the smoldering flames of the milkweed. *Seth never teaches me anything, and he teaches you enough to bring you visions in the smoke.*

My demons are my own.

Time passed. Somewhere in the night a cricket sang a hymn to our warm fire.

What was his name? I said.

He's dead now, she said. *They're both dead and it doesn't matter anymore what their names were. It doesn't matter what anyone's name is.*

It matters, I said.

My demons are my own, Zhan.

My grandmother lived in a small house with many children. Grandfather was the only man in our village with red hair, and Seth was the only boy with red hair. I remember that Grandfather's hair was sun-bleached red and brittle in sweat and snow. I remember Grandfather smelled like sour leather and milkweed smoke, even before I knew what milkweed smoke was.

I only remember the moment of seeing him once when I was a child. Though I had seen him many times, this ghost digs into the web and screams.

He put me on his lap when I was still young enough for laps. I looked into his face. I pinched his jagged nose. It was nearly as big as my hand. He laughed. *And whose little one are you?* he said.

I told him. I was the second daughter of his eldest son.

Oh, do you know who I am? he said.

I told him he was my grandfather.

No, not yours, he said. *Maybe I am, but probably not.*

My father had black hair and a thin nose. My grandmother had brown hair and a strong jaw. Then, she grew old and her hair faded into snow. I did not know what my grandfather looked like after the murders. His skin was tanned and leathery when I was a young child, but it was still too light for the Proliuxian folk.

I looked for him, too, in the city with all my heart. I wished I could find my grandfather and kill him quickly, before I found Seth. Then I could shove Grandfather's head into Seth's quivering hands. I could smile at Seth's gasp of horror.

I was supposed to be a rider. I was meant to drink blood and kill and die in the sudden, surreal thrill of battle.

Instead, I was a shaman's apprentice, and duty bound to hunt my grandfather with my Uncle Seth below the edge of our world.

A rider never places anyone's flesh before her duty, not even her own. Neither should a shaman.

My Uncle Seth was only six years older than me, and I never considered him a mentor. He was such a bad young man. When I knew him, before I left for the herds, he was my great-aunt's quiet shadow and did not listen to a word she said. He burned things, and kissed with village girls, whether they liked it or not. He got in loud fights with Baba all the time. I don't remember words. Words are never important in arguments, only how loud we shout them.

I never learned my great-aunt's name—or if I did, I forgot it long ago—because she was so old. We all just called her Baba. Everyone did. I remember her teaching us to read, a little. We children never sat still. She never stopped to discipline us. I think she was too old to hear us. While children grew Baba shrank. She leaned on a cane, and limped around the village.

Her hair was down to her ankles, and white. On muddy days, her hair would brown at the bottom. On dusty days, her hair would yellow.

Seth had long red hair, long and long down to the middle of his legs. Seth hated his hair. I see him in my mind, always tugging at his tangled red hair. I remember it better than his face. I braided it for him when the weather was too hot. That changed nothing. His hair crinkled in red frizz. His ragged braid draped down his sweaty back, and trapped the heat beneath. After he lost me in the city, Staf Sru Korinyes cut it for him right away. She couldn't stand how sweaty he got in the afternoons. I don't blame her. I blame him.

I did not yet have hair like that. The fourth thing that happened to me when I first met my sensei was my hair was cut back above my ears.

You must listen, she had said.

In the city streets, I looked for his red hair, or my grandfather's white hair. If my grandfather had white hair...

And my hair was longer, but still not long like Baba's.

I had not seen my grandfather since years before I had gone to the herds. He lived in the mountains, and came back once and a while with mounds and mounds of dead goats piled in a huge litter, tugged by bruised hands.

The goat corpses keep in the cold above the tree line. Sometimes the leather was ruined by cougars, rats, or vultures. Sometimes the body was too long dead, even kept cold. Farmers bought these bodies cheap, and buried them in their fields, hooves and all. The stinking corpses push the offended wheat out of the earth.

Before Baba was the shaman there was another, even more ancient, and Seth was young. When the ancient one died, Baba came for Seth in the mountains. Grandfather tried to send her away, and told her that Seth wasn't the youngest one.

Baba told her youngest brother, my grandfather, that Seth was both the oldest and the youngest, and it had to be Seth. *Laws of paternity and duty are very clear in the holy hymns,* said Baba.

My sensei told me she was sorry when the messenger came. I wonder if Baba told Seth the same. Maybe she said it after grandfather had his fit and fled into the hills to hunt away his rage. I can see her, red hair spilling around her like a cape. She leaned close to the boy. They smelled each other. She said it. *I'm sorry.*

And Seth, the boy didn't even understand why he couldn't go off with his father and the hunting forever in the wild world of rock, snow, and giant sky.

Adel bought me the finest liquor I had ever had in my life in the pub that she had so casually led me too.

(I still drink it now in goat milk to help my throat, and it still tastes wonderful, even though I can barely taste it these days and it burns so much.)

She said the drink was called *Kahli*. It was made with roasted beans and fermented sugar. I did not know what the word *fermented* meant, but I let it roll over me without question. There are more important things to question.

How did you get to this city? she asked.

On a boats, on a small water, and then a big water. I said, too drunk to speak clearly.

From the north? she said. Her hands lingered around the rim of her cup.

Yes, I said.

I have been north before, she said. She squinted at me. *I have never seen your people.*

Tall buildings, but not buildings. Made of . . . what plants go. What children throw, I gestured up with my hands, and painted the mountains in the candle smoke, *tall, very tall.*

Dirt? Balls? Oh, mountains! Mountains? Adel gestured with her hands. She held them high over her head and spread them wide. *Ocean to ocean, our continent has mountains in the north. Dirt, rocks, wolves, and goats. Gigantic mountains. No one lives in the mountains. It's too cold – too dry. You live past the mountains?*

I think . . . Yes. Far, far north. I felt an insect in my ear, humming and humming. I brushed at it, but there was nothing there. My eyelids drooped. My head looked up at the wooden ceiling. *Tall, tall things. Very tall. Very cold. Hard to go on.*

Yes, mountains! Adel poured me another drink.

I pushed it away. *Mountains. . . .*

Adel pushed it back. *Mountains!*

We fell into laughter. We laughed and laughed. We fell into each other laughing. I realized that she had only had one drink, and I had had many. She pushed me back against my chair and smiled.

She took another sip, and rubbed her neck. She chuckled to herself and said, *Past the mountains. . . .*

Seth and I broke the tree line on my grandfather's trail. We climbed a goat track south and south, then up the side of the mountains.

Uncle Seth made a fire from the milkweeds. Milkweeds were the tallest things that grew up here. Small clover hid around rocks, and occasionally a yellow flower winked at us in the wind. The milkweed was waist high and smelled sour. It felt like greasy, limp ligaments.

Seth gathered milkweed in clumps in the mid-afternoon and slashed the sides of them. He dried them on a sunny rock until all the white goo oozed from the slashes. Night came, and no tent or skin could keep away that cold a moment more without the demon fire from the milkweeds.

The mountains are so cold. At night, the wind grows, and the cold seeps into your mouth with every breath. Instead of true tents, Seth set the skins and sticks up as windbreaks, in a leather square around the fire. The wind came up or down the cliff, depending on the time of night. Seth angled the windbreaks to guide the wind a different way, around the fire and around our sleeping bodies. We slept with the stars in our eyes.

Seth piled the brown, dried-up milkweed in a circle of rocks and lit it on fire with two smooth stones. They burned long into the night, and very warm. Longer than pine, longer than cow dung, and warmer than both combined. He had made much milkweed, but only used half of what he had made during the day. The rest disappeared into the pockets of his clothes.

I still don't know everything he kept in all those pockets. Shamans have so many pockets.

Seth pointed at the fire. *My father taught me that,* he said.

When? I asked.

You were not the only one who had another calling first, he said, *I was going to be my father's successor until my great-uncle died. I was going to wander these mountains and hunt the goats, like him and like his father. Live in the snow, just like him. He always wanted me to follow in his footsteps.*

Seth looked down at the latest goat path we had been following his father on. Dried-up shit squatted beside a milkweed bush just off the path. The old man had used the milkweed to break the wind where his body was exposed, and hadn't bothered to bury the remains.

Funny, isn't it? said Seth. *That's what we're doing now.*

What? I said.

He yawned when he answered. He spoke through the yawn and it stretched his voice like wind. *Following in his footsteps.*

The wind changed and the milkweed smoke poured over my face. It was like breathing spirits. My eyes watered. I coughed and coughed.

Get out of the smoke, he said.

I barely heard him. He was far away. I looked at stars, not him. I looked at thousands of stars. All of them moved. They dashed away like fleeing fireflies. Now the sky was black.

He appeared in my face. Up close, his skin was a patchwork of pinks and browns. I don't remember if he was handsome or not. I remember he had blue eyes.

Are you okay? he said. *Are you hurt?*

What? No.

You passed out, he said. *I told you to get out of the smoke.*

I did. I think I did. Is it morning? I said. *It isn't morning? Where is the moon?*

You passed out a few moments ago. The milkweed smoke takes getting used to. The weed will burn hot all night, he said, *but the smoke can get to you if you're not used to it. That's why we can't have a tent over our heads. The smoke would kill us if we got it too strong. The wind will blow it up or down the mountain.* He paused. He examined my head for bruises or blood. He said in a whispered afterthought, *You should sleep next to the fire, not above it, or below it.*

Is it morning? I asked.

No, he replied.

When do we leave?

Tomorrow, he said. *It's not morning, yet. You will become accustomed to the milkweed. It's just your first time.*

His face was close enough to kiss. He had pulled me out of the smoke. He slowly lowered my head and returned to his side of the fire. He said, *You will dream of demons, too. You will not sleep well this night.*

I never sleep well, I said. *Riders don't sleep well. I didn't sleep well last night at all. I have a headache, too.*

In the pub, I didn't tell Adel that, but I was thinking it.

There are more eyes in the city than just yours, she said. *Why do you hunt your grandfather?*

I took a sip of the sweet Khali. I grimaced. *He has to kill men, women, and babies,* I said, *and the shamans to hunt them down them who to kill.*

Wait. What? Who is the killer?

My grandfather has to kill many others north of mountains, I said. *My father was to kill, my mother, many others. My grandfather to kill them.*

Adel sighed and pressed her hands into her temple. *A murderer, then. You and your uncle came here to kill a murderer.*

I shook my head. *No murder I do. We kill for Alastair. We are holy man, holy woman. We obey our Alastair word. We to kill a man who to kill.*

Adel cocked her head, and sipped her Khali. She put her drink down. Her empty hand touched a sword tattoo. *Justice, then. Law and justice,* she said. *I think I understand. I hope I do. I will help you. I know how to help with these things. Law and Justice.* Touch. A sigh, as long as winter. *Law and Justice.*

We were feasting, all the riders together. It was our last feast as apprentices. I drank sweetened blood wine, and devoured the boiled liver of a slaughtered buffalo. I sat between my two closest friends, also apprentices on the verge. Esumi, if the Goddess permitted me to tell you of our lives in that camp. If I could tell you how happy I was there training and hunting . . .

In the morning we would have all risen, despite our hangovers, to bring down a buffalo with only knives. It would be our last rites as apprentices. Then we would have received our saddles, and would have sung songs and would have rode out to war with the cannibals on the western shores this time of year.

No other holy duty could fall upon me, then. I would be a rider at last and forever, until my death in battle and ascension to the arms of Alastair. Once last rites occurred, my fate was set in stone.

Then, a messenger arrived at the far edge of our camp. We who feasted did not see him, since he was over a small hill along the plain. The guards did. Two riders circled the camp to guard our pleasures and they saw him right away.

The messenger was a tall boy about our age. Men of all ages were forbidden in our camp, especially tall boys about our age. The guards lifted their spears, but he held a scroll out instead of bare hands. The guards saw the scroll's green sash in the fading light, and snatched the scroll from his fingers. They told him to sit or die. He sat. A guard stayed with him, with her spear near his throat.

The message went to my sensei right away. She read it and frowned. The table silenced.

Zhan Immur, go home to your village right away, said my sensei, *You are not to be one of us. Alastair has chosen a new path for you. Your family has been murdered—all of them—except your uncle, Seth Immur. You are to be a shaman now. You are to be Seth Immur's apprentice, not mine, and not a rider after all.*

The words sank into the silent, mostly drunk crowd. I sobered.

Sensei pressed a finger into her temple. She closed her eyes. She said, *You came to me with a spear, a bow, and a cloak. You will leave with only these things. Alastair exists in ways we cannot foresee, and cannot contain. Her law is greater than our desire. Go now.*

The whole table numbed in those words. A hand appeared on my back. For a moment it was comforting. Then it pushed me.

I fell. I jumped to my feet. I said, *What?*

Sensei frowned deeper. She opened her eyes. *Go now, shaman. Only riders live here. You are no longer welcome.*

Then she said, as a soft afterthought, *I'm sorry.*

When I arrived at the rider camp as a young girl, I cried and fainted. Now, I didn't cry. Now, I didn't faint. I left with the guard, who took me to the messenger.

This messenger was the first man I'd seen in five years. He sat cross-legged in the grass, and picked his nose. He had the numb face of a farm boy, or a shepherd, or an unpleasant memory. He didn't know how close to death he came this holy night.

I nodded sadly at the guards. I knew the secret names they called themselves in the white heat of battle. They had taught me how to live, how to find my own name in that same heat. They and their sisterhood had taught me how to be a woman.

The two guards turned their backs on me, and left. They didn't look back. In the raucous distance, an apprentice laughed. Someone sang a song too loud while someone else banged a drum without any rhythm:

> *My spear is your key to the afterlife,*
> *I shove it in your hole and turn!*
> *Kiss good-bye to your kids and wife,*
> *And bend over for the burn . . .*

The messenger was a shepherd's son, near my age, and tired from the journey here. He stood up. *Seth said to get you back right away. I came as quick as I could. You think we got time to eat. I'm pretty hungry, myself.*

I fell into his arms. He staggered backwards in surprise. My legs collapsed, and I collapsed into him. I cried and cried, and howled and howled. I dug my fingers into his back with my agony. Goddess, I was in agony. Goddess, I can still feel that pain. I can still feel it . . .

The farmboy remembered at last the news I had just heard. His hand came up to my back. He let me buck and kick my pain into his body. He stroked my back as if I were a spooked sheep. He said, *Shhh . . .*

Uncle Seth and I spent a whole morning trying to communicate with the small town. We pointed north. We spoke. They looked at each other, and at our weapons. They pointed at a river boat. They shouted at us slowly in their harsh language of angry cats.

At the boat, a sailor grabbed at my cloak. Seth pushed him off. He fell back and laughed. He shook his head at us. He removed his own jacket and held it out to us. He smiled a toothless smile, and took it back. Then he gestured to the boat.

Uncle Seth took my spear and used the tip to draw a picture in the dirt. Two circles. He pointed at one of the circles and pointed at himself. He pointed at the other circle, and pointed at me. Then, he drew a third circle. He slammed my spear into the center of that circle.

Seth pulled the spear out of the ground, and then he struck the circle again. He pulled the spear out. The sailor cocked his head. Seth drew small lines from the two circles that represented him and me, and he pointed them at the circle he had attacked.

The sailor nodded. He smiled, and muttered something. He hopped onto his small skiff, and pulled out a goatskin cloak.

He held that, and pointed at the third circle. He pointed at the cloak, and the circle, and then the boat.

I think we understand each other now. Give him your cloak, said Seth, *It's what he wants.*

Give him yours, I snorted.

He doesn't want mine, said Seth

Offer it to him, and see if he takes it.

Seth harrumphed and took off his cloak. He held it out to the smiling sailor. The sailor snatched it with another toothless smile. He gestured onto his boat. Seth and I followed him on.

That night, I shared my cloak with him, both of us pressed together and my arm over his shoulders, to keep us both warm. *Are we going the right way?* I said.

If the Goddess wills it.

We traveled with six bags of grain, a large hog, and three sleek black birds in cages. The birds sang only one note in the morning mists, a long note like a dark bell.

What bird is there that does not hate the cages? he said. *What man is there who lives in such a small world as that cage so happily?*

The sailor looked at us with a big, stupid smile. He said something unintelligible.

He does, I said. I nodded at the man. I shrugged. I pointed at my ear and turned away from him. I looked Seth in the face.

Yes, said Seth, *the man who owns his own cage will sit in it and even die for it. Just like the cage of flesh. We would do anything to protect our fleshy cages because we think we own them.*

Duty owns my flesh, I said, *and it owns yours, too, oh magnificently brilliant shaman. This journey is our prison, and it is not of our making.*

He smiled and snorted a small laugh. *If this is your cage*, he said, *give it up. No jailer will stop you here. You hold your own keys.*

I shook my head. *No*, I said, *tell me a joke instead. I'm sick of all this gloomy, important nonsense you always talk about. Riders laugh in the face of death, theirs and everyone else's. Tell me a joke.*

Right, he said, *what do a flea and a man have in common?*

I don't know, I tossed a small pebble at the birds. It bounced off a beak. The creature shook its head and squawked.

They both hop from one bitch's back to another, said Seth.

That isn't funny, I said.

You just said to tell you a joke, he replied. *You didn't ask for it to be funny.*

Can you tell me a funny joke? I said. I threw a pebble at Seth this time. It hit him in the throat. He ignored it.

I don't know any, he said.

The pig ambled up to the cages. It snorted at the caged birds. The birds flapped their wings, and the pig pulled away from the wind.

Neither do I, I said.

I didn't talk to the dull-witted messenger the whole journey to the village. He spoke, and sometimes he told me to do something. I did what he asked of me or not without explaining. The journey that took me three months when I was twelve and alone took him and me four silent weeks.

My baby sister was supposed to be the shaman. If she died, I had a younger brother. If he died, it was only me. My youngest sister was six months old when I bled and left. I had held my mother's hand when the pangs came, and the tiny lump of flesh broke through to life.

My mother's groaning, twisted face and wild screams were like someone else's face and voice.

I held my mother's hand even though my mother nearly broke it, and I mopped her face dry of sweat. Baba was between my mother's legs. Baba sang hymns to the Goddess. Incense burned in a corner softly. Seth stood there, next to the incense, boiling water, and handing over warm, wet blankets. He looked at my mother bucking and kicking and screaming. He yawned.

I had watched my mother's belly grow for months like a miracle, and now the miracle was only pain. Even the baby girl was in agony. She emerged, screaming into the air, kicking and angry and cold.

I stared at stars at night during my journey back to my old village. I felt that same pain inside of me. That same pain. I bucked and screamed. The shepherd boy held me, and let me buck and scream. I felt a black ball in my stomach pushing through and pushing and pushing through.

And then, sleep came for us both after, and nothing at all had come out. My flat belly was as empty as my aching heart.

He drooled in my hair while he slept.

At least he snored, too. I could sleep a little when he snored.

My grandfather had murdered that same child I had felt connected to by a distant vein of life. This was my bond with my baby sister: I was there when she arrived.

I didn't even know her. She was too young when I left. Agony, I cannot describe for you, still I cannot though years have turned. I cannot. Goddess, agony . . .

Somewhere in the vast northern tundra, where the grass grows low and dense above the permafrost and day and night take month-long turns in the sky, my friends with my sensei charged into battle. Some of them died. At the end of the battle, the warriors of all the united lords came together to drink and dance and love because all of them were warriors, and might not have lived another moment after that one.

You were there, Esumi, and we could have drank and loved without the weight of empire on our backs.

Perhaps I would have died, in the kiss of a javelin thrown by a cannibal. My body dragged away, tossed into a pot and stirred with my sisters and brothers or eaten raw in the fields.

The beastmen cannibals would eat me, head first, and use my sharpened bones to kill my sisters. Or I would live, to train a new wave of sisters, and ride bison until my bones would be too brittle and I wouldn't be able to move.

It was the life I had grown to believe. My family far away was only a dream I dreamt at night under the darkness.

My mother's voice called to me in the wind, with the weight of the farmer's wife, whose child is bound by duty and birth to die far away, in a war she knew nothing about. Hands that smelled like challah bread. The mysteries of yeast and the mysterious wonders of winter in a small village and women's quiet solitude among the children's private worlds. Watching children grow. Waving the second-born off to war. Praying for a good harvest. A gentle husband with a strong back and heavy hands.

I dreamed about my childhood. Stirring pots in the morning with boiled milk to feed my father before he went to the farm. My father's veined hands—the strongest hands in the world—with the two missing fingers from a sick cow that bit him one bad day in spring. Those hands that ran down my head and were so huge. His tired smile at night, drifting in and out of sleep before the fire.

My mother laughed at his same old jokes all through the winter. They chased my younger brother and me around the tiny house when we were really snowed in. They pretended to be scary bears.

We giggled at them. My older brother scoffed, and sharpened his hunting tools. He killed wolves all winter with the other older boys, to keep the wolves away from the livestock. My younger brother and I giggled and giggled. We pretended our fingers were arrows.

My mother's thick face shook when she laughed. She had such a hearty laugh. At night, she snored to knock the snow from the eaves. When I first came to the rider camp I couldn't sleep, no matter how exhausted I was, because I couldn't hear my mother snoring. In the end, I listened to the singsong snoring of the crickets, and this worked enough until my sympathetic tent-mate picked up the snoring habit for herself.

And my grandfather had come down from the mountains after three years away.

He came down from the mountains with clothes on his back and nothing else. The village had believed him dead, at long last. The day—the very day—that my grandmother was declared free, the old hunter arrived to wide eyes and not a single smile in the whole village. Not even his sister, Baba, smiled at him.

My grandfather came down and saw the many children in his house, who had no goat to eat this time. Some of the children had been adopted by other families.

The younger children heard that the adoptions were a mercy. This poor woman had too many mouths to feed, no land to farm, and no livestock to raise. Her older children barely got by themselves. So many children to feed.

Two weeks journey south, seventeen winters old, and staring at the cold stars. Staring at Alastair's blind eye: the moon. I saw for the first time that my grandfather was not truly my grandfather.

He had killed everyone that was not of his blood, but of his name. He left behind only my Uncle Seth and me. I was too far away to kill, and surrounded by riders who kill uninvited men on sight. If he even remembered I was alive at all.

And Seth was his only true son.

And my whole childhood fell into a box the color of the night sky, and the box slammed shut. The dream fell to pieces, and I couldn't sleep anymore. I stared up at the cold stars and felt the rising and falling agony like a sickening ocean.

All of my dreams—all of them—had died.

I did not tell these things to Adel, yet. I couldn't. We did not have the words between us. We would when we would be dashing across the white tundra to Ilhota in the winter darkness. We would in the dungeon. In the dungeon all we could do was sit and wait and listen to Partridge singing the same songs over and over again.

Until then, we did not have the words to tell each other our own stories. All we did was look for Seth, and grandfather. Then, we carried the urgent message of imminent invasion to a land that did not even know Proliux existed.

3

Adel got me a room in an inn next to the pub. I took a bath. I hadn't bathed in months. I complain of city stench, but I smelled like the city. I was a walking pavement stone, covered in muck and puke and dust.

After I bathed, the water was as brown as the dusky skin of the locals. I imagined how skin could get so dark, and I thought it was cinnamon. The cinnamon seeped through the body, and out of the skin, and the skin turned brown.

(Is your skin brown yet, Esumi?)

I dipped my finger into the soapy water, and collected some small flecks of dust. I sniffed it. I touched it with my tongue. It tasted like soap.

I slept in a bed behind a locked door, and I tossed and turned all night. My back swelled up like an over-used tongue, and I slept worse than if I had gone back to my alley. I was unaccustomed to beds.

In the morning, Adel knocked on my door. Neither of us had a hangover. I don't know why we didn't. Maybe we both never really slept. Adel wore loose, cool clothes, and threw a dress at me. *I think this is your size,* she said. *I just had to guess.*

It wasn't but I wore it anyway. The dress was brown and rode high on my legs and hung loose in my chest. We had sweet rolls for breakfast, and drank cool cinnamon tea. Adel paid for everything.

In the street, people stared.

Adel stopped a street walker, and lifted a coin in the air. *Pardon me, Madame, but I was wondering if I could borrow your eyes for a moment,* said Adel. *We are looking for two men with light skin like my friend's here. One has red hair.*

The woman rolled her eyes and snorted at us. *Always you people asking us what we have seen. Would anyone find wayward sons if not for the scorned women? Go away, ugly. I don't serve your kind.*

In an inn, the innkeeper pushed spectacles up his fat nose. He shook his head, sadly. *A good man is hard to find, these days for sure,* he said. *Ran off on ya, huh? I'll keep an eye out for 'im, for sure.*

A beggar sipped an unidentifiable liquid from a filthy cup. He shook his head and cautiously took the coin. *No.*

Adel and I walked around, asking people who tend to notice people. We talked about food while we walked, because I could speak of little else yet.

She hated cinnamon in everything but tea.

So did I.

I loved the Khali.

She smiled. *Everyone does,* she said.

Seth and I ate goat in the mountains. He had a rope that he used to lasso them around the horns. The goat jumped back every time, testing the power of the strange rope, and then jumped forward to the source. Seth held a spear out. The goat collapsed when the spear burst into its chest.

We did not have time to strip and clean the skins. We dug into the meaty bellies and legs. We cooked the flesh over milkweed fires, and the meat tasted burned and sick. We left a trail of goats for the wolves.

My mouth went numb, eating the milkweed smoke in the meat. At night I had visions of a darker world.

When we reached the other side of the mountains—after the canyon—the trees returned, and we stopped using milkweed. I had a headache for days.

Seth said it was . . . *the angry ghosts of the mountains that never want you to leave.*

He said that after we found the trees, though. We wandered the mountains first. We found a canyon first.

We found the canyon before we found trees. Seth and I stood on a small outcropping of rock. We had just followed the trail over a ridge. Grandfather marked his path with dislodged roots and rocks, and the refuse of eaten goats. He marked his path well. I touched Seth's arm. *He wants us to follow him, doesn't he?*

Seth shrugged. *If he even thinks he's being followed.*

Mm, I said. Neither yes nor no. A word I learned from Seth.

If it is the will of the Goddess . . . said Seth. Then he stopped and pointed down below us at a cliff. He said, *We seem to be following him to that rift in the rock. I don't remember ever seeing a canyon like that with my father.*

How long has it been since you were here with him?

Long, said Seth, *Perhaps he never took me here. I don't know. Look at that thing.*

We stood on an outcropping that formed a goat path. My right knee was bent high because the path was steep. My left leg was tired and sore. I kept thinking about all these angles, and how easily it would be to misjudge a rock and break an ankle, and fall, and fall, and fall.

If it is the will of the Goddess . . .

Below us, the mountain dropped away to a steep slide of pebbles and rocks. A patch of milkweed clung to the rock face alone, like green acne on the white. The goat path wound around the middle of the jagged peak. Then, the path followed the stone skin between two fat fingers of mountain. The path looped down to the valley, a day's journey at least, and down and down into an even deeper place.

A canyon.

From where I stood, I could see how jagged it was. A single sliver of igneous rock that cracked and held apart two great, sharp peaks. A canyon that moved in a direct line into the center of the mountains, like a thunderbolt of Alastair carved into the stone.

Grandfather had moved in as straight a line as he could through the mountains for the last few weeks moving to this strange path. Weeks ago, he did this since we were weeks behind him and his shit had time to harden like white stones.

I followed Adel in the city for days. We learned to speak to each other. We talked of anything we could, and I taught her pieces of my own language. *Fish. Winter. Night. Run.*

We traveled all day long and talked to beggars, hookers, and innkeepers. All through time, the same stories over and over again. The same contempt or the same sadness poured from the mouths of the brown faces. Cities are full of people who say the same things to strangers. I wondered if there was a conspiracy.

Adel and I stopped a woman in a bright red dress. She had a feline face, and a squishy body that pushed against the seams. Her brown skin spilled over the green fringes like a flood.

And this woman smiled and said, *I never discuss my customers for free.*

Adel smiled and lifted a small coin in the air.

This prostitute reached for the coin. *An old fella with the oddest round eyes*, she said. *He wears nice clothes and he always has a little money to throw about. He talks to me in a weird language. He is a rough fella. You say he has white skin, and I reckon he do. He do underneath his clothes. I stopped seeing him, though. He tired of me.*

I clutched Adel's shoulder. My knees trembled. All this talking and walking, and this one disgusting person.

Where did he go when he was done with you? said Adel.

The prostitute smiled. *You couldn't pay me enough to tell you that, deary,* she said. *I will tell you he is unfaithful, one woman to another, but I will not tell you where he goes after. I have a neck to worry about, too, you know.*

Adel lifted another coin. She said, *Are you sure?*

Aye, deary. My neck is priceless, no matter what the rest of me happens to go for. The prostitute looked past us.

Then do not tell me exactly, said Adel. *Tell me how big.*

She walked away without the coin. She looked over at a man passing by with his mercenaries and fine silk robes and fine, thin jewels. She coughed at him.

Adel nodded.

In a riverboat, riding downstream, three men sat above us all.

Sometimes the river was wide, and a sail captured the morning breezes. Other times, men with long poles walked up and down the deck, pushing us along from the river bottom. The world was no longer sweet pine. It was short oak. It was long grasses. It was strong winds in the mornings and evenings, and dead calm in the afternoons. The world smelled like the muddy, yellow water beneath us.

We passed thousands of other boats, too. Like ours, but piled with different things or different people. We passed small villages and farmlands. Large dikes sprouted up around the villages, and men walked up and down the dikes with long poles in their hands, measuring I guess. Past the dikes, fields of corn and wheat. Farther south, we saw rice fields for the first time in our lives in muddy swamps full of mosquitoes and alligators.

The three men above us all sat up with the captain of the riverboat—if a riverboat of six sailors can call themselves captains. Those three men on the high deck wore blue and red, with intricate graffiti sewn into their sleeves and necks.

They spoke little to us, except for one. One was curious about us. He was a military commander once, and liked to get to know new kinds of people.

At the shipyard where we had negotiated passage, he had watched us from the bustling herd of man and agriculture.

I had only seen him because the crowd had parted for him. I don't know if it was respect or contempt. Maybe both. The crowd had split, tugging at their pack animals and crates of possessions, falling over themselves into the street mud. Burly men with sacks of grain on their backs had dropped the grain into the mud instead of standing in this one man's path. This man had passed by us casually enough, but he had stopped and had taken a second glance at us. He had heard our strange accent attempt to negotiate passage on a river boat. He had seen our strange eyes, our strange skin, our strange clothes.

He had made a brisk motion to his companions following in his wake. A mustached man had nodded. He had dashed forward to the riverboat captain.

On the ship the scorned one liked to talk to us, but Seth and I didn't really understand him. This encouraged his desire. He tried hard to make us understand. We learned as much as we could from this stranger. He never sat with us, or ate with us. He just talked to pass the time while he was still sober enough to talk. He stopped when he got too drunk. He smelled like damp flowers and bad alcohol.

I learned that he was the youngest son of Proconsul Argarax, and he had been thrown from the army for cowardice. I learned this from the captain. The captain stayed with the men on the raised deck, laughing and drinking and talking. At night, he joked about the special guests with his five sailors. I listened. I could hear better than I could speak. As the days passed, I pieced it together.

This Lord Argarax was guilty. He smelled of drink, and his body had recently disintegrated. Once strong arms now only got exercise under the heavy bottle of cheapest wheat liquor. His round belly pushed against his fine cloth. His fat face was sweaty and pimpled. His eyes were deep brown, and very sad.

Mid-morning, and Argarax, was slowly turning red where he had collapsed on the deck. Brown skin takes long to turn red. No one had pushed him into the shade. Seth and I kept to ourselves in the shade beneath the walls of the riverboat.

I mentioned the sailor's laughter to Argarax sometime along the journey. *They to laugh by you,* I said.

He sighed and held his head in his hands. *I know,* he said.

Seth placed a hand on young Argarax's back. Argarax stood over us on the raised deck and it was awkward for Seth to touch the young man. Argarax pulled away from Seth's hand. He walked to the other side of the raised deck, and another jug.

I can still see him, leaning against the rail, drinking and singing war songs with his two somber companions, who together drank less than half of what Argarax did alone. They were young men, like Argarax, but they rarely spoke. When they did it was usually to the other, not Argarax.

(One of them had a mustache. We would see that one again, in a café in Proliux. I wouldn't recognize him until years later, and I awake in the night with a start at what I know now. If I know now. The web drifts and faces merge and fade and a man in a boat is a man in a street café is a man in a castle is a woman in a red dress tossing filth from a window and it isn't a mustache at all but a line of soot and messy hair . . .)

One of our last nights on the riverboat, Argarax drank himself into another wild stupor. He shouted battle cries at sailors and tossed broken jugs like spears. He staggered around the top deck. The captain tried to calm him down. Instead, young Argarax jumped back from the captain's touch. *Do you know who I am? Do you? How dare you touch me! How dare you!*

And at the rail, at the back of the little boat, he took one long drink of his last bottle. He threw the bottle at the captain. The captain knocked it away with his hands.

And young Argarax fell back over the rail.

Seth and I ran to the edge of our deck. We leaned over and shouted that he had fallen overboard, in our best imitation of Proliux. We could not swim, so we did not dive in after him.

The captain shrugged at us in the moonlight. *He wants it, so let him have it.*

A sailor touched our backs and pulled us from the edge. Seth and I didn't understand.

The rest of the journey was a day passed on in silence. We slept. We woke. No one spoke unnecessarily. Every day is like this on the languid riverboats.

The men who had been with young Argarax disappeared fast, and no one really spoke to us while we journeyed to the city, on the trail of my grandfather.

Adel and I looked for Seth the same we way we had always been looking, with beggars, prostitutes and businessmen.

Adel and I found a beggar's corpse in the evening. We approached an alley because we saw a beggar in it, and we had not found another beggar on this particular section of street. The beggar's body sprawled in a long heap like a forgotten statue. The low fog of flies forever at the ankles clumped over the corpse. The hands had been gnawed by larger beasts.

She prodded the foul-smelling heap with a stick. The body rolled over. The body was stiff as stone, and crawling with ants. The ants had already removed part of his face. His skull was whiter than my skin.

Adel and I gathered water from a nearby fountain, and we carried it to the body. We dumped it all onto his face and chest. Ants shipwrecked in the little flood.

We pulled the body away from the ants' path. Back in the street, Adel stopped an older black man passing by. I didn't understand how we could get this man, of all the men passing on the street, to help us with a corpse, but he would.

The black-skinned men did these things. They were all mercenaries, from the distant deserts past the western sea, who had migrated east.

Adel paid the man to take the beggar's body to the nearest temple and pray for the lost soul to whatever God was convenient.

The man nodded at the corpse. *Why is he so wet?*

Ants, she said, *we washed them off.*

Do you know his name? he asked.

No, she said, *do you?*

He shook his head sadly. *No. Poor man, to die alone.* A long pause. The mercenary blinked. *My name's Fest Fasen.*

Adel, she said, pointing at herself. *Zhan,* she said, pointing at me.

I will help you with this man. His voice was as deep and rolling as ocean thunder. But he was from the desert. All mercenaries are from the desert. *He has been stabbed.* Fest stuck a finger into the man's chest, and showed us the wound. The blood had dried it solid days ago.

Fest wrapped the body in his cloak. *I will buy another cloak with my fee,* he said. *This is an honorable thing to do. I applaud your honor, Adel and Zhan.*

The corpse crackled when it moved. Fest hefted it onto a shoulder. He sighed under the weight and carried it down the street. People parted at this sight of the cloak-wrapped body on black shoulders. A stiff hand bobbed like a fishing rod behind Fest. The hand was tinged brownish-green. A large black ant crawled over it.

I shivered.

Adel took me by my shoulders. She looked me in the eyes. She said, *Sorry about that.*

Is good, I said. *I am good. Is good for killed man.*

Adel had astonishing eyes. From afar they seemed merely blue, or green depending on the slant of the sun or the fire. But close, I saw the individual cells of color, of all colors. Her eyes were kaleidoscopes.

Your eye is very good, I said, *yes, very good eye.*

She blinked and cocked her head. *Thank you, I think.*

We talked as we walked. I tried to tell her about the sky of the mountains. Down here, near the ocean, the clouds are gigantic, and far away. In the mountains, the clouds are close enough to touch, if you stand on a tall man's shoulders. At least, they feel that way.

Adel said that clouds were the same everywhere, and only the ground was different.

As we talked, a low, gray cloud wept gently for the beggar. Fest was praying for the poor beggar's soul, and the heavens answered. Soon, the cloud wept harder and harder, until the streets washed vacant. We ducked into a public house and drank a little Khali until the storm passed.

After the rain, the city streets seemed a little cleaner. The quick torrent pushed much of the filth into the gutters and the sewers.

I heard a cry from a high window.

Adel and I dove for the middle of the street. Wet slop splattered onto the cobblestone where moments ago we had walked. I looked up and could not see where it had come from. I think it fell from the clouds.

The mercenary we would meet again, after Adel and I found Seth.

When I think of that, I think of how small the city must really be. We pass a man on the street, and we see him again later on.

He told me that his city was small. He lived inside a few buildings, where black skin goes to relax, or to work.

Adel's city was large, because she was rich.

My city was large but lonely, since it was the docks, and all the alleys, and all the streets, and only the beggars and the prostitutes ever talked to me.

Adel took me to where she lived in the city. She lived in a small building over a tailor's shop, alone. The old tailor stopped us and demanded to fix my dress. His hands looked like wet tree bark with veins and moldy hair. They trembled when he worked and he pricked me thousands of times, like ants. I didn't flinch at the pricks, and afterwards, my dress fit well.

His shop was covered in colors I did not know existed beyond the summer butterflies until I saw them here, in Proliux. I had seen in many windows, and all the houses are like that here. Little objects with bright colors cram into the corners of every room. Each blank space on a wall has a picture or a statue. Every citizen was a king in a palace of colors and light. The palaces were small.

This tailor shop was as delicate as a collection of insect wings. I stared at the counter with the window behind me. The old man carefully hemmed my new dress at my feet. A counter with paper and quills. Fabrics upon fabrics upon fabrics.

He turned me to face the window. I watched another rainstorm outside while he worked. Lightning crashed, and the unsteady hands pricked me, and Adel talked of the sudden rainstorms in the long plains of Rhianna. I asked her where Rhianna was. She said, *West*.

That night, I slept on the floor next to the divan. Adel had offered me a blanket and a better pillow on the divan. I shook my head, and lay down on the floor. I told her that I had spent so much time in alleys.

I dreamed of oceans, and in the morning Adel told me I snored to wake the dead. It took some time to figure out what she meant, so she had to mimic snoring herself. We laughed at that. We sipped cinnamon tea, together. We looked out at the clean city. On this pleasant day, we would find Seth.

A few days with Adel, and I achieved what I hadn't been able to do for months alone.

Seth did not want to be found.

Shamans are powerful with the mysteries of our faith. They combine the elements of Alastair to create the mysteries of Alastair. I had not learned these things, yet. Still, the mysteries are powerful things. Smoke that burns blue in the spring feast. A pink cloud of dust that spreads through the waters and brings sleeping fish to the surface. A green leaf that stops bleeding. A red stalk mixes with sheep's blood to kill wolves, or mixes in strawberry pie to taste like sweetened wolf-bites to keep a child from vomiting.

These mysteries I had not learned. He had, though. He abused the mysteries of the Goddess for months, and dreaded my face in the crowd. He wore a mask to hide from me. He had cut his hair.

I lost him—or he lost me—and I had remained in the docks where we had arrived. My docks were at the far south of the island city. He did not stay for me to find him. He followed the surging crowds, and disappeared into the city.

I do not know precisely what occurred. Later on, he told me that he had given up, and I would never give up, and so he had left me. I believe him.

So many brown faces, and so long of a journey south, and he felt the pull of the crowd, tearing us apart, and he decided that he would let them pull. I jumped and shouted and waved my arms. He looked back and our eyes locked for one moment. I knew, then.

Seth followed the people that pushed him. He followed the human herd and discovered himself in a marketplace. Bustling bodies bartering for beautiful and exotic things. Pieces of odd furniture from the wood of new forests. All he had ever seen before of wood was pines and occasional birch, and oak when he had journeyed to the coast.

A gigantic black man waved a fist in the air and shouted. *Buy something or move along, friend. If I catch you stealing, I'll bash your brains in.*

We had seen so few of the darkest-skinned men down along the river ships. In Proliux, they are everywhere, and all for hire. Korinyes and Adel told me the same thing. The dark men were an old army, who took over the mercenary deserts and Rhianna, and they were allowed to stay in the city to pay off the debts of the generals.

Seth and I had thought the mercenaries were golems of the wicked gods, until we watched one's nose explode in blood.

Seth laid his hands upon the weeping black man, featureless in the moonlight. Seth pressed dried-up milkweed against the man's broken nose until it stopped bleeding. The black giant's shoulders heaved with sobs, but his eyes stopped leaking. Seth straightened the man's nose in one, painful crack. The man didn't flinch. His eyes rolled like drifting wheels.

Seth wiped the blood off the man's face with bare hands. He had nothing else he could spare for a stranger. Seth placed a sliver of old milkweed in the man's mouth, and said, *Dream well.*

The black man's opponent nursed his hand in a corner of the boat. Seth touched the hand. The brown man frowned, and cradled his hand away.

No move, said Seth, in Proliuxian. *I help.*

Seth gave a tiny sliver of milkweed to the brown man, and mimicked eating it. Seth said in a soft whisper of our language, *Go ahead and eat it. It won't kill you, but it will certainly calm you down. It will certainly keep you from feeling your hand for a while, too.* Seth touched the man's face like loving. *You fight over nothing, like dogs,* he said. *You are strange folk to fight over meaningless words.*

And we left him there, in a corner of the riverboat, holding his hand and staring at the stars.

I had reached into the black man's purse while Seth was moving away. I slipped out four coins before Seth sat down. Everyone else on our deck of the riverboat was awake and staring at Seth, who had soothed the wild beasts.

I stole again, quickly. Then, I sat down next to the brown man, and wiped drool from his face. With my other hand I stole from his nearest neighbor.

Seth stared at the black man with the broken nose. Seth reached over the boat wall, and washed his hands clean in the murky night river.

The black man drooled, too. I walked up to him. I ran a hand over his strange face. It felt like human skin. I wiped blood from his mouth with my sleeve. Someone handed me a rag. I said, *Thank you*, and I used the rag to wipe the blood away. When I handed the rag back, the owner tossed it over the side of the boat. It didn't splash.

I washed my hands in the river, too, and as much of my sleeve as I could.

Then I sat down, and stared at the black man, just like Seth. We studied the dark anatomy as best we could in the moonlight.

Golem no more. Definitely human.

Seth, in one of the island city's marketplaces, heard the giant black man command him to leave. He moved along. He saw piles of fish, in the next stall. The fish had shining scales and a fierce stench in the afternoon sun. Seth moved along again to vast piles of nuts and fruit and vegetables. He held out a small coin, and pointed at a piece of fruit. The vendor took the coin and handed two fruits to Seth without negotiation. Seth placed one of the fruits into his pocket. He ate the other one.

Seth moved along while he ate, his eyes as big as his fruits.

Seth told me about that fruit later on, and said it tasted like moonlight, dark and sweet.

Fest Fasen told us it was a plum. Fest hated plums.

We sat at a table in a public house, eating dinner. The growing hills hunched over the village outside our window. An army of mercenaries ate around us. Some of them stared at us, the only women for miles around them. We were in northern Proliux, at last, near the mountains.

Fest lifted the bowl of soup to his face and poured it down his throat. He puffed up his chest and bellowed out at his brethren whenever he burped.

He slammed the bowl down and it nearly shattered. When he spoke, his steel fangs sparkled in the candlelight. Fest said, *Plums taste weak, and rot quick. You need lemons or oranges. Those'll do you on a ship voyage good. Plums are a waste of money.*

Fest took another long drink of wine.

Seth loved burning things. He was thirteen winters old, and setting fire to ants with his own homemade matches. Baba slapped him when he did this. She was too ancient to hurt anyone with her slaps.

Seth burned leaves, too. He burned bushes. He piled pinecones up and set fire to them. He never flinched when the fringe of the pinecones cracked and popped, and the pile fizzled in explosions.

He didn't smile, either.

He burned outhouses a couple times, but they stank to raise the village against him.

He stopped doing these things, where people could see, after about a year. I never asked why because I was young, and he was old, and I didn't care. I don't know if, or why, he had stopped.

I just know that he carried those matches and that vial of burning liquid all the way south. He sold his ceremonial hunting gear and his heavy clothes to eat. He did not sell the vial or the matches. To impress a pretty gypsy girl, he breathed fire in her face.

Seth pulled at his curdling red hair. The sweat and heat pushed away the frizz like paint peeling from a humid wall. He had a few coins in his pocket that I had stolen for him, and he thought about buying something. Anything.

A prostitute approached him because of his dreamy eyes. He decided that he was definitely buying. I was not standing next to him to challenge his infidelity to Alastair. His coins were not enough, though. The prostitute walked away.

He saw a building as tall as the tallest pine he had ever seen and he stood at its roots, staring up at the white plaster and black timber that reached up to the center of the sky. He kept walking through this city, eyes as big as the sun, until nightfall.

He didn't sleep that night. He walked. He told me all about this later, and said he didn't sleep. He told me that he believed he was dreaming, and if he slept he'd wake up in the mountains and the demons of the milkweed would laugh at him. He walked and walked, until his feet burned like hallucinations. He sat down and watched the purple sunrise warm into the full morning flame through the tall plaster and stone.

Alastair-of-the-Wheat had awoken, but he ignored her eye for all the little things beneath.

Days passed.

He saw street performers in the marketplace juggling, performing magic tricks, and dancing. The street performers were mostly gypsies with darker skin, but still slanted eyes. Sometimes a gypsy had the kinked hair of a mercenary. These vagabonds were refugees from Rhianna, the defeated nation. The gypsies danced with whirling ribbons, like painting wind.

On an overturned cart with absent wheels, one gypsy woman danced with red, yellow, and green ribbons. She spun her lithe body like a tumbling cat, and her feet kicked high. Her light dress rippled. Her shoes had hard soles that thumped out a rhythm on the overturned cart that was a steady heartbeat pounding away: *ba-thum*, kick, *ba-thum*, kick, *ba-thum* . . .

A crowd moved through the marketplace, and paused a little to watch her dance. They tossed coins onto the cart. The gypsy woman spun and whirled and kicked her legs high in the air, and the ribbons painted love letters to the crowd. Sometimes she stopped to catch her breath, but her arms still spun the ribbons. She caught the eye of a man and smiled. She had the thick lips of a mercenary girl, but the high cheekbones of a Proliuxian. Her eyes were huge and round, like river mud crystallized into dark, clean jewels.

(Were they green? Were they brown? Blue? Her eyes are black now, but they used to have a color like clean jewels.)

She jumped down from her cart, and spun wildly at the crowd. Her feet snapped in the air, and the wind of it pushed men back. She found the shoulders of a young man. He smiled and let her guide him into the whirling dance. He let her dance around him. The ribbons licked across his body. When the gypsy girl spun away, he reached into his pocket for a large coin, and tossed the coin onto the cart.

This gypsy is Staf Sru Korinyes. She danced in spurts, stopping to drink cheap wine, and gather the coins on the cart. The coins disappeared into her magnificent, rippling dress.

Seth pushed his way to the front of the crowd. Instead of tossing coins, he reached into one of his own pockets. He pulled out a vial. He popped the lid off, and poured the liquid under his tongue.

In another pocket he kept long matches. Long matches were an item only shamans carried. Everyone else used flint. Even Seth used flint when he traveled.

He told me in Tsuin when I asked him about the matches that he kept the matches on him all the time with that vial, because it would scare off thieves.

Really? I said. I didn't believe him.

He made a sound in his throat: *Mm.*

Staf Sru Korinyes began her dance. Her ribbons whirled in the air.

She danced like this for a few minutes, and then jumped from the wagon. Down to the crowd, she moved toward a rich old man, who had paused to watch. He smiled at her approach and let her pull him from the crowd.

Seth stepped in, and swiped the match across the old man's scabbard. The fire flashed to life. Staf Sru Korinyes kept dancing, but jumped back and around to get the old man away from the white stranger.

Seth held the lit match in the air. He lifted it up, and blew over it. A ball of orange flame blew next and the sick smell like dry grease poured from the smoke.

The crowd gasped. They had never seen anyone breathe fire before.

Staf Sru Korinyes stumbled and fell and jumped back onto her wagon. She looked angrily at Seth. Seth smiled at Staf Sru Korinyes. He blew again and fire shot up into the sky. Then Seth placed the burning head of the long match inside of his mouth. He pulled it out and puffed a giant black cloud of smoke. He bent his head back, and stuck out his tongue. Tongues of fire danced, harmlessly.

Coins flew in Seth's direction. The crowd cheered for more. Seth gave them more. He turned with a smile to Staf Sru Korinyes. He gestured with his hand at her, beckoning her closer to him.

Staf Sru Korinyes threw a sharp rock. It smacked above Seth's left eye. Seth touched his eye with shock. He pulled his hand down and saw blood. He cocked his head and looked up at her. She threw another rock. Seth blocked that rock with his hand.

During the new moon, shamans dance and breathe fire and belch smoke to urge the Goddess to keep her blind eye open. Did you know that's why they do it? Seth told me that and I laughed at him.

It never worked on the Goddess. We do it anyway. So many ceremonies never work, but we keep doing them. Seth never had the chance to do that dance.

Seth knew how to make matches from wood, particular kinds of dirt, and manure. He knew how to make the liquid from coal and alcohol and fatty roots.

When Staf Sru Korinyes ran out of rocks, she tried cursing. Her hands gestured in the air. She approached with flailing arms and a whirling tongue.

Seth tried to speak but he didn't have the words. He couldn't remember the Proliuxian words. He tried soothing her with gentle coos.

She punched him in the eye.

Smoke still simmered from his lips. He spat a small spurt of fire, and she jumped away. She took off into the marketplace, and he ran as best he could after her.

He couldn't run well. He had a whispering limp when he walked, and the limp shouted when he ran. The market crowd pressed in fierce, though, around their fleeing entertainers, and she couldn't get ahead of him. Her ribbons moved out and in from her body like drapes, never given the chance to fly like a bird's tail.

And Seth still had enough liquid in his mouth to spurt small bursts of fire in his path. The crowd parted in shock and awe, cheering each little puff of smoke.

Seth grabbed Staf Sru Korinyes. He remembered enough Proliuxian to shout, *Wait!*

She slapped him with one hand, and stole his coins with the other. She spat in his face. Seth smirked. He had felt her fingers in his belt, and saw her hand slipping back into her own with the coins.

Even as a young girl I had heard about the older boys. Some will take a no, and leave you. Some will hear no, and laugh at you.

An old friend, whose name I have forgotten, had an older sister. This sister watched out a window to see if Seth was gone yet. She told me, *Go out there and see if Seth is still around. Walk around a bit. He's sneaky.*

Why? I said.

Because you're his niece and he won't bother you, she replied. *You're too young.*

Why will he bother you?

Because I am a girl who is old enough to bother, and I hate what he does.

Seth couldn't have been older then sixteen.

He wrapped a hand around her waist and pulled her close. His breath still stank of brimstone. *Wait, please,* he said. *Pretty girl.*

I am not for sale! she shouted. She slapped him, hard. Seth's head whipped to the side, but he turned back to her, unfazed.

I buy not, he said. *I talk. I talk with pretty girl.*

Your breath stinks, she said. *Get off of me.* She slapped him again. Seth's cheek was red as a sunset.

I will buy talk, he said. *I will buy talk, no more. Just talk. I want talk.*

His arms were strong, even if his breath stank of fire.

Staf Sru Korinyes was trapped in the arms of a dragon from the far north. She knew it, too. *We talk then,* she said. *Let go.* She sighed. I do not know how many times an insistent man has demanded her affections, but none had the terrifying breath, and alien white skin.

Seth let go. *You are pretty girl,* he said.

She rolled her eyes. *Can you afford me?* she said. *Conversations are expensive.*

Seth cocked his head. He said, *What?*

Money, said Korinyes, *Do you have money?*

Seth smirked. He pointed at her hand. Seth dipped his hand down into her belt. She squirmed and slapped him again.

Seth wanted to tell her that as a man with many pockets, he knew when one had been invaded, and knew where it had gone.

No taking, he said, *don't take me again, just talk. Just pay money for talk.*

Staf Sru Korinyes frowned. *You scare me.*

You scare me, he said. Seth smiled. *I want to show.* He opened his dusty cloak. Dozens of pockets with dozens of mysterious objects, sewn into the lining, and the cloak looked like a peacock's tail in dusty gray. Korinyes was surprised at that. He reached into a pocket and pulled out his vial of fire and another match. He took a small bit of the liquid in his mouth. Then he lit the match with his thumb. Staf Sru Korinyes trembled at this, and backed away.

Seth wrapped an arm around her, and forced her to stay. He

planted his lips on hers. She bucked and kicked. Seth stayed only for a moment.

Korinyes pushed back and slapped him again. She cursed and cursed.

Seth placed the match near her angry lips. Little spurts of fire puffed into the air.

You talk bad, said Seth, *You make fire words.*

She jumped back. She covered her mouth with both her hands. Her eyes opened as wide as her gasping mouth. Her heart raced in her ears. She cocked her head. She dropped her hands.

Seth held the match in the air, casually. Korinyes leaned forward and blew on the match. Little tongues of fire flew out from her breath. The fire fell like rain on the cobblestones. She opened her eyes in wonder.

You are pretty girl, he said, *pretty fire girl.*

Seth placed the match into his mouth, and his mouth lit up with fire. He puffed burning rings that drifted away like ghosts. Korinyes took the match from his hands and blew on it. Fire arced out from her lips. It caught the edge of one of her ribbons and began to burn. She yelped and tore it off her dress. It smoldered on the street.

A crowd had formed. They cheered Seth's display. Seth swallowed fire, and spat it out again, a miracle. More coins appeared.

Staf Sru Korinyes watched as coins piled up on the ground, more than she had ever made dancing and picking the pockets of the dazzled men.

Money, then. She saw the fire pouring from his lips, and the sparkling fire turned into coins upon the ground. Could a street woman like this see anything else in a man?

Seth looked at Staf Sru Korinyes and saw something else, though. I don't know what. A woman can never understand a man's heart. Maybe he fell in love.

I doubt it, considering what happened later, but maybe he loved her body, dancing. He probably loved that, even in the end. I think she even loved him, if only because he was around, and she wasn't used to having a man around more than the night.

But this is all a waste of time. Both of them are dead now, and I am forcing meaning on their ghosts so you and I, dear Esumi, can say their love is not like ours. Darling, I cannot write of these two without your face in my heart. I love you, Esumi. I love you so much. And you go away from me. Would you kill me too? I hope you wouldn't. Korinyes thought she knew he wouldn't.

And now I think they loved each other, and the world tore them apart. That's what I think right now. When I get there, I don't know what I will think.

A man danced awkwardly, with white hands and a black mask, wearing black robes that stood out against his white skin, and breathing fire. A woman as vivid as a beautiful girl danced around the flames in red and orange ribbons. The two kissed and she breathed fire for a time. She wrapped the fire around her ribbons.

I wrap a fire around the cold in my room. I roll over to dream of you and smoke. My chest burns, but I think it is really only that you are away from me, Esumi. It isn't disease. It is distance.

My cough is thick with blood. I discard a whole sheet of vellum because I cough a gob of my thick, pink blood onto it. Words it isn't, but a story is told. I may not finish writing all the letters I desire, and the blood tells the story of Alastair-of-the-Wolf, sharpening her teeth on my pages.

We found him—I found him—at a marketplace, in a black mask. He spat puffs of fire into the air as casually as pipe smoke. He hopped about the crowd, splashing weak fire into thrilled, squealing bodies. Staf Sru Korinyes danced, too. Her fire moved in and out of her ribbons. Sometimes her ribbons caught fire. She let them drop from her body, and singe and twist in the ocean breeze. More ribbons appeared from her mysterious pockets.

Adel and I were passing through this marketplace. We stopped at every vendor and asked about a light skinned man, with red hair. The conspiracy of silence continued.

At a nut stand, I turned to watch the street performers. A juggling act tossed flashing blades in the air. A thin man with a fat mustache laughed and laughed with the flying swords.

I looked a little further at a larger crowd down the street. I saw smoke in the air.

Adel pointed at Seth. *I saw that one already,* she said. *He wears a mask and breathes fire. Quite spectacular. I've never seen anything like it. A human dragon, they say.*

I cocked my head and walked toward the black puffs of smoke. The crowd roared with laughter and gasped with shock. The crowd collected like sediment in the human river. It clung to the fringe of this clump, and other particles drifted away, back to the flow. I pressed forward.

I pushed and shoved my way through the crowd. I saw him. I saw fire. I saw a perversion of our winter solstice ceremony. Him dancing and dancing on his limping leg with the flames and a woman who is not Alastair.

Adel was behind me somewhere, in the crowd. The weight of cinnamon-stained bodies pressed into us both. I shoved and shoved. People shouted.

I shoved.

I fell into an empty circle. Seth spewed a red rainbow into the sky. Staf Sru Korinyes gathered coins while her feet danced into the sky.

He looked down at the crowd, all of them and him, all smiling.

Not me. I stared with my sensei's eyes. His gaze fell on me.
He dropped the match. He ran.
I chased.

StafSru Korinyes lived at the top tower of a ruined temple, unreclaimed by the amorphous city. She grew up on her feet, I think. She learned to dance from her mother, she had said. She had no father that she knew. All Korinyes knew of her father was her kinky black hair, her deeper brown skin, and her full lips.

Adel might as well be a gypsy, too. Adel left Proliux and their arrogant dragonslayers to Rhianna and the service of the dragon. She joined the paladins and hunted murderers and fought against those black monsters that appeared in waves at the city gates. The swords on her arms tell the story of her initiation, and the scars and the burned ear tell the rest of her work in the war.

Rhianna fell, and Adel was in Proliux, wealthy and alone. That story was too painful to wear. Too painful for me to even attempt to describe to you, Esumi. I can only tell you later about her own words.

Korinyes came to this city for a painful reason, too. Her mother knew too much pride to raise a child of rape in a raped city. She could not bear to kill the child.

This was long ago, before the Rhiannan nobility sold their dragon to Proliux for the arquebuses of the island empire, and the empire's own mercenaries, at such a high cost of blood. This was a time when the villages kept watch with the temple bells to ring and flee when black bodies emerged from the cliffs. She talked about these times and Adel nodded. Adel's eyes stared into the fire.

Fest frowned. *Your people's weakness is not our concern,* he said. *Do you think Proliux never hired their own black men to tear down your villages? And their armies conquer you, and take over, and miraculously the mercenary wars end?* Fest balled up his fists and pounded them on the deck. My grandfather's golem looked up from his bonds at Fest, saw conversational anger, and returned to his blank stare and a small dinner.

Fest shouted in a whisper, *Empires are dirty things. Men are dirty things. If you think so sadly of these few bad, black men, you are naïve.*

Adel brushed hair from her eyes. *Empires are only dirty because of the filthy men at the top.*

Korinyes touched Fest's tense arm. She stroked his arm, and his fists relaxed. She looked into his dark eyes. *Violence is never an answer,* she said. *Violence makes violence makes death and sorrow. After so much violence, at least the dragonslayers bring a peace. The emperor ordered his own death, or so we are told.*

Seth said nothing through all of this. He ran his hand through Korinyes's hair. He nibbled the blackened fish the sailors had caught in a net. The sailors had tossed a net over the side of the boat and trailed it around the boat while the ship stayed at anchor. The fish they had captured they sold to passengers. Adel paid for everything we ate. Adel paid for everything.

Seth stared at Korinyes's flickering profile in the firelight.

My grandfather didn't say anything either. He stared down at his ropes, or down at his dinner. I had tied him down to the deck enough to paralyze a full-grown bison, even though he would never run away. I did it so the other people on the boat wouldn't toss him overboard in the night.

He ate fish with his hands lashed together. His purple legs would probably hurt, if he was still alive. He wore a high collar to hide the death blow in his throat. Grandfather's golem tossed bones into the fire with the flick of a wrist. I asked him why he never spoke.

He looked up at me and grunted. *In the mountains, I had nobody to talk to. I lived alone,* he said. He took another bite. He tossed another little bone. *Leave me be, girl,* he said, *Kill me for good, or leave me be.*

Seth shook his head at me.

I nodded.

The ocean was around us. Other passengers on the sea voyage sprawled around their own fires, having their own conversations. They docked at their little islands of light on the dark night deck, and drifted away, unanchored, into dreams.

I asked Fest why, on every ship, everyone lived on deck.

Too hot, he said. *Below deck, it gets too dirty, and too hot. On deck, in shade, we can get by. We toss our trash overboard and stay clean.*

Oh, I said.

He looked up at the moon. *I used to fight on the oceans, when I was young. An awful place to fight. Nowhere for anyone to run away,* he said. *Nobody knows what the battle really looks like. Too loud to hear your own Mardar coming. A horrible place to fight.*

I sat against a wall. Fest sat next to me. Seth and Korinyes were on the other side of the fire. Adel sat between Seth and me. Grandfather's golem was farther back from the fire, between Fest and Korinyes. Fest sat sideways to keep grandfather's golem in the corner of his eyes. The ocean rolled beneath us. Our ship cut at the night waves like my dagger through black foam.

Adel had given me a dagger by now. I twirled it just to do something with my hands. I sipped very bad, watered-down red wine from a large cask that emerged from belowdecks like a parade float with sixteen sailors holding it on their backs. That is the flavor of sea voyages. Bitter, gritty, and warm. I missed the dagger. Fest had snatched it from the air above my hand.

Fest Fasen looked at me. *This is not a toy, girl. Put it away or kill someone,* he said. *Don't drink and play with it. You'll lose a finger.*

I snatched the dagger from his hands. His fingers clenched over empty air. I sipped my wine. *If you tell me what to do again, or call me a girl again,* I said, *you'll be the one losing fingers.*

Fest laughed.

I sipped my wine. I twirled the dagger in the air to keep my hands busy.

My grandfather's golem stared into the fire. He never spoke unless spoken to first. He ate fish and tossed bones into the flames. He smelled like rotting meat because he was dead. This was the last time I remember seeing him eat.

Staf Sru Korinyes followed Seth out of the marketplace, and followed me as I chased him. She was astonished he had up and left. She was behind me. She saw my brown hair bouncing in the wind, my white skin around the edges of my dress.

Seth ran for the broken tower, Korinyes's home. I was at his heels. I was so close that I smelled the fire in his wake. I reached out for the seam on his hood. I reached out my hand a little farther. He turned fast. He ducked around a fat woman. My hand touched her hair. She turned. I was gone, past her. He leaped around a cart. I slowed at the side of the cart. Oranges. Seth leaped into an alley. A door slammed in the alley. I jumped around the oranges. I found myself in the same alley. He was already gone.

I was between two buildings, both decayed, both solid stone, both temples, once. Staf Sru Korinyes placed a small knife at my throat. *Who are you?*

I grabbed her wrist. I threw her over my shoulder and twisted her hand to release the blade from her grip. I didn't break her arm. *Where he go?* I said *Seth!*

She squealed. I pressed into her wrist more. She pointed at one of the buildings, of decrepit yellow stones. I let go, and dropped her knife. I jumped past her.

I never trust a stranger in a wristlock. I entered the building that she hadn't pointed at. This one was a crumbling marble tower.

A temple once, to a fertile god. Gargoyles around the rafters had giant phalluses, and horns. They held things in their hands, fruit or animals or people, all eroded together into stone. Some of the phalluses were snapped off and lay on the floor like fossilized caterpillars. White ants carved into the stone covered the walls. Some of them were real and crawled along like tiny black dots. I think they were ants. I didn't get close enough to see.

A single stone phallus at the altar, in the center of the old temple, was cracked down the center. Half of it lay on the altar; the other half teetered precariously in the sky. Past that, wooden stairs swirled up to a tower. Of course, this temple would have a tall tower.

I climbed the tower up and up. Beneath me, I heard Adel, calling my name. Staf Sru Korinyes called out, too, to her lover. I ignored them both.

At the top of the stairs, the tower opened up into a wide room, with broken walls. A cool wind blew off the ocean. I could see the ocean over Seth's shoulder. Past the ocean, I could see land: the continent. Seth stood before the destroyed wall, facing out to a long fall. He had removed his hood. His hair was short and chopped back to barely the length of a child's thumb. It was rough cut, and un-flattering.

You found me, then, he said. *You found me.*

A breeze lifted my hair off my head, and around my eyes. It was so cool. I said in our shared language, *I have looked for you every day I have been here.*

Why look for me? he said in Proliuxian. *Why waste your time like that?*

It is my duty, I said in Alamedan.

Zhan . . . Zhan . . . His lips still stank of fire. *It's hopeless. We'll never find him,* he said. *How can we follow anyone's trail in this gigantic city? We're already dead to our village. We're already replaced. Kyquil has already sent to Tsuin for another shaman. We're dead. Let's just stay dead. Look at this place.* His hand gestured to the gaping hole in the wall. *Look at this amazing place,* he said.

I found you, I said.

Adel and Korinyes came up from the stairwell.

Get out of my house, all of you! shouted Korinyes. *You too, Seth!*

I looked around the room. A bed of bright colors. A small fountain of fresh water. Piles of belongings, in messy heaps. Seth looked down below him, on the other side of the window. A small vein of smoke slipped from his lips, dancing like Korinyes's ribbons into the sky. He coughed fire.

I hate you more than I hate him, I said.

I know. I wish you would just leave me here.

The shepherd boy who was the messenger left me after we reached the village. Have I ever told you my village's name? We always called it the village, but in the codices and maps of Lord Tsui's libraries in Tsuin, our village was called Bear. I had never seen a Bear but once in my life and I saw it with Adel and not with the village.

The shepherd boy walked me past the first house. Then he shouted out that he had returned with me. He sounded like a cow lowing in pain, and he loped ahead with long, awkward strides. *We're here! Seth! Tellis! Kyquil! Da!*

People emerged from their little houses. In Alamedan villages near mountains, all the houses of everyone stayed close together, to help each other through the winter. Farmers and herders left in the frigid dark of early morning for their fields far away. Bodies emerged from houses: women. Women stayed home. Women watched me, unwaving, unsmiling. Hearty women, with heavy hearts.

Partridge was here somewhere, tending sheep and singing. I didn't see him. Later on, when we came back to the village and found him alone sleeping in an empty house and too hungry to sing, Seth would cock his head. Seth would try to make sense of the fool's words. I didn't see him until then.

Now, at that moment in time, when I came home to my village with the shepherd boy, and the women emerged from their houses, I looked at the houses where no one emerged. These houses used to be my family's.

My mother's house. I walked toward it with heavy feet. My heart bumped into my ribs and rattled to break free into the empty rooms of the house. I could hear it in my ears. My house was a small cabin. Three little rooms, and a door that hung open. It swung gently in the breeze. The hinges creaked like groaning.

I peaked into the house. My eyes adjusted for the dark. I did not enter.

On the wooden floor, old stains. Blood in brown footprints. The large brown outlines walked casually out the back door. I did not follow them, yet.

Staf Sru Korinyes and Seth lived in this crumbling tower over the city. In a soft feather bed they slept pressed into each other. His hands across her back in the morning. Her hands across his face at night. In the wall, a chipped marble fountain. Once, I imagine priests and priestesses washed their faces in this small fountain. Now, Seth and Korinyes splashed this water on their bodies to wipe the sweat away. They both drank.

The night wind sent shivers up their naked backs. The hole in the wall had a view of the dotting street lamps of the city all the way to the sea. On the other side of the ocean, the land and more dotting lights.

Where do the stars begin? she asked. She wrapped her arms around his waist. They stared out this crumbled hole at the top of the tower.

I know not, he said.

He could smell her everywhere. Long strands of black hair curled like serpents with broken backs and wandered the room in the sea wind. He could smell the ocean, too. He could watch the boats in the morning, before the two lovers went to the marketplaces to breathe fire and dance. He sat near the hole in the wall. He mixed his potent potions over a small candle with pig fat and dried mountain herbs. He had a second vial, for her. She used to keep perfume in it. He had poured the perfume out onto her body one night. In the morning, he had picked the vial up, and had filled it to the brim with his fire potion.

When did love occur? At what precise moment can I say they must have believed in their own love, through this haze of lusty routine? I heard them describe their time together at nightfall in the mountains. We still had Khali left from the city. We hadn't fought snow yet. We drank Khali and huddled against the biting cold around the first milkweed fire. Instead of demons, Seth Immur and Staf Sru Korinyes saw love. The fires in their bellies and their noses recalled to other fires. They spoke in pieces, one drifted off into the haze and the other picked up until drifting off. A pause. Then more.

I listened. Fest fell asleep right away, holding the rope of my grandfather's wide-eyed golem. Fest snored and his steel teeth flashed green in the milkweed firelight. Adel sipped a little Khali.

Staf Sru Korinyes told me about when she knew. She had wrapped his hair into a long braid, as I had done before, but this time, she had pulled it tight, and had snipped the hair away. Then, she had glued the two ends together with heat and ship's black pitch. She had created a loop of red hair rope. She had placed it over his shoulders.

He had smiled at her. He had picked it off his shoulders. Then, he had placed it upon hers. *You keep it,* he had said. *I am yours.*

Adel listened to Staf Sru Korinyes tell her story. She sipped her Khali, and stared into the fire with her astonishing kaleidoscopic eyes. They fuzzed and blurred behind the milkweed smoke. Demons. *A gift? A little gift is all?* she said. *You, beggar, fell in love because he gave you a gift, and men did not give you gifts before without wanting your body in return. Had he had you yet? Had he?*

Staf Sru Korinyes frowned at Adel. For a while no one spoke.

Seth whispered something into Staf Sru Korinyes's ear. They kissed softly. His hand reached under her shirt. Smoke blew up around us, despite our windbreaks. Demons. I looked away.

Seth spoke so all could hear. *I fell in love when I saw you dancing. I fell in love right away, Korinyes,* he said. *I saw you dancing and I had never seen anything so beautiful. I could see your soul in your dance. I loved it right away.*

Adel said nothing. Her eyes fell shut and she fell back to the ground, and slept. I stood up and tossed a blanket over her. She nestled underneath it. In the morning I asked her of what she dreamed. She looked at me with a frown. *You told me I'd dream of demons,* she said. *I did. My demons are my own, Zhan. You wouldn't tell me of your demons, would you?*

I would if you asked, I said.

I never do, she replied.

Kyquil's wife barely fit through the doorway while carrying a baby on each hip. She wore no sandals. Her hard feet were accustomed to the beat of rocks and sticks. She had a mole on her bulbous nose, with giant black hairs growing out of it.

I choked up when I saw her adjusting through her doorway. She was a mother.

She said that Kyquil and Seth had already started on my grandfather's track as much as they could. They took it out to the edge of the fields, and journeyed a little farther every day, to keep after his trail. They'd be back at nightfall. I could wait for them in her kitchen, and warm my feet by her fire. I could warm my belly with her food.

I sat at her table. She talked about the funerals. The bodies were all burned together, and Seth sang hymns and danced. He had the old limp that bugged him after a while, but he could dance better than Baba could.

Then Kyquil's wife hummed to herself one of the songs sung to babies and corpses. Alastair's lullaby. Her voice was gorgeous. The road had been long. My eyelids drooped while a baby gurgled in her arms. Just before I lost sight of them all, I thought the child was my brother, and still alive. Kyquil's wife began to sing . . .

> *Sleep comes for us all*
> *Eyelids always fall*
> *Make your days thick*
> *To lose them quick*

I hummed the song to Seth to remind him of home. He was still awake. We stayed, all four of us, in that ruined tower. Staf Sru Korinyes slept in her bed, alone. Her hand lingered over the empty space beside her. Adel slept in a chair near the fountain. I slept on the hard floor. I woke up once in the night, because I slept light and I felt him walking over the floor. I saw Seth at the window, staring and pacing.

I stood up silently. I hummed the melody. He turned to me.

He nodded. *We have to find him*, he whispered, *don't we?*

I kept singing. I nodded.

And after that, then what? he said. *Will you hound me forever?*

I shook my head. *No*, I said. *Just fulfill your duty. Find him. Kill him. The village has a new shaman by now. Adel and I had a good hint from a woman. She told us he was working with a very powerful family. We can find him.*

Powerful family? he said. *I've heard about the dragonslayers. We'll get killed.*

Dragonslayers? I have not heard of them at all. Maybe we will get killed, I said. *We'll see what Adel thinks we should do.*

Where did you find her? he said. He pointed at Adel's small body. Her face hung loose in her sleep. Her scarred skin hung off her face like it didn't quite fit on her bones.

She found me, I said. *I trust her.*

Maybe she'll kill us first, he said.

Maybe . . . What's her name? Orynpis? Yesniriss? Maybe she will.

Korinyes. Staf Sru Korinyes. He shrugged. *I trust Korinyes. I'll watch your back if you watch mine.*

Don't give up this time, I said. *Never give up, Uncle Seth. I'll kill you if you give up. If you give up, you get in my way, and I'll have to kill you.*

I'm surprised you didn't kill me this time.

How do you know I won't?

You don't bargain with people you're going to kill, do you? he said. *I don't imagine you would.*

In the morning, Seth and Adel were awake, talking in low murmurs. Korinyes had migrated across the bed, into the territory Seth had abandoned. She was still asleep, her beautiful face at peace upon Seth's pillows.

I don't think Seth slept at all that night. He had rings under his eyes, and an edge like drunkenness to the tension in his walk.

I woke up from the floor. I frowned at the last sleeper. We needed to start hunting. No hunter dared sleep in so late. I prodded Korinyes. She moaned softly. Seth and Adel looked at Korinyes and me. Korinyes stretched and sat up. Then she opened her eyes and saw us all. Her body sank. She pulled the covers back around her and bit her lip.

We plotted over breakfast and bitter cinnamon tea. We needed a mercenary, because courtiers always had mercenaries—Adel said that, and Korinyes agreed. We would hire the bodyguard to present ourselves as foreign nobility before the courts. Then we would demand knowledge and see if we could find any.

Staf Sru Korinyes had spent a long time alone in this tower before Seth forced himself into her life. Back then, she woke up alone, with the sun on her face. She stretched her arms and yawned. She bathed herself in the pool of water that poured from the fountain that never ran out. She drank cool fruit juices from the venders' stalls and ate fresh bread, alone. She was never really alone, because of the things inside of her. She moved around the city, searching for new places and new corners. She looked both ways before placing a hand upon a wall. She left tiny pieces of herself everywhere she traveled, in secret.

I will tell you about her, after you know her like I knew her.

When Korinyes woke up and stretched her arms over her head and saw all these people in her room, she ducked back under her covers. She looked over at Seth. I watched one of her hands slip under the mattress for something heavy. I thought it was a knife. I casually walked over toward her bed to go to the fountain from the gap in the wall. I looked down into the sheets, ready to take the knife from her, but it wasn't a knife.

Underneath the covers, she clutched a silver hand mirror. When I looked down, my reflection looked back. Around my face, silver ants chased each other in a circle, and down the handle. Silver ants sparkled where the sun slipped through the silk sheets. She looked toward her lap, quickly adjusted her hair, and then slipped the silver mirror back under the mattress. She was hiding it from us, expecting thievery. I suspect that she hid the mirror from Seth, too. He never mentioned it.

Korinyes listened in on Seth and Adel speaking of mercenaries. She agreed that one was necessary to make any appearance among nobility. She kissed Seth. She ran a hand over his short, red hair.

I took a long drink from the fountain, my hands cupped tight. Afterwards, I looked down at my reflection in the rippling pool. It still looked like me. I hadn't seen my own face in a long time. I ignored the silver mirror where it hid, and I don't think I ever saw it again through the whole journey.

Adel asked Korinyes for tea. Korinyes frowned. *I don't keep tea here,* she said.

Why not? said Adel.

Korinyes leaned into Seth. *We don't need it. No one ever bothers us. This is our little world, and we don't drink tea.*

Adel shrugged. *Well, we shouldn't stay here long, anyway. Please, get dressed and we'll go get some tea.*

Korinyes shook her head. *I am dressed. I'm no rich one like you, with many fine clothes to choose from.*

Then, we shall leave immediately. We are near a fine tea house.

They won't let me in, said Korinyes. *They won't let Seth or me in. We're gypsies.*

If you behave, they will let you in, especially if you are with me, said Adel. She looked over at me and gestured toward the door. *I'm not going to stand here in this ruin a moment more when I could be drinking tea. This tower could collapse at any moment. Every breeze is dangerous.*

It's fine here, said Korinyes. *I've lived here for years.*

I'm sure it suits your needs adequately. Since it does not have tea, it does not suit my needs at all. Do you even have food here?

I have what I need, and you are not a welcome guest, so I will not share it with you.

Then we shall leave immediately, said Adel. *Seth, I presume you will be joining me?*

I'll be right there, he said.

Adel gestured at me. We stepped into the stairwell. We closed the door behind us.

Once in the stairwell, Adel pressed her finger over her lips. I nodded. We both leaned into the wooden door, listening through the cracks.

Who is the girl, again?
My niece.
And the other one?
I don't know.
Are you leaving me?
No, Korinyes. I could never leave you.
You're lying.
I want you to come with me. I want to stay with you forever.
Forever is a long time.
It isn't enough time for us. I wish I could be with you more than forever.

I rolled my eyes. Adel did nothing. She kept listening.

Esumi, you have promised me forever, too. Where are you now? You choose an empire over your own heart. This pain that I endure everyday, where you are missing, is more painful than any cough.

We are divided at the heart. When we hold each other, we are slowly healed. When we are apart we bleed to death. I cough blood, and I cough blood, and I cough blood.

Do you remember these lips? They are red all the time, like fresh spring berries because they are always covered in the blood of longing.

In Kyquil's house I dreamed of blood and blood and blood. I dreamed of all my rider sisters swimming in blood, bathing in it, and diving down below into the red depths of the blood. I don't know where the blood came from.

I walked on top of the blood with Baba's walking stick. I looked for the source. Each person I encountered in the sea smiled and laughed at me. They claimed the blood wasn't theirs.

In the end, I brushed a hand across my stomach, and it was blood from my navel. I was bleeding. The blood was mine.

I couldn't seal the source. When I woke up, it felt like I was dying.

I had the same dream in Korinyes's house. This time, though, the sea was full of Proliuxian people. The street vendor who only fed me his worst spat thick gobs of blood at me. The other porters full of spite splashed me with the blood before I could ask them anything. For miles and miles I walked across the blood. I saw everyone angry at me. Seth, Kyquil, the shepherd boy, Adel, Korinyes, and everyone.

I used my hand to catch a dagger thrown by Seth himself, and I found the source of the blood. It was me. I woke up, and felt like I was about to kill Seth for stabbing me.

I saw Seth and Adel standing in the sun, speaking in low murmurs. Korinyes was still asleep.

Korinyes had no tea in her room. Adel took us around the corner and down three blocks to a street café. Suddenly we were in a wealthy neighborhood, surrounded by folk who wore trimly tailored clothes. The women revealed only their faces to the street. The men wore vests, in all manner of shape, size, and color. Each man or woman was followed by at least two others, dressed in steel and black. These jangling dogs were armed. Nearly all were the darkest-skinned mercenaries.

We lounged casually in a café. No one sat next to us.

Adel quickly flashed her sword tattoo to the waiter. He nodded. The swords disappeared up Adel's sleeves. The waiter offered us a strip of paper with writing on it. Adel glanced at the paper, and pushed it back toward the waiter. That was the menu, but apparently it was rude to order off of the menu. I think it was the menu, anyway.

Bring us all tea, she said. *Also, some break fast. Something light. Whatever you think is best for us, darling.*

The waiter brought us tiny sweet rolls with thick fruit frosting on them. They tasted like honey and spring.

Staf Sru Korinyes sipped her tea slowly. *Who's paying for this, Paladin?* she said. *And why am I allowed to sit in this café with you?*

Adel shook her head. *Shh. Drink your tea,* she said. *Don't call me Paladin. Call me Adel. That's my name.*

Staf Sru Korinyes nibbled on a roll. *Too sweet,* she mumbled, and put the roll down onto a cloth napkin. *Is that your only name?* said Korinyes. *Haven't you got more to it than that? Just Adel? I mean, my name is Staf Sru Korinyes, and I'm a gypsy and not a paladin.*

Adel cocked an eyebrow. *How fortunate for you. Jardan Bosch Adel is my whole name.*

Staf Sru Korinyes leaned back. *Jardan, you say? And a servant of the dragon?* Her rapturous voice twittered shrill. *What do you do with these two strangers?* she said. *What gain is in it for you, Jardan?*

You ask such questions at a meal I provide for you, gypsy? said Jardan Bosch Adel, *Drink your tea, girl, before it gets cold.*

Korinyes placed the tea on the table. She pushed it away. *I'm hardly a girl for at least a decade, paladin. And, I do not like cinnamon at all,* said Staf Sru Korinyes. *I only drank to be polite.*

At least you are trying to be polite, said Adel. *What do you like to drink in the morning?*

I prefer not to drink anything, said Korinyes. *I prefer to have an honest conversation first thing in the morning. Instead of breakfast, I prefer to wonder at what my morning company is up to.*

In your case, I can see how morning company can be a more pressing concern than breakfast, said Jardan Bosch Adel, *since your morning company may often desire you for breakfast.*

Staf Sru Korinyes scowled. She stood up and mashed her unfinished roll into her plate.

Seth raised his hands at the two women. He shook his head. *Why fight? Why?* said Seth. *Sit down, Korinyes. She talks of me and true, I do like you for breakfast. I prefer you to food always.* Seth gently coaxed Korinyes back into her seat.

Korinyes crossed her legs and raised her hand to the waiter.

The waiter with the mustache appeared next to Staf Sru Korinyes. *Is there a problem?* he said to Adel.

Adel nodded. *My guest does not like cinnamon or things that are too sweet. She was going to eat them anyway to be polite, but I insist on bringing her exactly what she wants.*

My apologies, madam, I chose wrong for you, said the waiter. He bowed his head and looked genuinely sad.

Your choice was excellent for everyone else, said Adel. *Only she did not like it.*

The waiter turned to Korinyes. *My dearest apologies, madam. I should have known you would prefer something less saccharine. Here is a menu.* The waiter handed a sheet of paper to Korinyes. *Please, select whatever you want,* he said. *I will bring it out to you as soon as it is ready.*

Staf Sru Korinyes took the paper and sat down. She looked at it. She pointed at one of the globs of strange letters. *Bring me that, then,* she said. *I'm sure it will be better.*

The waiter cleared his throat. *Madam,* he said, *I thought you said you did not like cinnamon tea.*

Oh, said Staf Sru Korinyes. Her face reddened. She handed the menu back. *Please, just bring me something else. Something plain, please.*

Seth took her hand and kissed it. *What just happened?* he said. *I don't understand. You fight, and then you try to order cinnamon tea?*

Adel took a bite of her roll and swallowed. *Gypsies often can't read*, she said. *Now, are we ready to discuss the problem at hand? Seth, you are a holy man charged with the duty of justice, yes?*

My father, he said, *yes.*

I cannot take you into the council myself. I may be able to get you in. Do you have any holy vestments? Any particular uniform?

Not anymore.

Well, we'll just have to make one up. Nobody's ever heard of your people before, anyway. You will need a bodyguard, too.

I sipped my tea. The words I understood, but I did not understand enough to speak quickly.

He said, *What is a bodyguard?* Seth pointed at me. *Can't she be the bodyguard?*

A mercenary, said Adel, *You will look better in the court if you hire a mercenary.*

A what? said Seth.

You remember what I told you in the room, yes? The men who are very dark skinned, said Adel. *Black. A mercenary. He will protect you and your interests*, she sipped her tea and frowned. *I cannot buy one for you. He will be loyal to me. He must be loyal to you. How much money do you have?*

Not much, said Seth.

Then you won't get much of a mercenary, said Adel, *Still, you need at least one to preserve your life in court. Finish your breakfast. I know where we can find a mercenary. Hopefully, he won't be too old.*

Old? I said.

Adel ignored my question. *Korinyes, I'm sorry if I threaten you.*

I feel threatened because you are a Jardan and a paladin, said Korinyes, *You think me so shallow? I think you are a noble, and you have no motive for this, or for the marks on your arms. You should be in Rhianna bowing like a dog to an empty throne.*

So should you, gypsy. Justice is my motive, said Adel. Rhianna, before the dragon's death, returned to her. She looked at Korinyes with sad eyes. *Always justice. I am a paladin, and I fought for your people with all of my heart and all of my might. It is my hope that my fellow nobility will see past this history and let me in, since the surviving paladins are puppets of proconsuls.*

Who is your puppetmaster, I wonder . . . Don't tell me. I know you would never tell me that. Justice is the motive of heartless people, who protect their gold with the sword, said Korinyes, *and your might was not enough.*

Adel sipped her tea again. She took a long bite of her sweet roll. She chewed slowly. We three looked in her scarred face. She said nothing for a long time. She took another bite. Then she sighed. *I will not argue with you a moment more,* said Adel. *I am tired of the past, and there is so much to do in the present.* She turned to Seth. *Do you desire my assistance?* she said.

Yes, he said, looking at me.

Adel nodded. She sipped her tea. *Then you will need a mercenary to do it my way. I know where one or two can be found cheap,* said Adel. She put her tea down gently and reached for another roll. *He will probably be maimed or old or something like that,* she said. *He probably won't have much fight in him.*

I do, I said.

Everyone glanced at me and blinked. I sipped my tea.

The waiter returned with something pitch black that smelled like a stronger, bitterer Khali. He plopped it in front of Korinyes. He also had a different kind of bread in his hand, which he placed on a napkin next to the new drink. He looked down his nose at Korinyes. Korinyes looked at the two new things, and frowned at Adel.

The rest of us ate breakfast, and drank tea.

Korinyes's warm black drink cooled, untouched. Korinyes picked at the roll carefully.

We talked more, until no more food or tea remained. Adel placed large, sparkling coins on the counter and the waiter bowed at her.

I woke up in a bed in Kyquil's house, after I had fallen asleep at his kitchen table to the mother's song. Kyquil had solid stone walls—white rock and jagged clay mortar with clean glass windows like a rich man. I awoke, and I reached a hand to the wall at my side. I touched the cool rock.

Seth and Kyquil and two other men talked in the next room. I sat up and looked around. I was alone. My things were on the floor near the door. My spear, my cloak, my bag of food.

I hadn't seen Seth in years. I crept out of bed. I peeked around the leather flap between the rooms. Kyquil sat like a meaty burlap sack at his table. Seth sat across from him. Seth looked thin next to Kyquil, even though Seth was never thin. Kyquil drank and coughed. Seth ran a finger in and out of the flickering candle flame.

They talked politics in the village. Seth was in charge now, with Baba dead. And Seth had to leave, too. Seth probably would not return.

Kyquil listened to Seth saying these things. He held his head in his hands. He said, *And you want me to take over for a while?*

Yes, said Seth.

Why me? said Kyquil.

Seth shrugged. *Why anyone?* he said. *The women have talked to me, you know. They seem to think you're the one who should do it.*

Just because other people want me to do it? said Kyquil.

It's as good a reason as any, said Seth. His fingers paused above the flame until the fire burned him too much. He pulled his finger away. *I don't know. You don't want to? Don't do it.*

It's just such a huge . . .

No it isn't.

What?

It isn't a huge responsibility, you know. People take care of themselves, said Seth. *All you do is marry 'em, and meet the merchants in spring and fall in Tsuin. If someone dies, you say a few words over somebody's pyre. People take care of themselves, Kyquil. Nice words is all this is.*

What about the ceremonies? he said.

Skip them or have them as you see fit. Do you think the Goddess will frown upon the community for doing its best? You won't have a shaman, at least for a while.

I leaned back in my room. I leaned against a cold stone wall. I listened.

You'll catch him quick, said Kyquil.

No. No, I won't, said Seth. *Those are his mountains. He's had weeks to get ahead of us. I won't catch him. We have to go, but we won't catch him.*

You'll catch him, said Kyquil.

No, my friend, said Seth. *Don't wait long for a new shaman. Don't wait three winters.*

I won't because you'll be back in one, said Kyquil.

You won't because I won't be back, said Seth. *Don't be so naïve.*

Don't be so cynical. Seth, you'll catch him. I know you will. And when you come back with his head we'll all celebrate.

He might come back with mine, you know. I'm no killer. Baba never taught me to fight, if she even knew how. She never needed to. I just hope he lets Zhan live.

Pause.

At that moment, I snatched my spear from the ground. I tossed aside the cloth curtain between rooms.

Kyquil looked up at me.

Seth kept talking, kept running his fingers in and out of the candle flame. *Zhan had no part in this mess,* said Seth, *I hope he lets her . . .*

I threw the spear. Seth blinked. The flame snuffed out beneath his hand, with the top half of the candle. The spear thunked into the wall and trembled.

I scoffed at him. *You're lucky I let you live,* I said. *We'll catch him. I'll catch him if you don't. Get your things. We're going now. We'll return with his head soon.*

Seth stuck his bleeding finger in his mouth in shock. I had barely nicked him, but I had surprised him.

I stepped into the room. Kyquil said nothing. I tugged at my spear. I had thrown it so hard, that it caught inside the clay mortar between the rocks. It took three hard pulls to remove the spear, and the point had shattered like an icicle. Seth sat at the table. Kyquil lifted his broken candle. He drank a cup of water in one swift swig.

The waiter swallowed the black drink with one sip and then one swift swig. I had looked back at him, cleaning the table. He lifted the drink, and sipped it. Then he smirked. Then he chugged. The bread went down in three swift bites. He saw me watching him and winked.

I looked away.

The story of the waiter who had witnessed the death of Argarax is a story I cannot tell you. His ghost isn't here. His face slips in and out of the shadows of the city. An alley cat with new clothes and a new face, watching us move through the streets slips between the cracks of the web, immune to the pull of memory.

I can't remember his skin, or his hands. I don't know if I saw him everyday and failed to see him, or not.

Maybe I only saw him those two times. After the young Argarax was killed, the man was released from his duties and joined his family at their street café among the rich. A simple story preserves Adel.

But when did she call for Tycho's carriage? This could be when she reached out to Tycho with new information. Two foreigners just like the gruff hunter, and in Adel's company, talking about an appearance at court.

I don't like to think about that, but I can only speak with the words of the ghosts. My teeth sink into the husks in my head, and the stylus moves. I must turn to another song.

Someday, when I am dead, I will know Lady Jardan Bosch Adel.

The wolves howled all the first night. My face was pale and I kept my spear in my hands. Seth tossed dried flower leaves onto the fire. They sizzled. He pared away a root with a small knife, and nibbled at it. He gestured to the fire. *That'll keep the wolves away,* he said. *Wolves hate the smell of those herbs, you know. If we live long enough, I'll tell you all about that stuff. Sleep well, Zhan.*

Earlier that day he had gathered chunks of dried meat into a large pack that he then handed to me. We stepped into the sunlight. Kyquil offered us some doe elks to ride. Seth shook his head. *As much as I wish we could, the law is clear on this. We go on our feet to hunt,* he said. *Always on our feet because he moves on his feet. We go to the ends of the earth on his trail.*

We walked past farmlands, and shepherds. They waved sadly. Some of them offered us things. Seth turned them all away. He did it silently. They all nodded silently. The law is clear on this.

When we got to the edge of civilization, one last hill until the mountains, Seth stopped. He turned around. *Look, girl,* he said.

Don't call me girl, I said. *I'm not much younger than you.* I pressed on.

I was a boy to Baba the morning she was killed, said Seth. He reached a hand to my arm.

I shoved it off. I pressed forward. *Baba could call the earth an infant,* I said. *Don't call me girl.*

Zhan, then, said Seth. *Look, Zhan.* He jumped in front of me and pointed. *Get a good look at your home.*

This isn't my home, I said, *and I didn't get to say good-bye to mine. Get your fill of this nonsense. We are on the hunt.*

Fine, said Seth, *the wolves don't stop to enjoy the scenery.* He fell in stride beside me.

Yes they do. A wolf will stop to savor the wind. I've seen it, I said. *Wolves don't discuss it, though. They savor, and they move on quick. After they have captured their prey, they howl and howl.* I didn't look him in the face when I talked. I stared at my boots. *That is when the wolf discusses the beauty of the wind. After the hunt.*

You are my apprentice, girl. Do not try to teach me of the wolves.

I am the wolf. You are the pup.

Don't call me that, I said. *I'm not a girl.*

Girl, I will call you whatever I want, he said. He grabbed my shoulders hard. He spun me around. *Stop. Look.* He pointed at the valley with the village. *We will be dead before we see this again. You're a fool if you think otherwise.*

I don't care what I think, or what you think, I said, staring at him. I refused to look back. *Our duty does not care either. Let's go.*

Look.

No, I said, *I move quick. See if you can keep up with me.*

Hunting men is different from hunting caribou, girl, he said. *Do you know what to do?*

Do you? I said.

I ran away from him. I ran. I rushed past the hill, the whole village at my back. I could feel the whole village watching us leave. I could feel their eyes crying tears to me. I wanted to turn and look and wave. I wanted to scream. I wanted to cry, too.

I had caught a slight glimpse of the village through my lens of anger. It blurred from the corner of my eye. Rolling fields of wheat and corn cut into the woods. Sheep drifting like clouds across open fields of grass in the lower hills. Fruit trees with young children plucking apples and nuts from the branches.

I will see this place again, but Seth was right. We would both never see this again. When next we came to the village.

When we next came to this village, Esumi, only Partridge remained, and stone houses with no windows and no doors and no mothers.

In the woods again, past the last hill. The world curved up toward my face. It seemed to urge me backwards. I wasn't following a trail. I wasn't following anything. I was moving up hill because it pushed me down to the valley and the village. I cried softly. I was alone. I moved as fast as I could through the forest and up the hillside.

I cried and cried. I ducked around trees. I ducked around rocks. I stepped over roots and lizards and past the chirping birds.

I moved around a white boulder. Seth stood on the other side, and I bumped into him.

You're going the wrong way, he said.

I choked back my tears. I couldn't choke back my tears. *Where were you?* I said. I was trying so hard to stop crying.

Seth put a hand on my shoulder. *Zhan,* he said, *I'm sorry. I'm so sorry.*

I threw it off. I punched him in the face.

He fell. His nose bled. *I'm so sorry, Zhan,* he said.

Well show me the right way! I shouted, *Let's go! Where is the right trail?*

Seth pointed west. *He camped out not far from here,* said Seth, *but then he turns east a bit. It's easier to move up these hills from a different angle. There's a wolf trail over there that's a bit easier. Might find some company if the pack's around, but the trip is much easier. Baba taught me to hunt in the woods, for moose and for martins. I've been doing the hunting for her for a long time. I know how to read the tracks of men in the woods and the mountains, too.*

What will you be doing with those horrible women?

I . . . We have to kill someone.

I don't want to kill anyone.

You can come with me. Everywhere I go, you can come.

What did this one do to you, that you must end their life?

He killed many people, many good people. He slaughtered women and children and innocents. He killed his own family. He deserves death.

But, then you will be a killer for killing a killer. You will become what you have destroyed.

No, I just have to find him. Zhan will kill him.

Who? Why her? I don't understand. If this is so important why have you been hiding with me? Let's get out of here!

I wasn't hiding, Korinyes. I was, but I wasn't. Do you trust me?

What?

Do you trust me?

Adel gestured at me. Together we walked down the stairs. We knew he would come down the stairs. We knew he wouldn't try to escape with her. We dashed into the alley outside the ruined temple. We leaned against a wall. We watched the tower for any sign of his flight.

When the two came out from the door, fresh and clean from the little fountain, it was an anticlimax. We took to the streets, and they followed us to the café.

I glanced over my shoulder to make sure he was following us. I watched him walking through the street, unmasked and quiet. Korinyes held his hand, and held my gaze unflinching.

Neither one of them looked happy.

Adel led the three of us to a low building near the docks. She told us that older mercenaries worked on ships, and in the low marketplaces near port. The building was made of cheap pine, and stank of cheap hops. Inside men laughed and laughed, ceramics chinked and shattered. I heard it all through the cracked door.

Adel walked in calmly.

The room did not care, and continued to howl.

Seth and Staf Sru Korinyes remained in the street. Korinyes shook her head. *This is a mistake,* said Korinyes. *She's up to something.*

She's helping us, said Seth. *You don't have to stay.*

Neither do you, said Korinyes.

I have to stay, he said.

Why?

It's my duty, he said.

What are you talking about? Let's just go, she said. *We can go to a new town. They'll love the fire. We can see the whole world with your fire.*

No, Korinyes, he said. *No. I can't go. You can. You can go.*

Please, Seth . . .

I stepped through the door and left them arguing.

Adel winked at me. *About time,* she said. *Is our nobleman coming?*

I shrugged.

Adel was chatting with a sturdy fellow, bald with hefty legs and a round belly. He was familiar to me.

He offered his hand in peace, up in the air. I took it. Our hands swung down.

Fest Fasen's my name, he said. *I've met you before. There was a body in an alley covered in ants. You paid me to take the fellow to a temple and pray for him. Those little bastards bit me all over my shoulder. The body was probably infested, and that's why he was killed.*

Probably, but that is no reason to deny some honor for the dead.

Not if you're in Rhianna, said Fest. *Anyway, I hear you travel with someone who needs more strength?*

I looked behind me. The room howled so loud. I couldn't understand anything. Snippets of jokes and languages all alien floated through the air like pipe smoke. *I . . .*

Seth stepped through the cracked door. He walked over to us. Staf Sru Korinyes came in after.

The black men turned and whistled at her as she walked. She cringed and took Seth's hand.

Seth flipped a match in his hand. It burned. He looked around him. He smiled.

Adel said, *There he is.*

Seth lifted the match to his lips. The match exploded into the air into a huge fire.

The whole room stilled.

I am looking to hire a man, said Seth. *I need protection.*

Fest Fasen raised a hand in peace. *From what,* he said, *the water?*

Sometimes, said Seth.

Fest laughed. *How much?*

Seth held up a bag of coins. *Not much,* he said, *but how often do you get to work for a man who breathes fire?*

How long? said Fest.

I don't know, said Seth. *Long, I guess. Very long.*

Adel placed a hand on Seth's shoulder. *This man is a noble from another country we have never heard of, like I told you,* she said. *He needs to appear at court. He'll need you to keep him alive there, as well as in other places.*

Fest smiled. He snatched the money from Seth's hand. He pulled out a small, tarnished sword. *My body is yours,* he said, *and so is my blade. I haven't been to court in a long time. It'll be nice to give those young bucks a blow or two.*

I had a closer look at Fest this time. His skin was tight as leather. His hair was missing. In his mouth, he had bright steel fangs between brown, mottled teeth. I had seen others of his kind with this odd feature, or some other odd feature. I didn't stare at his teeth.

I looked at his hands. They were ancient hands, covered in veins and white hairs. His knuckles were crooked. They had been used many times. His eyes looked right at me, straight on and declared duty as casually as the next drink with a tarnished sword.

I glanced at the old black wolf, smiling in the streets as we walked. His steel fangs sparkling in the sunlight. He met each passerby with a cold stare.

The sun fell slowly. We had already huddled up against a fire. These summer days, the sun crept across the sky. In winter, the sun will run away from us.

The wolves howled into the fading light. Seth smiled at that. *Things that are empty must be filled. The world is full of quests,* he said. *Our quest, wolf quests, mountain lion quests, bear quests, soldier quests, lover quests, squirrel quests, cannibal quests . . .*

I held my spear close. Seth tossed dried flowers onto the fire and whittled with a small knife upon a root. He kept talking about all the creatures in the world on quests. The wolves howled and howled. Sunlight limped away, and still the wolves howled. Seth ran his mouth while throwing the flowers. (I remember Partridge doing the same with songs. Singing and singing all day long until Fest wanted to strangle him. And in the dungeon, the foolish boy was bruised with Fest's fist.)

At night, I could feel wolf breath on my face. I could feel their frozen breath off the mountains. The night creatures sang away the fears of darkness. So did the fire. I slept as close to it as I could. I slept as best I could. I still felt the black ball of mourning inside of me. Seth slept silently. I listened for the night noises of the insects and owls.

I felt alone with the stars. I might as well have been alone, I thought.

And I was on a quest.

In Alameda, our castles are made of stone and concrete and mud and they pile high up into the sky. They take generations to build. Each one began as stone walls to keep out the cannibals. They grew and grew. Towers upon bedrooms upon barracks upon storerooms. Now a castle can survive two long winters on their stores alone, unless an army invades and devours the food. They are all made of gray granite. The wealthier nobles of Tsuin and Ilhota and Pascanus put thick glass in their windows.

Of course, we never had dragons in our lands. Only cannibals. Perhaps someday our nations will cross the oceans and find more of these mysterious dragons, and we will take to the underground as well with the old ones.

Adel tried to explain dragons to us, and we did not share the vocabulary. She shook her head. Korinyes tried. We simply couldn't grasp what a dragon was. We knew it was large. It was underground. It was old. Proliuxian men killed the dragons and called themselves noble. They usurped the caves of dragons as the palaces of the nation. That is all Seth and me knew. In the streets above, people talked little of dragons. That war was so long ago. Why speak of dragons? Why not speak of dinner, or coins, or the elusive ecstasy of love?

Adel scratched her tattoos while she spoke of the dragons. She looked out to the horizon. *Ancient creatures they were*, she said. *A shame we killed them all.*

What is words, I said. *I know not the words you speak.*

No matter, she said, *as long as the words are still true.*

I didn't like the sight of the mercenaries outside our window. I remembered an alley and one of them who would not tell me which castle was to be invaded. He wanted to invade only my own.

And the mountains past them. I hated the mountains, too. The fires and fires of hundreds of tents. Dark mercenaries, polishing arquebuses and preparing for the long journey through the mountains.

I slept in an inn. We were nearly at the northern edge of Proliux. The mountainous dales and valleys pressed into the sky. We would find our way north again with my grandfather's golem. Seth would speak, and the golem would answer.

Fest never did anything Seth told him.

I touched Fest's hand. It felt like an old boot, and it looked like veins beneath black leather. *When I first saw your skins,* I said, *I thought you were golems.*

When I first saw yours, I thought you were too pale, he said. *I thought you were sick. Either sick, or a ghost.*

I looked up at Seth. *I am sick,* I said. *I am sick of mountains.*

I'm sick of the dead one, said Fest, *I can't wait until we don't need him anymore. Yet, we will need him a long time. We will need him as long as we fight my brothers.*

I took the rope from his fingers. *I will guard him tonight, Fest.*

He looked at me and saw the killing circle in the dragon's lair. He let go of the rope.

Really? said grandfather's golem. *Aren't you scared of me? Everyone else is.*

Aren't you scared of me? I'm the one who killed you.

He smiled at that and leaned back into the wall. His glossy eyes stared at me all night long.

After we hired Fest, we went shopping for clothes. Seth wore a long white robe, with a silver rope around his waist. I wore white leather. I placed a steel belt around my waist.

Adel asked me what my best weapon was. I told her spear.

She asked if the spear was hooked or straight.

I didn't understand that question.

She showed me two spears. I took the straight one.

In the evening twilight, we ate at the street café again, with the same waiter with the same mustache. At night I shared the floor of Korinyes's ruined tower with Fest. Adel said she had to make some arrangements to get us past the wall.

In the morning she had circles under her eyes and wore a gorgeous green dress. In the street below us she had a carriage waiting, with gleaming white stallions and a gypsy boy at the reins.

She gestured for us to enter. I went in first.

Inside, a thin young man in black velvet robes held a gnarled cane and smiled at nothing. *Hello,* he said. His nose was jagged. His eyes were brown. He held the metal cane like a delicate flower. He gestured next to him.

I sat down.

Who are you? I said.

He looked out the window. *I'm the one who owes Adel a favor,* he said. *You'll never get inside without me.*

Seth stopped too, when he saw the man.

The man gestured across from him. *Please, sit down,* he said.

Seth sat down. *My name is Seth Immur. What is your name?*

Tycho, said the man, *and you, Seth Immur, are a lucky man.*

Why am I lucky?

Korinyes entered with a cocked eyebrow. She sat down next to Seth.

Why ask such a silly question? said Tycho.

Because I must, said Seth.

Adel helps you, said Tycho.

Adel stepped into the carriage and pressed into me.

Tycho leaned forward to nod at Adel. He turned back to Seth.

Adel pulls in the longest nets to save your life.

I don't understand, said Seth.

It's an old expression, said Adel. *This one will get us in. You won't get past the gate without him.*

I've already told them that, and my name, said Tycho.

I've told them mine, as well, said Adel.

I know, Lady Jardan, he replied.

Streets passed in silence. Korinyes reached out for Seth's hand. Seth clasped hers. Tycho stared out the carriage window. His face was flat as moonlight. Adel stared out the other window. I was wedged between them enough to make breathing an embarrassment.

I couldn't see out the window at all.

If I could I would have seen new city, far inland from my port.

My hands cranked and cranked on my spear. It stood up between my legs and aimed at the sun through the leather roof of the carriage.

Adel touched my hand. *Stop that,* she said.

I had seen so few carriages in this city. I wondered whose it was. Adel's, or Tycho's.

Seth snatched up a flopping fish from the deck. He held it in one hand, with the tail pointed to the sky.

Zhan, did I ever show you how to make golems?

No. You never show me anything.

I don't, do I? I should show you how to make golems.

He squeezed the fish. Purple blood oozed out onto his hand. Seth placed the fish down on the deck, and wiped his hand clean. Then he pressed a small stick into the gills of the creature. He poured a drop of blue liquid down the little shaft of the stick.

He frowned. *It didn't work,* he said.

What?

It should've worked, he said. *Hm. I'll have to try it again on something else.*

Try what? Making a golem?

Of course.

He dropped the dead fish into the fire.

What was that blue liquid?

Fire water. Made from the fermented blood of a sheep, and the blood of a bug. A few other things, too, each mysterious and rare. It's supposed to turn things into golems.

You never tried it before?

He smirked. *I have tried it before. I have succeeded before.*

On what?

A person.

Who?

Not you, don't worry. I haven't done it in a long while.

Right, I said. *How did you do it?*

Magic, I guess. His eyes looked up at the empty sky. *Faith, perhaps. I don't really know how it works. I'm no theologian. I am a simple shaman for a simple little village.*

A simple shaman who makes golems.

Yes. A simple shaman who makes golems.

I didn't believe him at the time

The carriage came to a stop. A sharp knuckle rapped on the window. Tycho opened the window and poked his cane out, handle first. He gestured with it. The carriage continued.

We swayed back and forth. I felt a little sea sick in the carriage because of how it moved. I didn't puke.

Seth looked at Tycho with creased eyebrows. *What are we doing now?*

We're being patient, said Tycho. *The trip takes some time,* Tycho looked out the window when he talked. He never looked anyone in the face when he talked. *She tells me that you are a paladin from a foreign land.*

Not quite, said Seth. *Yes, in a way, but not quite.*

Mm. So do you or don't you serve the dragon? asked Tycho.

No, said Seth, *I don't even know what a dragon is. I serve the Goddess.*

Mm. It doesn't matter. All the dragons are dead now, anyway. We finally killed the last of them when we took Rhianna.

You didn't kill that dragon, Tycho, said Adel, quietly. *Maybe your armies did, but you were no dragonslayer.*

I said 'we', didn't I?

You had nothing to do with it, said Adel.

I had everything to do with it, said Tycho. The corners of his lips crept up his face. He pushed them down with will alone. *And so did my brothers. And so did you, dear heart.*

Don't call me that.

Do you want in my carriage or not, dear heart?

Adel stomped her foot. *Please,* she said, *don't call me that.*

I will call you whatever I please. And I will stop calling you dear heart because it displeases you. Adel, I'm sorry I displeased you. I never meant to displease you.

Please, stop talking, said Adel. Her eyes closed. Her fingers reached for her temples, and she rubbed slowly. *I'm so tired of talking with you, Tycho. Let's just get this day over with and then we will go our separate ways again.*

Mm. We'll see.

Tycho turned out to the window again.

I leaned forward to see past his face. All I could see was a sliver of cobblestone fuzzy in the ecstatic motions of the carriage.

Seth and Korinyes said nothing at all. I quietly swallowed small chunks of bitter vomit. I was sea sick in a carriage. I didn't want anyone to know.

I would kill my first man soon. His blood would be the reddest blood I had ever seen and it would be splashed all over my face and hands. An old woman would hand me a towel. I would take the towel and wipe clean. Tycho would say something important to another man. That man would say something important back.

Black skin would fade to ash from my killing blow. His eyes would roll back into his head. His cocky smile would fall off his face like an avalanche of black snow. His voice would whimper out to me, too late. *Please* . . .

The carriage came to a halt not long after Tycho and Adel talked. We stepped out into a garden lined with cobblestone. Trees hewn into geometric shapes, and three beach trees merged and crossed and cut to grow together before a large, torchlit cave.

Men moved with a calm bearing of the heavily armed. Many of them had skin as black as midnight, and stepped behind a person of cinnamon-brown and narrow eyes. They moved through the hedges of red roses and purple grass.

Fest stepped next to me. He smiled. I blinked. I had forgotten him from the other dark men. I remembered in an instant.

Keep your feet on, girl, he said. *This is a dangerous place.*

My name is Zhan, not girl, I said. *What is so dangerous here? It's beautiful.*

Adel placed a hand on my shoulder. *He's right, Zhan. The law here is not of justice, but of power. And men kill things they cannot subjugate. At least, they try to. These are the children of the dragonslayers. No one is their equal.* Adel spoke without contempt. It was simply a fact. The sky is blue. The ocean is salty. Men kill what they cannot subjugate.

Not even the children of the slayers of the cannibals?

Fest shook his head and cooed. *It doesn't matter what truth is here, girl,* said Fest, annoyed, *Zhan, I mean. Truth doesn't matter. Truth is created by the power of a noble word.*

Adel nodded. *Astute, Fest. You surprise me with your truth.*

No I don't, he said. *You told it to me.*

Then, I am surprised you listened. Keep an eye on Korinyes, said Adel, *I'll watch Seth and Zhan. I don't expect anything out here as long as we're with Tycho, but nothing holds true down below.*

Aye, he said.

Seth and Korinyes watched everything pass around them. Tycho stood near them. A dark man stepped from the rose bushes and walked toward Seth and Korinyes. Tycho raised his eyebrow. The dark man smirked and walked away.

I see, I said.

I spun my spear in the air. I lifted my body into the easy air on the balls of my feet. I listened to the sound of bodies passing through rose bushes, and boots on cobblestone. I watched for shadows trying to sneak up on me.

Tycho sighed. *Let's get this embarrassment over with, shall we? If I am to ruin my reputation, I'd like to do it quickly.*

Seth and Korinyes smiled at the roses. Did they ever know how close they came to their own death? Only one eyebrow.

Tycho sighed. *Please, let's move ahead, people. They are only plants. You have seen plants before. Have you ever seen a dragon cave before?*

Seth and Korinyes walked forward. A narrow-eyed man with cinnamon brown skin pulled a dagger from his sleeve. *Tycho, surely you jest bringing a gypsy here. How do you know she isn't one of the infested ones? Did you check her skull yourself?*

I do not jest, Suli. And I don't care if she's infested or not. That's not how family members treat each other. Put your knife away, dragonslayer. You wouldn't attack my family over a foolish little gypsy.

The man nodded and put his knife back up his sleeve. *I would only attack the gypsy and the . . . strange ones. Never you, dear friend, Tycho. What a strange family you have these days.*

A man may not choose his own family, said Tycho, *dear friend. A man may only choose his friends.*

Suli laughed too hard at that. His belly rocked and his back bent. No, they aren't friends. Suli walked away into the garden.

I should tell you about our weapons.

I carried a spear with a straight edge.

Fest carried a sword and various smaller blades underneath his clothes. They chinked lightly while he walked. He had his teeth, too. He had giant steel fangs that stayed as sharp as new talons.

Seth carried a small stick. We had offered him a blade but he had turned it away. *I have plenty of fire,* he had said.

Korinyes bit her lip and took the dagger from Adel's hands. *I know,* she had said to the dagger.

Adel carried weapons, I'm sure, but I don't know what they were, or where she kept them. I think she might have carried no weapon at all, too. I don't know.

Tycho carried his gaze like a suit of armor. He walked like he was bored by the mysteries and the honor of the location. I doubt he ever truly approached this place in boredom.

The rest of us were afraid, or astonished, or a strange combination of the two.

In the first passageway stalactites and stalagmites were smothered in jewels. The torchlight flickered in the rubies and the pearls and it was like light teeth chomping up and down. The hall was bathed in the orange light. Bronzed by the light, men and women walked around. They looked at Tycho, and at us.

We went deeper.

We turned a narrow corner. A cold steel brushed my neck. I turned, but too late. Fest already had the offender in hand, pressed into the dazzling walls. The offending mercenary smiled. He had white teeth and his ears were carved up in some ritual symbols. *What strange skin she has,* he said.

The last skin you see, I said. My spear touched the offender's throat.

Fest pulled out his sword.

Tycho sighed again. Always sighing we do, at the line between our life and death.

Go away, you, said Tycho. *They're with me.*

I shall leave, Lord Tycho, said the mercenary. *I didn't know.*

Tell your friends, said Adel. *And be sure to let Lord Xaxu know. Send him my regards.*

We pressed deeper. The hallways grew taller and taller. Women touched Tycho's face. He pushed them away with his cane. *Not today, my lovely darlings. I am a man on a quest for blood. My wife has returned from the dead in the service of justice, and I wish to show my father.*

He reached out a hand and took Adel's arm.

Hello, said Adel.

One of the women snarled, *Jardan Bosch Adel is still alive? Weren't you a traitor to both of us? Don't you serve the dragon now? Your arms . . .*

I serve my husband always, said Adel. *He who killed the dragon.*

I apologize, but this is not a matter for now, said Tycho. He raised his eyebrow again to ward off the danger. So much power in one eyebrow. *Please, my lovely darlings. I would love to discuss all of this with you at a more opportune moment. I will be throwing a ball soon to celebrate the return of my wife. Then we will discuss such matters.*

The woman frowned. She had a small face, like a clamshell, and it scrunched up into a sudden veracity. Her hand tensed around something beneath her dress.

Tycho touched her forehead gently with his cane.

She fell back, her eyes sealed shut. Her head hit the stone floor, hard, like a large gourd landing.

Tycho smirked. *When she wakes up,* he said, *get her something cool to drink, and also my apologies.*

Seth lit a match and blew a puff of fire that flashed in the gems. People gasped and stepped back.

Pardon me, said Seth, *I think I ate too much spice in my breakfast.*

The strange women stepped back from us. They left the sleeping one where she had fallen. A thin line of blood trickled over the stone where her head had landed.

Korinyes smiled and let go of Seth's hand. She had her dagger somewhere. I watched her walk. The weight of something swung in her dress. We pressed deeper into the cave.

The jewels took shape and swirled into mosaics of emerald men in long phalanxes charging toward a great creature. The beast breathed rubies into the sky.

The men held arquebuses in their hands, though I still didn't know what those devices were. They were small silver funnels and smoke and fire shot out from them in tiger's eye and obsidian.

Small couches and divans lined the halls. People in decadent gowns surrounded by armed guards talked in thrilling voices about nothing and everything both at once. The world bends to these tongues, and their version of realities.

This is all from the dragonslayers' original deed centuries ago. They did the impossible. How does anyone overthrow such a visceral, vengeful god?

The surface dwellers have such safe lives, with shining coins and bakeries and marketplaces and Khali and cinnamon tea. The tall buildings that scratch the surface of Alastair's blue mask were all made by men who have thrived in this realm of the dragonslayers. These fingers point to the heavens and declare war upon the Goddess, and upon their petty gods and goddesses. The dragons who had for centuries demanded tribute were defeated by our lords. Next is to be You, O mighty Heaven.

The noble dragonslayers burrow underneath the ground in the dens of the defeated. They commune like brutal sheep with the jewels of the dragon's horde pasted onto the walls in scenes of victory. Each voice says nothing and leads an army. Each army unites under another and another and another until the power cracks. They kill each other with the ease of fornication. Each little death is a rebellion.

Adel told this to me in the mountains. I had asked her why everyone called her a servant of the dragon. She concealed her forearms
and snarled at the dragonslayers. Her eyes burned with the demon
fire of the milkweed.

She cursed Tycho, and all his brethren.

And we passed through this underground palace in safety because the son of the most powerful, honorable man in the entire realm of Proliux stood with us and stated, *This is my family.*

And this lie was as firm a truth as falling, though everyone knew it to be false.

And he took us to the throne room. A single chair carved from the ivory tusks of the giant, defeated beast. No one sat in the chair right now. The chair was gilded with the crackling dragonscale leather. The skulls of dragons lined the walls like the signet shields in our own Alamedan castles. Like narrow-necked whales with shark teeth, gigantic black holes for eyes, and a lean, lizard face.

Three other chairs, there were, with three men. These thrones were smaller, and lower. They formed a triangle around a circle of silver on the floor. The three men's thrones aimed at this circle. They did not look beyond each other, yet.

A man, as fat as two good harvests, clopped Tycho on the back. *Hello, my dear friend. I hear you are in the throes of a family reunion!*

I am, said Tycho, *This is my long lost wife Adel, and her relations.*

Ah, I see, said the man, *is the old one of her line as well?*

My ears perked up.

Seth coughed. *This old one,* he said, *does he look a little like me?*

Hardly, said Tycho.

Adel took Seth's shoulder. She pulled him down and whispered into his ear. His mouth opened silently, *Oh.*

I said, *What?*

Seth shook his head at me. (*The dragon,* he would say later, *the old one is the dragon. They were attacking Adel, the paladin.*)

Adel brooded. Her fingers twitched and popped. She was ready to kill everyone here. I saw it in her eyes. The swirl and mash of colors in her pupils are only green eyes in this dim torch light. Green eyes, and white knuckles. Bones popping.

Deeper we crawled down the long, gorgeous halls.

Korinyes stayed close to Seth. She felt a hand near her. She stabbed it. A black hand clenched and pulled away. I watched the blood drip down his silk sleeves, flickering in torchlight. Adel finished him off fast. I don't know what she used because she came from behind him, and the mercenary tensed and released. I think it was her strange daggers, weighted odd for the paladin games.

She leaned the body back against a wall. None of our noble counterparts said a word. None of the other mercenaries moved a muscle.

Adel's hand was clean when it appeared again. No blood at all. Tycho caught her eye and smirked at her.

Seth took a deep breath. He had the vial in his hands, ready for flames. He had other things in his pockets. He had so many pockets.

And the caverns were magnificent and flickering jewels in the torches filled the caves with the stench of kerosene and tar.

Deeper. Down a long stairwell crowded with bowing servants and silent women. Black men, mercenaries and giants among their own kind line the walkways with twitching eyes. Each waiting for the precise moment to overwhelm the other lords.

Along the walls of the lowest chamber in the caves hung the bleached skulls of dragons, like serpentine sharks. Giant jaws, and giant teeth, and narrow heads like lizards. Their other bones were wrapped around their heads like mosaic tiles in imitation of the living.

We saw once more in our whole lives, when we came north again, the village where we had come from.

Bear was the official name, though I'd never seen a bear my whole life.

We passed over the mountains at last, with Grandfather's golem in tow.

And the fields were fallow, the rooftops sunken or sinking in. Seth ran to the edge of a rock to get a better view.

Get down, idiot, I said. *What if it was the army?*

No smoking ruins, he said. *And we got ahead of the army. I don't see anything.*

The songbirds of home sang in the trees around us. The familiar cries of home, and nothing remained but the birds and the woods.

We pitched our camp in Kyquil's abandoned home, were I had warmed my belly and my body, with the heavy woman's hospitality. Where I had heard her sing a beautiful lullabye.

All the iron things were gone. The stove. The smokepipe. The pots and pans. The furniture nails.

Chunks of abandoned, rotting wood piled in heaps at the fringes. Our firewood.

Adel stretched out next to the fire. *It's still so cold. How can anywhere be so cold?*

Seth touched the panes of the window. The glass and the shutters had been removed carefully long ago.

Seth sighed. *It wasn't always cold here. This was my friend's home. He had a wife who kept feeding and feeding you. Wonderful woman. I left him in charge of the village when we left. I told him to get a new shaman right away.*

Grandfather's golem sat at the edge of this all. He stared at the fire.

Fest tugged at the rope around the golem's neck. *What do you see in these fires, you? You stare in all of these fires.*

The golem's face was a stone. *What do the dead see?* said his tongue, without moving one of the frozen lips. *I cannot see much anymore. My eyes are rotting out. The fire is bright enough to break through.*

Seth's knuckles whitened on the windowpane. His lips curled. *Quiet, you! I am tired of you. I think we'll leave you here for the wolves.*

The golem looked up at Seth. *You don't know tired like I know tired, boy. I am tired. I haven't slept since I died. Cut off my head and burn this flesh. Leave me for the wolves. You don't need me anymore.*

Seth nodded. *You will sleep soon enough,* he said. *Goddess, what happened here? What happened to our home, Zhan?*

Silence. The fire crackled. The golem turned to the open doorway. Outside, the wolves howled so close to the village. They chased after the dead stench of rotting meat dragged with us on a rope.

Korinyes touched Seth's arm. *A bad harvest, and a long winter. This can kill all villages. Your whole family dead, and their harvest no longer helping the families. And Kyquil can't feed his people as good. And they tear away the edible unnecessaries—things like cloth and pets. And then, they kill their flocks. Some of them die from hunger. And then, when spring breaks in again, the ones left strip away the things worth trading, and that's it.*

Adel's eyes were bloodshot in the fire. Her voice silent. Her gaze deep into the fire. Her lips pale white, like the white scar tissue on her brown face.

Korinyes shrugged. *That's the way of villages. Someday, new people will come, or your fields will fade into forest. It's like this with ants, too. Ant mounds die, and new ants find them or the mounds disintegrate into dust.*

Seth's knuckles were still white. His rage still pure.

Fest smiled, and his fangs glimmered. *We will need your anger if the wolves come. If the scouts of the army find us fleeing and hunt us down like wolves hunt rabbits. Our armies move fast over the forests and the open fields. We sleep too much. We'll never beat them.*

Adel spoke at last. *Quiet, Fest. Go to sleep while you can still wake up.*

And where were we? I don't remember. There was a fire, though, and he said that. Someone was angry. Was it me?

He was right, though.

And then my eyelids dropped and all that mattered was this forgotten dream, quietly.

The crack of wood on wood, the clean line of blood on a spear head, and drops of it on my white leather jacket. This, too I remember from the palace. In the center room, where I danced the dance of wolves with a gigantic mercenary. Where I shoved the spear into his body and his eyes opened, surprised.

*A*re *you awake, Zhan?* whispered Adel.

I sat up. Adel's silhouette in the darkness. Her black hair and mangled ear. Her hot breath.

Zhan, take the golem, quickly. There's something we must do before Seth wakes.

I rubbed the sleep from my eyes. I pushed my blanket off my body, and it was cold. Goddess, it was cold again. No seagulls laughing overhead in this village.

Grandfather's golem leaned against a wall because he had trouble holding his putrid head up straight.

Korinyes slept hard, and snored a little. Her arm draped over Seth. Fading embers glowed. His drool glistened in her long hair. Fest was gone somewhere. I don't know where. Adel didn't seem worried, and so I didn't worry. When we returned to the hut he was back.

Grandfather's golem could barely speak. The cold hit him harder because he had no blood keeping him warm. He walked with a heavy limp in both legs. His arms hung like anchors in the air. His head lolled about like a flag.

I grabbed the rope and pulled him from the wall. He staggered forward. He didn't speak.

Adel stepped out into the village square. I went with her.

Zhan, this used to be your village, but you weren't here when the murders happened, correct?

Yes, I said.

Do you remember who lived in what hut before you left?

Maybe a little, I replied. My footsteps were sure, but I was not. I concentrated on each of the houses, trying to remember what they were like when I was a child. I tried to remember when I came back from the riders.

Golem, show me everyone you killed, said Adel, *Start at the first. Zhan will cut your head off if you are lying.*

I can't lie. Cut my head off anyway, his voice slow, soft. *Leave me for the wolves to finish.*

The black sky was starless. Too many clouds. The night sounds of home and winter. The howling wolves. Nothing but the light of our torches in the early morning twilight. The insects were silent. Our footsteps sucked our boots as the three of us stepped through the muddy mixture of old snow and dirt.

Grandfather led us to my father's house.

Zhan, whose hut was this?

Mine, I said.

Partridge was in the empty village all along. He was too afraid to come out of hiding, or too stupid to know we were there. He didn't know who we were. My husband was still far off, yet, in Ilhota.

And in Proliux, in the court of the dragons, I killed a man for the laws of men and not the laws of Alastair. My husband assured me I was not guilty of murder.

I try to place the man's face—the first one I killed—into the web. His empty eyes and ashen skin are there, lingering in the rafters with his haughty brethren. His husk is too far gone. His ghost felt no anger in death. It stays with me only as a guilt.

I have killed too many of his kind to remember the angle of a cheek, or the curve of his nose against the jewels. He is every one of the mercenaries up there. He has every face, and every scar. I cannot place him.

But I remember what it felt like to kill him. It was horrible, and I loved every moment of it until he looked up at me with those eyes.

Yes! Brown eyes! He had brown eyes! I can remember a little of it, I hope.

A very old man wrapped in layers of gorgeous cloth and a crown bigger than his whole body pointed at Seth. Seth blinked. He looked at Adel. Adel pointed at me. I said, *What?*

You will fight for our right to stand here, Zhan, said Adel.

Why her? said Fest, *Why not I? Isn't that why you bought me?*

No, said Adel.

That little girl? said Fest, *She looks strong, but . . . But a girl against a prime mercenary? You send her to die.*

Better her than you, said Korinyes.

I will not shirk my duty! he growled. His hand found the pommel of his blade. His chest puffed up.

Your duty is to do as you're told, said Adel.

Tycho touched my white leather shoulder. *You should hurry,* he said, *You're wasting their time.*

I moved forward. I didn't think anymore. I couldn't think. I could only breathe, and feel the wood in my hands, and the ground beneath my feet. Between these things was the emptiness of me. The spear was made of wood, which grows from the ground, and metal which also comes from the ground. Men took these things from the ground and made the spear. I was the emptiness between the ground and the spear. I was a gust of wind. I was only a breath.

Inside the silver circle, between the three thrones, a gigantic black man already stood, swaying side-to-side. He twirled a hooked spear in his hand. And I took my spear into the circle. Mine was straight as an arrow, and the shaft was a heavy wood I didn't know by name.

Everyone around me stared at this girl on the killing floor. The flickering mosaics stared. The crowns like the eyes of a peacocks' tail stared.

(Have you ever seen a peacock, Esumi? I saw them there. Women carry them as pets, and wear them like crowns at their feet. When the peacocks call out, it's a cry for help. That is what the three men's crowns looked like, I think.)

The mercenary on the floor with me smiled. He had white teeth and black skin. His red and orange garb rippled in the wind of his motions. The sound of cloth on cloth is all I heard. I added my calm breathing to the sounds. I twirled my own spear.

Tycho slipped a knife in my belt as I passed. The flat of the blade pressed against the small of my back while I walked into the circle. He patted my back above this secret weapon.

Whose side was Tycho on? I said to Korinyes.

His own, of course, she said.

I don't remember where we were, but I asked her that and that's what she told me.

I killed them four first, said the golem, slowly. *I didn't mean to with them. I was eating there because my wife wouldn't let me into her house. His wife said something mean. I hit her. Then he hit me, and I stabbed him. It felt good. I stabbed the rest of 'em, too. Can't remember their names, but the man was supposed to be my son. Didn't much look like it, though.*

Adel looked at me. *How many were here that you killed?*

Four.

I had more family than that, I said. *Who did you kill here?* I let him walk into the house. I followed him on the string. Adel came in after.

Let's see . . . he said. *I killed the woman. Can't remember her name. The man. A little girl. A boy, too. An old boy. Maybe as old as Seth.*

What about my other brother? I said.

Oh, he wasn't here, said the golem, *He was at another place.*

Where was he? I said.

He was at one of them other houses.

My home was empty. The wood floor still had the old blood stains, brown and covered in dust.

Adel looked at me. *Show me how you did it, please?* she said. *Where were you?*

Goddess that room was so small. I could jump and hit a wall. The floor was full of termite holes. The mortar between the stones was crumbling while the wood beams disintegrated. And the house was so small. I don't remember that. Six easy steps to a wall.

Grandfather held a hand out. He started to speak. His voice was too slow for me.

I spoke for him. *A table. Our table was right here. This is where we ate dinner. He was sitting there.*

I looked down at the blood. The burnt sienna outline of my father's blood was still there, telling the story of the hunter's prey. *Yes, you jumped up from the table when you hit her. He hit you, and you spun away.* I moved like the killer. My hands held imaginary intentions. I grabbed at the phantom knife upon the table and followed the trail of boots and blood. *You grabbed the knife from the table, and then you turned around again and you stabbed my father in his liver, and then his belly, and then his face.* I closed my eyes.

I only stabbed him once, said the golem, *Only in the chest. He died nice and easy. I know how to kill, girl. You got it wrong.*

I stood where my father had stood when he died. I put my feet on the bloodstain.

He stood right here when it happened, I said. *This is where my father died, Adel.*

Adel was very still. She was standing where my mother had stood. I could see their death in my mind. The old goat hunter angry at them because he hated them and he hated their contempt over a meal. He hits my mother hard, and she falls against the wall. My father is a farmer not a warrior. He swings, too, with his big, slow hands.

Grandfather doesn't play with death. He kills. He spins in the strike, and the knife is just under his hand. The kitchen knife I had used when I was just a girl, cutting my summer sausages . . .

And the knife lands in his heart. My heart. I look down at my heart. It beats underneath my heavy furs and cloaks. And I can see the knife jutting out and burning. And I turn and look at Adel who stands where my mother stood when she watched her husband die. And the knife came for her next, too.

First, she reached a hand to my face. I was crying. I didn't want to cry in front of the golem. And Adel reached a hand to my face.

I'm sorry I needed you for this, she said. *We can go back, I can do this alone, and come back over it with you later. I've already gone over it with Seth while you were asleep. I know this story well enough. I just wanted to be thorough and I didn't think I had time to do it alone with you.*

My father died right here, Adel, I said. *He was standing right here.*

The golem coughed and leaned into a wall. I wanted to kill him again.

Little girl, said the Hawk on the killing floor.

I circled him. He hopped and spun. He was twice as tall as me. We were three spear lengths away, and he could reach his hand out and cover over half the distance with a spear in hand.

I circled closer. He circled with me, hopping on his feet.

His eyes flickered. He moved in quick.

Fest told me about mercenaries while we were in chains because I wanted to hear someone say something, and I asked him to tell me again because I had forgotten. He nodded. He brushed an ant from his arm.

He told me about the tribes. Fest had sharpened steel teeth and no hair because he was of the serpent tribe. The hawks grow long nails, and cover them with sharp steel. The camel tribe cut grooves in their front two teeth. The sidewinders shave half their heads, and let half grow long. The beetles burn their hair and beards away.

He said, *That one over there is a hawk.*

Partridge, who I haven't told you about yet, mumbled at the sounds Fest made. The foreign language was lost to the boy. *Hawk hawk hawk hawk. Hawk hawk. Hawkie.*

Fest smacked Partridge in his limp, potato face. *Quiet, fool.*

Hawk. The boy's nose bled.

Fest smacked the boy again. *I said quiet.*

The hawk guard said, *Leave him alone.* His voice was like needles in my ear. His rough Alamedan cut like his sharp fingernails.

Our leader hasn't picked yet, has he? said Fest in Proliuxian. *He hasn't decided.*

What are you talking about? I said. *Picked what?*

The guard reached out his claws and scraped them over Fest's forehead. Blood welled up in the broken lines.

Fest licked his blood as it drained across his face. *You'll see,* he said.

I smashed the mercenary's spear up to the ceiling. I whipped to the side. My spear spun with me, slow and heavy. I pulled it around and up to reach for the beast's skull. I caught him on the shoulder blades with the heavy shaft.

He was in mid-swing, and his swing failed. He reached a hand out instead, and grabbed my arm. His steel claws dug into me like a hawk's talons. His eyes flared.

I did not scream at pain. I dropped my spear and jumped in. I pulled the knife from my belt, and sliced inside the mercenaries' elbow. His spear whipped around, and my knife deflected it.

I slammed the knife just above his wrist. It broke through bone. The talons wilted. I tore away. He swung his spear one-handed at my navel, hard. I jumped into him and the spear, and caught the shaft at the axis of the strike. I shoved my shin into his groin, and pounded my head into his nose. I twisted the spear from his hands when I bounced away from him. I collapsed to the ground and rolled away. I had his hooked spear in my hands.

(The world spun around me: the many men dressed in fire at the fringe of the circle, silently. I paused to choke down vomit. I was seasick. I was scared.)

He pulled the knife from his hand. I heard the sucking, scratching tug. He didn't even whimper at the pain. I was on my knees now, with his spear.

I looked up at the beast. He picked up my spear in his hands now, and one of his hands clutched the spear limply. I could not see my dagger. I could see blood seeping down the spear handle.

He smiled. *I like you, bitch,* he snarled. *Maybe I let you live to bear my brats.*

I jabbed with his spear lightly. He slapped it away. Wood on wood. I jabbed again. He blocked again. He stepped back away from me. He backed off.

I stood where I was. Behind me men stood against the edge of the circle. To my right, the three thrones stood, with three old cinnamon brown men.

The beast tore at his shirt. My knife appeared in his good hand,

and cut away a line of cloth. His muscular belly was exposed, his protruding belly button like a coral worm. *I like you, bitch. If you had bigger tits, I'd cut them off and keep them.*

What do you remember about the holy books, Zhan?

I remember nothing. I have learned nothing. You are a horrible teacher.

You are a horrible student. You think too much, I think.

And you think too little and pretend it's wisdom. What are we doing, Seth? The mountains are behind us. You say he went farther south. You point to his tracks. I say we are beyond the mountains that he knew so well. I say we have entered the land of the dead. Why are we here?

The question every shaman asks themselves someday. Someday we will not be here. The more important question perhaps is where will we be when we are not here.

Do you think it makes you look smart when you don't give a straight answer to a straight question? I think we will go home.

One can only hope.

The mercenary stepped forward. He lifted the spear up in the air to swing down. I slammed my hooked spear blade onto his good hand. Pieces of finger fell to the ground. I spun, and smacked the spear out of his hands. My dagger appeared in his stabbed hand. It came down fast. He stepped forward to reach me with the dagger. His body leaned sideways for longer reach. He expected me to jump back.

I darted sideways, to his open body, with the hooked spear turned for my killing blow. I shoved the long talon of the hook up into his throat. It passed his teeth and found the bottom of his eyes. His eyeballs filled with red like twin sunsets. I twisted my arms back down to cut into his skull bones. I heard them twisting and popping inside of him.

He mouthed the word. I heard it like a guttural grunt spoken with the blood of a quick death. A red whale cry. *Please ...*

He spoke too late.

His body exploded in it, messy and frothy. He coughed, and bubbles of blood blew through the air in a perfect arc right onto me, across my ribbons and my face. My hair. My hands.

I had never killed a human before.

Between the two lovers, I did not know what to expect from their pockets. I saw them once playing a game with sticks and a ball. We were on deck. They tossed the ball, and let it bounce twice. They placed their hand on top of the ball the moment it touched the ground, on the second bounce. They picked up the sticks underneath their fingertips.

The swaying ship made the task more difficult.

Adel handed me her dagger. *That game is dangerous. Paladins play it with daggers.*

I spun the knife in my hands. It was weighted too heavy to throw well. The blade was thick at the bottom and the top, and weighted too strange for my hands. These weights were strong enough to puncture beast bone, she would tell me.

First we scatter the ground with animal bones. Then we toss our blade as hard as we can into the ground. We want the butt of the weapon to crack a bone. Then we want the blade to imbed into another bone. We want to catch the handle the moment it touches the bone, so we can force it through. All the broken bones are then ours to divine.

That's impossible, I said.

It's just very difficult, she said.

She held out her hand. I traced the scar lines in her palm. I traced the scars. *Why do the paladins play this game?*

She smiled. *So we can see our own death, in the bouncing of the bones and the cutting failures of our abilities.*

The game between the lovers ended abruptly. Staf Sru Korinyes gathered the sticks and ball into her pockets. I saw no bulge in her dress. I never saw the sticks or the ball again.

Adel leaned back on the deck of the ship. The heat was powerful, and no buildings shadowed our heads. It was as hot on these waters as the mountains were cold.

I sipped warm, watery wine.

These ships were nothing like each other. The riverboats were low and flat. The sailors held long poles and walked along the edges. Or they rowed. Or they furled brittle, yellow sails and rode a convenient wind.

The sea ships looked like the submerged tips of a proconsul's palace. I watched them in the horizon, at the edge of the planet. The gigantic white sails billowed like harnessed clouds, around the heavy stone center of the whaling ships. In their wake, oars of the long boats revolved like insect legs.

I had heard about whales, but I didn't see them until the ocean. *We didn't see that when we came down,* I said.

We take a different ship, said Adel, *Faster, and much more expensive. It goes out farther and catches the faster currents north. We will ride the current to the peninsula, and then we will go aground again.*

The golem was unpopular with the crowds. Green skin and red eyes. Hair like red sand. He smelled like the rotting monsters of the deep. They plotted ways to throw the golem to the whales. He wouldn't have minded.

These men who kill the dragons kill the deep ones, too, said Adel. That's what she called the whales. *That's what the dragons called them,* she said. We leaned against the side and watched the sea of blood, the sharks. Men with arquebuses fired down into the wriggling bodies of the water. This was the first time I'd seen arquebuses fired. I wouldn't forget.

Blood and blood and more blood. A red sea. And men in long boats dragging up the dead sharks. Some of the sharks were dragged onto our own boat. That night it tasted like bland pork. Fest ate lemons raw and said he couldn't taste the meat afterwards.

I told him the meat wasn't too bad.

He said that the important thing was the fruit. I took a bite of a lemon. I grimaced. I held the shark in my mouth to ease the pain.

Fest laughed. He told me that he didn't have too many taste buds left from so many oceans.

I asked him about the war.

What is there to tell? he said. *I don't know what I was doing. I was down below, with a cannon. When a flag raised, I fired the cannon. When it fell, I stopped. I couldn't hear a thing because my ears were sealed with heavy wax. Adel and Korinyes know it better.*

How long ago was it? I asked.

Not long, but very long. It was in the western seas. I came from a land over that sea to fight. He picked up another lemon abandoned by a sailor. He squeezed it into his mouth and tore away the meat of it. He tossed the rind over his shoulder. He didn't pucker at the fruit.

Why did you go? I said.

He picked at his teeth with a nail. He didn't look at me when he spoke. *I had no choice.*

Korinyes helped me with my hair. She wanted to cut it. I told her no. She combed it for fleas and lice. She braided ribbons through it.

Seth used some of the warm, gritty wine to make a sculpture of fire during the new moon. The sailors were terrified of the fire. They wanted to put it out right away. Then the flames began to dance and shape. Seth lit the fire in a metal bowl on the main deck, shielded from the strong wind. It was blue. He whipped his cloak and turned the fire into a howling wolf, and then Seth whipped his cloak and the fire was a sleeping bird. He tossed a piece of paper and a yellow and black beak smoldered awake like a scream.

He shaped the fire until the fuel died.

Sailors paid him money for new demons. He kept the coins in his pockets.

A young sailor broke his leg falling from the topmast. Seth pushed the ship barber away. Seth poured a liquid down the sailor's throat and called out for seawater. Fest tied a rope around a bucket handle, and pulled some up. Seth poured the water all over the man's clothes and face. Then Seth slammed the broken leg in place with a fist and a firm grip. The sailor didn't scream. The young man stared up at the night sky. Seth lit a match and set fire to a ribbon. He placed the ribbon on the man's body. The fire burned up the ribbon with warm heat against the cold wind.

Seth never told anyone why he did anything. Not even me.

The wind tugged the ribbon, but the seawater clung to the ribbon until the burning crept up the man's body, and even over the wetness. When the ribbon burned up entirely, the man with the broken leg stood up and walked below deck. For seven days he remained down there. No one went after him.

The deepest room was silent as death. Even after the mercenary's body collapsed onto the circle, it was silent.

Adel whispered in Seth's ear. Then she shoved him forward. He looked away from me, and up to the three men on thrones.

He said in clean, rehearsed Proliuxian, *I come as a representative of a foreign nation, to request the return of a dangerous criminal who may seek asylum with your merciful, and fair triumvirate of procunsuls.*

Two dark men with clawed fingers dragged the dead body away. Three little gypsy boys scrubbed at the blood with sponges and pails of water.

I toweled off as much blood as I could. It didn't stain my white leather hardly at all. It did creep into the grooves, where the seams soak in the red and stay. This is the way of killing, I think. I pressed the towel hard to get at the blood. It wouldn't all come up from the bonds.

I crept down at night when most were sleeping. I saw the sailor, holding his leg and crying. He sat in a hammock and sobbed. I saw his heavy, brown back shuddering in his weeping. I don't know how he ate down there. Someone else must have fed him. Or Alastair's blessing fed him. Or he ate his own pain. Or a thousand things I could tell you. None of them mattered. All that mattered was Seth doing it. I wish he was useless. I wish he didn't know anything at all to be useful, and we could cut the gangrenous limb off. Abandon it to burn like the golem.

The sea voyage was awful for me. I tried not to let people see it. Every rumbling of the world beneath me, and I felt it in my stomach. The unstable geology of the waves beneath the boat. The brown and white flavor of the shark's revenge.

The peninsula was next. We docked. It was a little cooler up here. It would be another month before I wore a cloak.

A clean line of blood slowly crept down the spear's shaft, to my hand. The blood nibbled my finger, like a small red insect. I flicked it away.

Proconsul Argarax raised his hand. The other two crowned men looked at him. Proconsul Argarax pointed at Seth. *I know of you, shaman. My son has told me of you.*

Her, said one of the other two, *The white one next to him. I recognize her. She's a porter at the Kura Docks.* This one was tall and lean. When he opened his mouth his thin skin barely contained his old skull. He seemed to crumple into his throne. The jagged jewelry weighed down his fingers. His shoulders sagged. (This old man was Adel's father.)

Seth looked at me. He looked back at the two men. His mouth opened. He took a deep breath.

Adel raised her hand. *My most honorable father-in-law, Proconsul Argarax, and you, two, other most honorable proconsuls, I know of this girl's previous deeds. These two chase a criminal in a nation that does not recognize her native currency. A quest cannot be fulfilled on an empty stomach. Armies march on their bellies, as do court appointed executioners.*

Proconsul Argarax lowered his hand. *My friends,* he said to the other two men on the thrones, *I, too, know of them. I shall handle this matter personally, with your permission,* he said. He turned to us and spoke, with bored eyes and a strong voice, *Please go home. I will give you more information when I am prepared to act.*

The same proconsul who had called me out grimaced. *My lord, Proconsul Argarax, I am astonished that you agree with so little evidence. Are our courts not also fair and just?*

My lord, Proconsul Bosch, said old Argarax, *My time is mine to waste as I see fit. I know of this affair intimately. The man who they claim as a killer is in my house at this very moment, seeking my protection. I already know the evidence against him. Your daughter came to me with this matter already, and I asked her to bring them here with my son. I wanted to get a good look at their nobility for, as you probably know, they keep such ignoble company.*

Lord Bosch shook his head. His lip curled in disgust. *Did you say daughter? I do not have a daughter, my lord. I have only shame.*

Adel bowed deeply. *My Lord Bosch, may I also say that it's a pleasure to see you again, and that you're feeling healthier.*

He raised his fist slowly at her. *Be glad you did not call me your father, ugly traitor. I would kill you if you called me your father.*

I will leave your sight, my lord, said Adel, *I do not wish to displease you with my presence, and our concern has been answered by the court.*

(Later on she would tell me how much she hated seeing him there, on that throne. *Men gain their thrones by selling their daughters, or sending their sons to die,* she would say.)

The three of us left quickly, the same way we came in. We moved fast on the way out. We paused for no one. No one tried to stop us, either. Up and up and up we climbed the dragon caves. The same torchlight and bejeweled bones watched us leave with black eyes and flickering shadows. People watched us pass. I felt their eyes like mosquitoes on my neck. I wanted to wash my hands of the blood. I felt covered in mercenary blood.

The carriage was waiting for us. Fest opened it first, and peered inside. He ran his hand along the seats. He nodded at Tycho. We poured into it, and rode away from the dragonslayers.

Tycho looked bored.

Adel rubbed her temples as if she had a headache.

When we passed the gate, I heard the sounds of a city outside the carriage. I opened the door and leaned my head out of the carriage. I threw up on the cobblestone.

Adel handed me a handkerchief. I used it on my bloody hands. I ignored the vomit on my lips.

Tycho smirked at that.

The next house wasn't so bad for me. Grandfather's golem told us how fast it was. The family was asleep. He slit their throats like chickens. Outside the snow began to fall again. Our quest was fading in the white face of winter.

And did Adel know it? I think she did. She knew the army was close behind us in the high hills. She knew the routes we took. She knew the two days in the village were more than just wasteful. They were a necessary evil, with winter falling any day now. And she dragged me around in morning twilight with grandfather's golem on a string to keep me thinking something else. She wanted me to only think about the past and not about the moment. This moment, where we raced an army to beat the drums of war, I was thinking about what I was going to tell Fest about Alastair when he asked for it. I was thinking about Korinyes's ribbons in my hair. I was thinking about Seth's failure as my new sensei. I was thinking about everything but the armies at our back, and at night the wolves howled close to the village because of the golem on a string because so much rancid meat so close to winter was a blessing for the ravenous wolves.

I wanted to grab Adel and tell her we didn't have time for this. I wanted to tell her that we had to hurry because the snow was coming and we had nothing to eat but mountain goat rotting fast. I wanted to tell her lots of things, but the lump in my throat would only tell her one thing if I opened my mouth. The lump would burst like a ball of blood.

And in this house my brother died. Half a bed was still in the room. Two posts, feathers from the mattress and one long board from the side of the bed. Grandfather's golem touched the wood. He ran a hand along it. He said, *This is where I killed your brother. He was sharing a bed with his cousins. I don't know why. Four were in this bed.*

We left that house. Outside were wolves circling us. They were mangy and thin. I saw more ribs than teeth. No farmers to cull their numbers. No sheep to fatten their bellies. They had overtaken the town square and paced in circles around us in white flashes of moving snow. Dark mouths in the moonlight, drooling. Adel frowned.

What do you recommend we do about these wolves? she said.

I recommend we leave the golem behind, I said. I choked down my tears enough to think about killing the body that did the deed again. I wanted to watch. Instead, I knew we would kill the wolves. Wolves are predictable. And these wolves were on the brink of death already. The astonishing thing was they had only now decided to attack us.

I have killed so many wolves in my life, Esumi. One attacks, and the other moves in right away from a different angle. Their teeth are sharp, and their claws are sharp, but they are an easy kill for the nimble. There were six wolves around us.

Come on, I said, *we're over the mountains and we don't need him. Let them have him.*

Grandfather's golem said nothing.

The wolves growled themselves toward their final fever pitch.

That isn't our decision to make, said Adel. We backed up to the golem, each of us letting the circle form around us with our backs to the house.

Is anyone making a decision? I said. *Or are we just walking?*

Seth has been making decisions the whole way, she said.

I jabbed at the wolves with my spear.

They yelped and snarled and jumped away. They crept in, looking for an opening.

Adel said, *Do you remember the game the paladins played?*

What? I said. *No.*

I told you about this one. She threw her blade hard. The butt of it slammed into a wolf's head. It crunched bone, and careened off the crumpling animal. The dagger was airborne again, and landed hard enough in the back haunch of another animal. That wolf limped away with the blade in its back.

I remembered the game.

The wolves moved in for the kill. I stabbed the first. Another came at me from the side. I fell to the snow and tossed him away over the center of the spear.

Grandfather held very still.

Adel killed two more before I could turn my head to see how. I looked up, and two wolves were dead. They didn't even twitch in the red snow.

The last wolf, that I had flung over my spear, jumped in again. Adel tossed another dagger. The butt of it slammed hard into the face of the animal. It collapsed onto me. The blade flew straight up into the air. It landed in the ground next to my head. Sharp wind in my ear.

I pushed the wolf off. I picked the weighted dagger from the snow. I stabbed the unconscious wolf in the belly. I held the bloody blade out to Adel. *Did you miss?*

Yes, she said.

I picked up grandfather's rope again.

I had never seen a dagger do that before, I said.

Adel smiled wistfully, *Even that skill is futile against the arquebuses of the mercenaries. We must move out soon, before light,* she said. *Dead wolves attract others. And the army will be slow over the mountains, but they, too, will move fast against the winter.*

The next house hid Partridge, whom I had never met until this moment because I was gone before his family had let him see the light of day, and he was terrified of Grandfather and Seth and Fest and Adel and even me.

Do you want to see the other houses? I said.

Do you? she replied.

Yes. I picked up one of the larger dead wolves and slung it over my shoulder. A foul meat, but it fills the belly.

Adel wiped her blade off on the white coat of a wolf. *Every deed,* she said, *every single violent deed creates another violent deed. This is a lesson of the paladin's daggers.*

All this time, you hardly ever told me about the paladins, I said. *You only asked about Alameda, where we walk.*

Zhan, I think I trust you and only you, she said, *and I wish I was worthy of yours. To the next house. Golem, lead us.*

Adel snatched the rope. Grandfather's golem struggled through the muddy earth to lead us into the next small house of death.

After our long sea voyage, we needed to head inland to reach the mountains. Then, we encountered the army.

Adel purchased horses for us. I was used to riding bison, or doe caribou. I had never ridden a horse. It was wider in the back than a caribou, but not as wide as a bison. I couldn't stand on it, like I could the bison. I couldn't drape my legs over only one side. I held onto the bridle and tried to keep the creature slow. I took to it better than Seth. Adel bought a cart and piled the golem in back with Korinyes and Fest. Two horses pulled the cart. Seth and I rode those two. Adel kept the sixth horse with her. Fest rode that horse now and then, until he got sick of riding and returned to the cart. We thought we moved fast. And then, we saw them in the night. The mercenary army.

We saw the smoke first. We moved during the day and slept at inns at night. And we saw their smoke from their fires first.

I had never seen so many black bodies in one place.

The cool late summer wind blew in our faces while we rode. We didn't press our horses too hard. Fest could barely keep his animal pointed in the right direction. He was a horrible rider. He was better than Seth. Seth fell three times. Unfortunately, he did not bump his head very hard.

At night our legs burned.

And the army burned their fires so casually. We came over a ridge and saw the source of all those little fires burning like fallen stars.

They looked bored. They laughed. They sat around. They polished strange weapons. Arquebuses always looked strange to me. They hooted at Adel, Korinyes, and me. Fest and Seth glared at them. The golem scared them all. They knew a corpse when they saw one.

I touched Fest's saddle. His horse stepped forward. Fest jerked the reigns. The horse snorted.

Fest touched my hand. *You're spooking my horse.*

I looked at him, and saw his dark face. His sharp teeth. His skin like black leather. His hands as cruel as an army and his steel serpent fangs.

In the public house Fest watched his brethren pass with no expression at all. He drank too much because he always drank too much, and he listened to Seth tell us about what Seth was doing when he first arrived in the city of Proliux.

Plums, said Fest. *They were plums.*

Outside the foothills grew and grew into great peaks and terrifying walks through an empty expanse of mountain goats and milkweed.

Inside, the laughter of an army descended upon an inn-keeper. The poor old man poured drinks and didn't seem to care what happened to his inn. He spilled ale because his hands were shaking. Only Adel, Korinyes, and I were women in this room. We sat against a wall, and kept the golem with us. The unwholesome stink of the dead body kept the men staring only. The innkeeper had more things to worry about than a gypsy and a golem.

Grandfather's golem didn't drink. He used to eat, but then he just stopped unless somebody forced him. He said that he couldn't feel his stomach anymore, so he stopped eating. For a while, I would force feed him some ale. Nothing happened. I had stopped even that long ago by this inn.

And like a fire of shadows, those mercenaries lifted their mugs in the torch and candlelight. They shouted and sang and pounded on each other for pleasure.

(Later on, I noticed that Korinyes had acquired a few more heavy places in her clothes. So many pockets, she had.)

Adel told us to stay close, and keep a watch that night. I took it first. I watched grandfather's golem from the corner of my eye. I leaned with my back against the bolted door. I listened to the night. Proliuxian villages sound just like Alamedan villages. Armies at night sound like villages on a lazy afternoon. Sudden bursts of inexplicable noise followed by long silence.

Did I ever tell you how our nation got its name, Esumi? Did anyone? It was so casual, and a whole nation receives a name that never goes away.

I was right there.

We were in the forest together, north of the mountains, but still in the high hills before the village. My grandfather dangled at a loop of rope, attached to the end of a heavy stick. Fest led him ahead. We thought we were ahead of the armies. Adel and I pointed at the trees. Korinyes and Seth walked together. She whispered something in his ear, and he laughed. They held hands.

Adel looked at the two, and creased her brow. She turned back to me. *Birds*, said Adel.

Birds, I said. Our language.

She pointed at the ground. She said to Seth in Proliuxian, *What about the crickets?*

Birds, he said in our language. *Everything that sings is a bird.*

She spoke in Proliuxian. *Even frogs?*

Yes, said Seth.

Korinyes said in Proliuxian, *But they're all so different. How can you call them all the same thing?*

I tried my well-practiced Proliuxian. *When you see with your eyes, they are different. When you see with your ear, they are the same. We do not hunt them down to look at them. We live our lives and hear them singing. Everything that sings is a bird. Different kinds of bird they are.*

What do you call your language, said Fest in Proliuxian, *you know, I mean . . . We call ours Proliuxian or Rhiannan depending on what we're speaking. Even we mercenaries call our language something. What do you call your language?*

It just, said Seth, *just is. We have no word for the whole thing.*

Why not? What do you call yourselves? What is the land called?

Alameda is where we walk, but our nation has no name. It is only our nation. For many years we knew of only one nation. We did not need a name.

Why is Alameda where we walk?

Grandfather's golem snarled, *Ask a shaman, get a steaming load of holy sheep shit.*

Fest snapped his wrists and the golem collapsed. He landed in the mud at the foot of a pine tree. Grandfather pushed into the tree. His hands were bound, so he had to push and scrape with his shoulder to stand up again. The bark broke against his vest and crackled into jagged pieces on the ground.

I spoke, in a very slow, deliberate Proliuxian. *Meda is the emptiness. Alastair allows us to exist in the emptiness. We are each of us empty inside, because we are our senses, and our eyes and ears and fingers all reach out. When we sense something inside, it is only emptiness. The world is* Alastair *and full. We are empty. This is* Alameda. *We who follow Alastair live in* Alameda.

Fest cocked his head and shook it. *Okay,* he said. *How about we call your language Alamedan?*

No, I said, *our words are not empty.*

Seth laughed again. *They're not?*

No, I said.

I disagree, he declared, *Alamedan it is.*

Adel didn't seem to notice our moral debate. She touched at the pine tree like the one my grandfather had pressed. In Alamedan, *And what is this called?*

And Partridge. In the last house Grandfather took us to the potato-headed fool, Partridge, lay in a heap next to a rotting sheep corpse. The smell of the corpse was not very strong. The creature was already a gray, abysmal dust castle of delicate architectures and brittle bones. The sheep had been dead at least a year.

Partridge was asleep. Grandfather limped and dragged into the room. And he stopped suddenly. Adel and I pressed in behind him.

The room had piles of roots and nuts, six or seven blankets, and the remains of a fire.

Adel looked at me. I shrugged, and shook my head. Adel looked at grandfather's golem. The golem didn't move.

The boy—he will always be a boy—did not seem to care that the brown stain on the floor was human blood. Of course, he didn't seem to care about the rotting animal next to him, either. He was asleep. He didn't snore. His chest heaved up and down slowly. In the moonlight his lumpy head was pale. Adel lit a torch. The dead sheep turned green and brown. The boy was still pale. His eyes opened.

Hello, said Adel.

The boy smiled and waved. He sat up. He said, *Hello*.

My name is Adel, she said. *What's your name?*

You talk funny, said the boy.

What's wrong with him? I said.

He's just simple. He can talk, said Adel. *Do you understand me?*

You talk funny, he said. He laughed. He said it again with a high yowl. *You talk funny!* It sounded like a kil-de-beer bird singing in a foreign language.

I frowned at the fool. *Tell me your name*, I said.

You look like Aunty Boo, he said, *but you're skinny. She's fat.*

I jerked grandfather's rope. *Do you know him?* I said.

This is Partridge, he said. *They left him here to die.*

Who? said Adel.

His family did, he said. *Look at him.*

Partiridge stroked the dead sheep with one hand and picked at the lice in his hair with another. *You talk funny, too. You talk slow.*

Adel looked at me. I shook my head. *I don't know him*, I said.

Seth told us about Partridge. Partridge was born this way. His soul was mixed up with a bird's soul. He chatters and sings and chatters and sings like the little folk among the trees. His parents called him Partridge and raised him like a pet bird. They kept him locked away in their home, and fed him seeds and bugs.

When the boy was older they let him follow the shepherds around. He liked the sheep. They liked him. He sat at our fire. Fest frowned at him.

We should put him out of his feeble misery, said Fest. *Let his soul find his bird.*

Seth took Korinyes's hand. *We can't leave him here. He needs our protection. He needs our help.*

Adel handed the boy a roasted root. The boy ate.

Seth kept talking. *It is my duty to protect the boy. Zhan's and mine. He's been mixed up. We have to protect him. We can't leave him here.*

You talk of duty now? I said.

I do, he answered, his voice a rock to be thrown.

Adel smiled at the boy. *Partridge, tell me how long you have been here alone.*

Partridge looked up. *You talk funny.*

I know, said Adel, *and you look funny. And that makes us even.*

I don't look funny.

Tell me how long you have been here, alone.

I don't look funny, he said.

You look fine, said Adel, *But please, tell me how long you have been in this village alone.*

I don't look funny, he said, *and you talk funny.*

Partridge started eating again.

Seth shook his head. *Don't even try*, he said. *Just listen. He couldn't have survived a winter alone. The village emptied recently. It emptied before this winter. He couldn't have been alone for too long. He just isn't capable of it. His family left a bunch of food in the hut, and left him.*

We'll take him to Tsuin, I said.

He'll hold us back, said Fest.

We'll take him to Tsuin, said Seth. *He won't hold us back. He's got nothing but energy. Just like a bird.*

I want Sheep, said Partridge, *He's my friend. He's so quiet. He stopped snoring. Please take us with you. Please?*

The room was quiet now. Everyone looked at Adel.

Partridge said again, *Please?*

Adel ruffled his filthy hair. *We won't leave you, Partridge. How could we leave anyone with such a beautiful face?*

He smiled. Relief poured over him.

One more would join us, in Ilhota. I weary of speaking of him already, Esumi. I would rather talk of Partridge forever, or Grandfather's golem rotting away.

Golem's don't heal. Every scratch or nick of living hangs gaping open in his skin. His body creaks with stiff joints that never heal right after a bad night in the mountain storms. The eyes burn and unfocus after so many stars.

And Partridge. He was a skinny runt, shorter than me, with a lumpy skull like a potato. His eyes never focused on you right. They drifted around like pebbles in white puddles.

And the stars, Esumi. The stars of winter are the coldest stars of all. They are so cold they want to wear the cloak of black clouds against the night winds. There is no darkness like a winter night darkness when there is not yet enough snow to last the day.

We lounged in Adel's room above the tailor shop. We drank tea slowly. Korinyes hummed under her breath. Then she stopped and blinked. She turned to Adel. Korinyes's voice hesitated. *That was your father?*

Yes, said Adel.

And you are a paladin?

Yes, said Adel.

Why?

Adel said nothing. She sipped her tea. Korinyes did not ask again. Instead, Korinyes opened a window and breathed in the sea wind.

Fest is my father, said Korinyes.

Fest looked up. *What?* he said.

Korinyes smiled and winked. *You might as well be my father. That way I can disown you. I've always wanted to disown my father. You were a terrible father*, she said, laughing.

Adel sighed.

Tycho glanced at Korinyes. He quickly shook his head, no.

Korinyes said, *Your husband wants me to stop and leave you be, paladin.*

Adel looked at Tycho. Her gaze was pure anger. Her nostrils flared and her eyebrows crinkled like bristling caterpillars. *Get out of my apartment*, she said, to him.

Tycho smiled without exposing his yellow teeth. He nodded. *It was truly a pleasure to see you again, Adel. I can hardly wait until our next encounter.* He stood up and gracefully strode from the door. I heard the tailor downstairs shout out words of cheer at the departing lord.

Korinyes held very still against the window. *Should I leave, too?* she said.

Adel shook her head. *Just don't mention my father again and you don't have to leave. Don't mention anything. Just sit down and wait quietly. Argarax will make his decision soon. He is notoriously decisive these days. He wants the throne before he dies so he can give it to Tycho. None of his other sons have survived long enough to take it.*

Korinyes nodded. *And your politics? Where do you stand? Your*

husband on the brink of a throne, and you are a paladin and spurned by
your own family? Your husband on the brink of a throne and here you are,
spurning him from your little apartment over a tailor's shop. Korinyes
ran a hand along the windowsill when she spoke.

Adel ran a hand over her forehead. For a moment all the scars
dropped away. The skin adjusted against her bones. Her eyes opened
up like two small crowns of bright jewels. And she was so beautiful. *I don't stand for anything anymore. I just do what I can to get by. I*
was there when the dragon died, Korinyes. I was in his lair, right by his
side. I threw my daggers and killed two with every throw. It wasn't enough.
And they didn't shoot me. They weren't allowed to kill me because of my
husband. I saw the arquebuses fire and fire and fire. The old one raised
his claws and breathed fire back at them, but he couldn't reach enough of
the soldiers in time, and he bled to death. I touched his maw in the end,
wanting him to take me and live. I was there when he died, and ever since
then, Korinyes . . .

Her hand passed through her long black hair. Her hand pulled
her black hair out across her shoulder like a fallen woman's wedding
veil.

8

After the last house, grandfather's golem fell down against a wall. Snow drifted down upon him quietly. The cold killed his joints. He could barely move after facing so much cold without a drop of blood in his body to warm him.

I had left the carcass of the wolf outside the last hut, and I picked it up and slung it over my shoulders. It had grown heavier in the weight of death, and the weight of a sickened stomach. I wanted to throw up. *Get up,* I said to the golem, *We're not finished. There's one more house.*

No more.

What? I said.

I didn't kill Baba, he said. *She was too old to catch me like you and Seth did. I figured I'd let her live and lose her to her death in the mountains. Then you showed up,* he pointed at me, a*nd I knew she was dead, before I got too far at all.*

Adel cocked her head. *Baba was the shaman, yes? Seth's teacher?*

You did kill her, I said. *You killed her and fled into the mountains. Seth and I followed the trail.*

I didn't kill her, said Grandfather's golem. *And I have no reason to lie about anything, anymore.*

You killed her, and don't lie, I said.

Adel touched my shoulder. *He isn't lying,* she said. *I know he isn't. I've gone over these houses with Seth already, and I saw it there, too, though Seth doesn't know what I saw with him.*

Who killed Baba? I said.

Adel looked at the hut where we all slept. She shook her head. *I had thought so,* she said. *I had suspected it since even the beginning. I looked him in the eye and saw it lingering there.*

What? I said.

Seth. Her voice was soft, barely a whisper. It was like a snowflake landing in my ear, and the chill of it cut deep.

No.

Ask him about it sometime without mentioning it. She blinked and shook her head. *That doesn't make any sense. Ask me to ask him about it sometime, and I will show you what I mean,* said Adel. *Right now, I desire a little more sleep. My mind is weary of death this morning. The boy will come with us, won't he?*

Yes, I said. Partridge was following behind us. He was looking at the dead wolves. He wasn't paying attention to us.

Good, she said. She stretched and yawned. *Have you ever met a murderer?* asked Adel. Her eyes were heavy and her posture bad. She looked up at me.

I think so, I said. I stared in her eyes.

You have met all kinds of men in your life. But you have never really met many murderers, said Adel, *At least, none that you know. They are selfish creatures, like animals with intellects. Seth is a murderer. I can see it in his eyes. I can hear it in his voice. I have come all this way, and I knew it from the start. Now I have some proof of it. That's all I wanted.*

I'll kill him for it, I whispered.

No, said Adel, *You need him alive now. He will go to Tsuin, while you and I journey to Ilhota. One more killer left alive will not change the cosmic order of your cold world at the moment. And in this case, it might even save your people. If we survive this winter you can have him.*

This woman told me more than I had ever learned in this whole journey in this one weary moment. I felt like her apprentice now, and not Seth's. Seth taught me nothing. Adel led me by the nose.

Esumi, she knew we would divide before we knew we were going to divide.

And Partridge we kept because she kept him. Because she knew we would deal with the mercenaries. Esumi, she knew everything, and we followed her because she said that she knew. And where was her proof?

I was a girl, Esumi. I was such a child. I was lonely, and she was there, and I took her hand. She told me what to do. She never asked me to do anything. She told me to let Seth live. She didn't even hint at a simple little *Please.*

Please, Esumi, come to me. Write to me. Do something besides think of me. Betray my husband and become My Lord of the Spring, just as she betrayed her husband and all of us in the name of... Something. A word I don't know, maybe it doesn't exist yet. I can't enunciate *her* reasons.

I don't want to imagine yours.

Staf Sru Korinyes and Seth Immur were still awake at a bed near a window. I don't know which bed, or which window.

The inns shrank and shrank as we journeyed north, and innkeepers seemed to shrink, too. Old men growing older in a world with no youth to step into their shoes. Children die young in the colder world. Young men work as sailors to flee south into the sunlight. And innkeepers shrink.

We traveled as hard as we could, and we still could not pass that army. They left earlier than we did most days, and they moved faster than our cart. Our golem couldn't ride a horse. The cart got stuck in wheel ruts, and stuck to roads and ferries. The golem slowed us down.

The army journeyed only part of the day, and we could not pull ahead of them. At night Fest or Adel or I stayed awake and held our weapon aimed for the barricaded door.

The army camped out not far from the village. All night the dark mercenaries drank and howled below us. Adel and I shared a bed, and she whistled softly in her sleep. Fest sat in a chair tonight—guarding grandfather's golem—but his eyes had drooped long ago. I wanted to kick him awake, but I had watched his eyelids droop in my bed. I would watch for him. And in the afternoon I'd volunteer for his next turn.

I shared a bed with Adel. I held still so I wouldn't wake Adel next to me on the dusty mattress. I stared at the ceiling. I stared at the door. I watched Fest breathe. I turned to Adel's mottled skin. This close there are even more scars, tiny ones like flecks of glossy glass. I tried not to sneeze. I listened to the soft words of Seth and Staf Sru Korinyes. I watched ants crawl across the ceiling like small black moles upon the plaster over Seth and Korinyes's bed.

Morning was just beginning outside. The icy dead of morning twilight to be broken in moments by waking birds, and waking lovers.

Blankets and sheets rustled. *Are you still awake, Seth?*

A kiss. *Yes.*

Good. I'm so scared of them when I close my eyes, she said, *just like a little girl. They look at me.*

Who? said Seth

Them, she said. *The soldiers.*

We will pass them in the mountains, he said. *They won't move as fast as we will. We will outrun them in the mountains, and reach Tsuin and Ilhota fast.*

They look at me, Seth, because they know that no one would stop them. They can see my heritage in my hair and my face. I could be one of their dark daughters. They want to make more dark daughters.

They can see how beautiful you are, he said. *Go to sleep, Korinyes.*

I don't want to, she said. Kiss. *I want to stay awake with you.* Rustle. *Do you want to stay awake?*

No, said Seth, *but I will, if you want.*

Fest is asleep. Do you think anyone else is awake?

No.

Rustles. Kiss. *I should have joined a choir.*

What?

You remember the choir Argarax had?

Yes.

That was a gypsy choir. We are very popular singers. We get in choirs and we sing the songs our mother's sang for us, she said. *They love it.*

Who loves it? said Seth.

The dragonslayers, said Korinyes, *They pay well. They offer security. It reminds them of their power to command the songs of the conquered. I'd be safe in one.*

Why don't you do it?

I don't know. No reason. Many reasons, she said. Rustle. Bones popping—they're stretching a little, I guess. *I don't know. I guess no one ever asked. I guess I wanted freedom to move around, just in case.*

In case of what?

Just in case.

Of what?

Nothing, she said. *It was just in case.*

The armies moved in the morning, and they moved fast. They jogged with heavy packs and kicked up a cloud of dust. We watched it in the distance while we rode our horses.

The army moved through the forest or along the road, whichever happened to be the fastest. In the mid-afternoon, they set up large square camps with wooden walls and deep ditches. At twilight, their many fires trailed long tongues of smoke into the air.

Dragonslayers killed visitors, and invaded. Their armies moved north to arrive at the edge of winter, to cross over just before the snow and reach Tsuin while our whole world huddled in our homes for the months of cold. Alamedan nobility journeyed home from Ilhota in spring. The armies returned from the seaside campaigns against the cannibals on their islands in the spring. Not even the cannibals braved this weather, or they died at our castle walls too cold to hurl a javelin. The mercenaries would move in fast, take Tsuin or Ilhota because those two castles are closest to the mountain pass, and they would hold the castles all winter, with Alamedan food stores, and Alamedan women.

We flew north as fast as we could to warn our peoples of the sudden war.

This was grandfather's doing. A lonely, cruel hunter from a tiny village, who was as illiterate as the goats he killed, discovered a new world and decided to play the fate of empires against each other.

If it is the will of the Goddess. . . .

An invitation arrived by two mercenary men with the same purple cloaks. They knocked on our door and Adel nodded.

Come in, said Fest.

And in they came, two men with kinky black hair like dead moss on their heads and few original teeth. They smiled big and flourished their arms. They stepped inside awkwardly. The room was crowded. I sat in a chair next to the door. My spear rested across my lap. Korinyes stood up from the windowsill when they came in. Seth took her hand. He had sat next to Korinyes, on Adel's bed, and he had kept sitting when the two men arrived.

Adel had been sitting on her divan, facing the door. Fest sat next to Adel, and glared at the two visitors.

Adel stood up. She ran her rough hands over her dress, to straighten the creases. A gesture as casual and meaningless as anything. As her hands passed down her dress, her body changed. It straightened. Her face hardened like death. She clothed herself in her own nobility. The reckless anger of moments ago lost on her face, and only a calm now. I think that would be the face that burns itself into the retinas of Tycho, when she would kill him.

The two messengers looked around the room. They looked lost.

Finally, one of them caught Fest's eyes. *Proconsul Argarax sends his greetings, and his invitation,* said one.

Fest nodded.

A village, at the quiet edge of an oxbow lake. We approached in a flat-bottom boat. This village was one of the last villages before the jagged mountains really and truly took over from the round foothills.

A sailor told us, *This is the village where the priestess died in the middle of a wedding. She was very fat, and her heart left her right before the two lovers kissed.*

Grandfather's golem grumbled. *That was years ago, I reckon, and all of them long dead, and it's the only thing worth talking about ever happened here. Another village. I hated villages. I hated them all.*

Seth leaned against the prow of the boat. *This is the village where they tried to kill us because we looked like you,* he said, *They tried to kill us because you had come through, and abused a poor girl. I left her mother some skins to trade to pay for the poor girl for a while, at least. She was badly hurt.*

And you believed her? said Grandfather. *You believed her without any proof didn't you?*

What evidence did I need? said Seth, *They were going to kill us. We paid to stay alive.*

They took advantage of you. I never hurt that girl. The golem growled like an animal. *She was hurt when I arrived and they played the same scam on me.*

The sailor could not understand a word the two men spoke, because it was in Alamedan. The sailor pushed a long stick to the back of the boat, then he walked forward to the front, and did it again. He spoke little. Sometimes he hummed snippets of familiar melodies. The other sailors did the same in their own private worlds of long workdays up the river. The pale passengers were only a mild topic of conversation before a well-earned rest.

I sprawled upon the deck in the cool afternoons, and I stared into the sun. I listened to the hummed sailor songs. A familiar melody caught in my ear like a spider's net. I heard the choir of gypsies in my mind, that I had heard in life just before I killed grandfather.

Proconsul Argarax kept two silver towers in his estate. He lived on the mainland, atop a hilly peninsula. Korinyes pointed at the high turrets, the silver steel balustrades cloaked in bright red tapestries. *I hear he keeps cannon pointed at the city, just in case*, she said.

Fest shook his head. *They'd never reach the island from there. Cannons aren't that powerful. They'd probably not even aim good into the water.*

We caught a ferry across the water. Sixteen men rowed the boat without caring much for organized directions. Over their heads, a giant rope, as big around as my skull, slid through two gigantic loops of steel. The ferry wobbled and cranked around on the swift waters, but the rope kept us in line with the shore.

An hour spent on deck feeling sick, I listened to Adel tell Seth what he needed to do inside. Let the old man live, or kill him fast. I assumed they spoke of grandfather.

We arrived at evening twilight, and my stomach had arrived as well, at the back of my throat. I think it liked the view of oceans, so it crawled up to see the black waters and the shoreline.

The ferry took us to Proconsul Argarax's front gate: a stone pier. At the end of the pier, purple cloaks with long, curved swords. Between the two guards, a large silver door, with an upside down dragon carved into it, spread like a hung, dead rabbit. His claws jutted out like knobs. The guards said nothing. They grabbed the claws of the dragon, and tore open the silver cadaver.

The gardens were next, with one long path lit up against the fading light by a chain of torches. The light was like a liquid brook of light spilling down from Argarax's palace. We walked up the stone pier, into the dead dragon's esophagus of gravel and smoke, the humid trees of the peninsula's swamps spread out in dark green shadows. We heard a bellows of bugs and night birds, and a steady cicada heartbeat.

I heard footsteps in the forest, but they were outside of the light, and I don't know if it was man or beast, or something else entirely.

Korinyes pressed closer to me. *Seth isn't a fighter, but you are. Will you keep me safe in there?*

I will, I said. *And Fest will, too. And so will Adel.*

Tell me that again sometime, she said, *and maybe I'll believe it.*

The next wall was silver, too. A dragon's skull was hammered into the metal. The nostrils were the flaming handles. The mercenary guards in purple cloaks twisted and pulled as we approached.

We walked to the head of the dead dragon: Argarax, in his palace. Past this dragon's head gate were low houses for soldiers and servants. Argarax maintained a village within a home. This I understood.

That was like Tsuin. Proliux was like Ilhota. Tsuin is where Lord Tsui lives, and it is a city. Ilhota is where the nobles go to speak with each other, and with the Shamans of Alastair. And Ilhota is a larger city of many loyalties and many houses outside the main wall.

Something heavy fell inside one of the huts. Korinyes touched my arm. I turned but saw nothing.

Korinyes snatched my hand from the air. We were outside of Tsuin. The dark gray walls of rock through the fast-falling snow were only visible in moments. A wind whipped the snowflakes like drapes out of our vision. Tsuin appeared and disappeared through the white fog.

It was so cold. I couldn't feel my feet. My nose was numb. Korinyes wore her bedroll around her shoulders for warmth. Still she shivered. When she spoke to me, her jaw could barely utter a sound around her shivers. When she grabbed my hand, I could barely feel it, and I thought, neither can she.

What are we doing here? she said. *Why are we doing this?*

I bit my lip. It stung bad in all this cold. I wrapped my cloth-bound fingers around her arm. I rubbed it hard for the warmth and the blood inside of her to move again. I looked ahead at Prince Tsui. *We won't survive the winter outside the walls,* I said.

But they've taken the city. We'll die in there, whether we get their leader or not. The Mercenaries won't stop killing just because they don't have someone in charge.

I glanced at Adel's back. Her black hair against her cloak in the strong wind. Adel leaned against the winter and pressed hard forward, always forward.

Adel will lie to them, I said. *She is a Proliuxian noble in a land without them. That's what she told us she would do. It's what she did in Ilhota.*

Korinyes frowned. She whispered, *If I were you, I wouldn't trust her. She has betrayed before, you know. She left her kin for the Rhiannan paladins. She told us as much. Don't you remember? And now she leads us into the arms of the Argarax army.*

Seth touched Korinyes's shoulder. *We aren't important people in this world, Korinyes,* he said. *We are not valuable hostages. Maybe the prince is, but we are not. Please, we don't have a choice right now. I'll keep an eye on her. I won't let her pull anything.*

Korinyes jerked away from him. *You wouldn't know what to do, if she did.*

The walls of the castle loomed ahead of us. Prince Tsui led us to the fractured front gate. He and Adel walked side by side, their cloaks whipping around them.

Seth tugged his own cloak around him hard. The wind grabbed at his growing hair.

This is the wind that steals children, he shouted, *This is the wind that carries the children into the mountains, where they are so smothered in cloud and snow that the boys become goats and the girls become wolves! This is the wind that has carried away Korinyes's heart! If love fails in this wind, so too shall we!*

Shut up, I shouted at him, *I don't want to hear it from you! I don't want to hear anything from you! I should kill you now! I should just break your legs and leave you here to freeze with the souls of the murderers!* I pulled my dagger from my pack and spun it toward Seth's legs.

Fest grabbed my hand. I don't know where he came from, but he was there, and he grabbed my hand. In his other hand he led Partridge. *In a war with mercenaries, every soldier counts,* he said. *Haven't I told you that already? I wish we still had the dead one with us.*

I pulled my spear from Fest's hands. I shoved it back into its lashes on my pack.

Come on, said Fest, *We're falling behind. We can't get separated in this mess. It's worse than a sandstorm. At least sand is a warm death.*

Back in the window, in the last inn on the last night. I drifted in and out of sleep until the creeping tide of morning washed in from the window. The rustling leaves in the autumn wind woke Korinyes and Seth, too. The birds sang. They talked so softly, I could not quite discern one voice from the other. I could barely make out the whispered words.

Are you still awake? Rustle. Kiss.

Yes.

The birds here are beautiful. I love how they sound. What are they singing?

They sing. People don't care what they say. Just like the choir of gypsies. They sing beautifully and no one cares what they say in their secret language.

No, not like the gypsy choirs. Those birds are free. They sing and soar and they are free.

The gypsies would sing if they were free. The birds would sing if they were in chains. Either way, the music is beautiful. Perfect music to kiss to.

Kiss.

Proconsul Argarax's main house was a castle of painted plaster and pink coral. Instead of crenelated turrets were towers with shingled hats. Even in the fading light, the bright red tapestries like wide runnels of dry blood blazed out against the pale pink palace.

The diaphanous songs of gypsies, a hundred gorgeous voices strong, dripped from the windows and clung to our ears. I had never heard anything like that before. Music like a choir of birds trained to sing together one pure melody of beauty.

Two guards in purple cloaks stood next to this door. The door was wide open, and solid wood. The brass hinges were polished to a mirror shine, and they leafed out in autumnal furls.

Inside the walls were bright white plaster, and paintings hung from the rafters like hard tapestries on steel strings. We stepped inside and I saw the plaster a little closer. The craftsmen had drawn designs of hills, flowers, and curling surf upon the walls, in tiny white cuts.

People were here, dozens of them. The grand entryway of this palace was so full of people. On a raised stage Rhiannan refugees stood, mostly gypsies like Korinyes, with mouths open and beautiful sounds spilling over the room of decadently dressed dragonslayers.

The singing stopped. A pause in the air. I gasped for breath. And then, no applause for the singers. A conversation only. The echoing room held the song in the air still, but soon the jabber of words filled the hole of sound.

Korinyes grabbed my shoulder, *Hey, are you coming? Are you paying attention or what? We can't get separated in here!*

I turned. We were being led past the crowd and the choir to a side room.

Inside of this room, Proconsul Argarax stood next to piles and piles of food, each mound as beautiful as a painting. The smell of good Proliuxian food will always come back to me. The strong spice smells of a royal feast. Cinnamon. Cardamom. Pork. Fruit.

And Proconsul Argarax, the tall, angular old man, stood between two beautiful women both young like me.

Inside of Ilhota we would find Prince Tsui.

In the center of the city, just beneath the holy tower, spears lined the earth with bodies impaled and left for the crows. The representatives of the kingdoms of the confederacy left to the sky and Alastair's blind winter eye.

Except for him. His fat belly did not give him away among the shamans. And they hid him because they know how important it would be after this was all over to have a nobleman left in the city. The other nobility fought hard. They died so fast. They thought it was cannibals.

And the invading force herded the people into the center square, and took all of the nobles' bodies and hefted them into the air on long pikes. Those that were still a little alive died slowly, screaming in pain.

Except Lord Tsui's nephew. He said that he was studying in the high tower when the armies came, and it happened too fast to fight back successfully. When he reached the ground he was captured before he could raise a shout. He had to wait and hide among the shamans and merchants.

Voices clattered just past our host's giggling and delicious distant cousins (he had introduced them as such). One had blue eyes. One had green eyes. Their faces peeled away from the same ambiguously pretty mold. These girls were bred for this place, on the arm of a dragonslayer, and they fulfilled that place adequately.

We odd outsiders passed into the ballroom, and one of the darling cousins—green eyes—touched my face. *Is this really your skin?* she said.

I nodded.

You are so beautiful with such light skin.

I harumphed in my best impersonation of a general. We pass into the ballroom. The whole world here is fluid as blue fire, as the milkweed smoke that brings the dreams of demons, as the ocean currents and the clouds. Here they are, all of those dreams: crowds of people dressed in shimmering demons, holding the shimmering demons in their hands and gnawing politely on the food. The smiling brown faces with high cheekbones. All of them brown and oozing that bitter, perfect odor. I smelled cinnamon in that room and too much perfume.

Are you a girl? said green-eyes in her golden voice, *You are a girl, aren't you? I think you are a girl.*

No, I said, *I am a woman.*

The choir stood on their high stage, men and women in rows wearing long white robes. They began to sing in another haunting, dissonant key. The pain of Rhianna falling was in their voices, in the dragonslayer's ballroom.

Korinyes never joined a choir.

After the village we divided. Seth thought it was his idea, but Adel led him to it.

Adel and I moved fast to Ilhota. The snow had started to fall steady now. We had about a month until the winter set in for good. We carried bits of burned wolf meat that tasted like sour ashes.

We didn't sleep much. We started a fire at night with leftover milkweed. We made small fires. We had little left. It was so cold. When we felt rested enough, we tied the burning milkweed to a stick with leather straps and we ran through the darkness until even that died. At night, we were warmer if we were moving.

And we talked, Esumi.

A conversation of her life. A marriage born before her. Two babies tied together in the womb by two men who each vie for the same empty throne where a dragon used to sit.

In Proliux and Rhianna, said Adel, *we believe that when we kill something, we become the thing we kill. A hunter eats the animal he kills and becomes that animal. A dragonslayer becomes the dragon he kills and eats the dragon meat and vies for the dragon throne. This is why I can let Seth live. He killed the shaman. He is a shaman now. And you are the dangerous one. You killed the killer. You are the killer, now.*

I am not Proliuxian, I said viciously, *and I want to kill him. When we go back for him, I want to kill him. He is a murderer. You know it to be true. I believe it in my heart, too.*

You can't always get what you want, she said firmly. *You'll understand later on, I think. And if you don't, then it won't matter much, one more killer left alone by law.*

Proconsul Argarax nibbled casually on a piece of white cheese. He gestured at the ballroom.

So many of my fellow dragonslayers are dying to witness the execution, you know. Your father has been ever the burden on us, socially speaking.

Socially speaking, said Adel, *you have ever been the burden on me as well. I will relish your execution someday.*

He laughed. *What? And this is how you greet your husband's father? You can't still be angry about the old nonsense with Rhianna. You simply can't.*

Adel reached for a slice of bread. She quietly lifted it and hefted it in her hand, as if it were one of her heavy daggers. She did not eat. *Paladins of Rhianna hate you always.*

He laughed at that. *Ah, but I have become the dragon. I killed your precious old one myself. I shoved my blade into his heart. I ate of his flesh. The paladins follow me, now. You should follow me. I am the dragon.*

Your armies did it, said Adel, *your dark-skinned armies did it. Your generals ordered the mercenaries to kill. They did it with arquebuses, thousands of them. And thousands of mercenaries died trying. And you weren't there. And those mercenaries aren't allowed in your ballroom as anything but soldiers, born to die for you.*

I was there, he said. He let go of the two women. He stepped forward to the paladin. *I was there when we killed him. It was my hand that drove the blade into his face.*

I was there, said Adel, *and it wasn't your hand that drove that blade. I don't care who you are. I won't let you lie to me again.*

Old Argarax sighed. *Hm. We can stand here and catch up all evening and anger each other or we can get this mess over and done with. You want to kill the old man. I have him in the ballroom. He doesn't know what's going on. I say good riddance. He's so very rude. As are you, dear daughter. Send Tycho my love.*

Adel looked over at me. *Tycho has never wanted my love, nor has he ever had it. And you know this already. And the killer is in the other room. Seth, do you remember what I told you?*

I do, said Seth. Seth reached for a piece of white cheese. He pulled it up to his mouth. He nibbled slowly. He sighed. *Lovely,* he said. *That is absolutely delicious, Proconsul Argarax. Thank you so much for your hospitality and cooperation with this issue.*

You're welcome, said Argarax.

Seth nibbled slowly. All eyes were on him eating cheese.

Argarax cocked his head. *Well, are you going to kill him or are you going to eat my cheese?*

We will kill him, said Seth. *It is our duty. Then I will attempt to turn him into a golem to guide us over the mountains again.*

Argarax and Adel spoke at the same time. *A what?*

Seth smiled. *I hope it works. If it doesn't work, well . . .* He took another bite of cheese. *We have come this far to kill him. We will kill him.*

Adel nodded. Argarax smiled. *Good,* he said. *Word got out about your companion here. My friends were hoping to see her in action for themselves. A regular paladin, they say. A woman warrior who can kill the most dangerous men. Not many women can do that. Even the paladins usually turn away most of the girls that want to fight.*

There are many more like her. An army of them, said Seth. *They ride giant beasts into battle and throw their spears into your throat. Every second born child defends us from the* cannibals. *The women become riders, or archers. They are ferocious warriors. The men are warriors, too, with heavy axes and long javelins.*

Paladins aren't soldiers, said Adel, *at least, not if they don't have to be. They uphold justice. They serve the dragon. This girl is no paladin.*

Adel flexed her fingers in and out of fists. She bit her lip and looked away from Argarax.

The dragon is dead, said Argarax. *They're all dead. We set men free from the slavery of the monster's stomach.*

It wasn't slavery, said Adel. *It was a freedom like nothing you could ever imagine.*

You would've volunteered to feed him, said Argarax. *You would've given yourself to him gladly, and smiled while he gnawed on your bones. You paladins die to extend the life of monsters. You should be happy I killed him. You don't have to die for anything anymore. You can live your life free, and die for nothing at all but old age.* His voice dropped with his gaze to the floor. Grandfather spoke now, to his daughter-in-law. *Look at you,* he said. *You used to be so beautiful. My son loved you once because you were so beautiful. He had others, I know, but he did love you. Don't you ever forget that. Before the war, and before you left him . . . And now, look at you. You have more scar than skin. You swore to die for a monster that would eat you alive. You serve it happily. You call it freedom?*

Yes, said Adel, *You will never understand freedom. You and your son will never understand true freedom. You think freedom is the throne of the world, where no one can alter your words, and no one can tell you what to do, and men live or die by the slight twitch of your eyebrow. That isn't freedom. That is a life of fear.*

I don't treat the question philosophically, child, he said. His distant cousins giggled. *Ah, but you are my guest, and I shall entertain your notions to be polite. Besides, I am curious about you, child. You are an enigma to us all. So tell us, what do you think is freedom?*

Death is freedom, said Adel, *and service of the dragon was freedom, and justice is freedom, and the world's truths unchanged by your tongue are freedom. And you did not kill the dragon. I was there. I watched him die. I know who killed the dragon. The dragon was betrayed by his own command. Even the dragon embraced his truths, Argarax, unlike you. The dragon ordered his own death. All the paladins knew it. The people know it, too, whether you tell them what to say they think or not.*

Argarax smiled. He looked out at his crowded ballroom. *These are old words of old things. We will never understand each other, dear daughter. I just wanted you to know that your husband did love you once. That is all.*

It isn't enough to love, said Adel. *Love is not enough. Only death is an end unto itself.*

An interesting philosophy, dear daughter. And the matter at hand, said Argarax, *the killer in my midst, masquerading as an interesting, if vulgar, foreigner who desires to open trade routes to the nation across the mountains?* Argarax and Adel still stared at each other, though Argarax was verbally talking to us now. The gaze between the two enemies locked together, a conversation unto itself, where no words can express the complexity of the mind. No language carries the thoughts of Jardan Bosch Adel into the mind of a man who believes that all he says is truth.

Seth glanced at me, then, when Argarax and Adel locked eyes. I think Seth was trying to tell me something. I don't know what.

Proconsul Argarax looked away with a quick flick of his neck. He released his distant cousins. He stepped into the ballroom. The two delicious women stayed near the food. They followed me into the ballroom.

One spoke to me.

No, I said, *I am a woman.*

I rolled my shoulders and popped my neck. All this way we had come. A whole new world of men and women, and our killer hiding among them in the largest city in the world.

And the best and brightest of Proliux stood with him in the ballroom. The choir sang. The food and drink flowed. All to see a foreigner die by my spear.

They were thinking about our nation's ability to fight.

Snow and snow and snow, the whole time it took to run to Ilhota. The sun rose late, and melted some of it. We didn't actually see the holy tower in the sky.

We saw snow clouds, and sometimes thunder. It snowed. Of course it snowed. We saw the walls a darker gray than the white horizon. Smoke, too, in thin, gray curves slinking up smoldering lines into the sky. The houses outside of the city had been burned to the ground, and still sat in ruin.

Adel and I had run along the road as best we could. The forest and the low brush had been cleared away from this straight path through the woods. We had stepped in snow and had felt wheel ruts etched into the permafrost. Then we had reached low brush and the pure grass we could only know by the shape of the carved hills beneath the falling snow.

The sun melted some of the snow in the short daylight, and it turned into freezing mud beneath our feet. And we ran through the forests until we saw the walls.

The city was already a smoldering ruin, by then. The outer walls were blown to pieces. The burned wooden huts were torn down, too, and lay in skeletal architectures poking up from the low snow like half-buried corpses. The snow was higher than any bodies, and for that I was grateful. I didn't want to see another corpse ever again unless it had dark skin.

The castle walls of Ilhota were still intact, inside the city walls. Adel gestured at the blackened wall. I said, *I don't know what happened.*

I do, she said. *But we need to get closer and see if it's my mercenaries or your cannibals. We need to get inside, too.*

It's not cannibals, I replied, *They've never breached Ilhota, and they never go so far inland during winter.*

We need to be certain. Her voice nearly cut me off. *It's important.*

I'm certain, I said. *And if you remembered what I had told you about the cannibals, you'd be certain, too.*

Adel touched my arm. *Then let us go to look for their general.*

Why?

If we kill him the mercenaries fracture with no employer, she said. *Do you know a way inside?*

No, I said. *I've never been here before.*

We ran along the inner wall, which was intact. The wall was high, and nobody was on it.

The wind, Esumi. You know that wind. It rides the winter like ice skates and it flies down over us.

Ilhota stands tall. The buttresses around the castle walls hold down against the snow. The holy tower stands tall. And our feet crunched in the snow. I touched Adel's shoulder. I shook my head and said, *Shh . . .*

Somewhere in the darkness a baby cried. Then it stopped as suddenly as it began. The wind blew. The charcoal wall was cold on my hand. On the other side of my hand a thousand people died, slowly, underfed, and with too few fires and too little charcoal burning on top of what could only be dried up shit.

In the elegant ballroom, Argarax raised his hands. *Hello, everyone, I have an announcement.*

The crowd silenced remarkably fast. Silence came like a candle snuffed to smoke.

Where is the foreigner? shouted Argarax, *The foreigner is here, is he not? Where is he? Friend Immur! Where are you?*

I held my breath. My hand tightened around my spear. My eyes narrowed into angry slits.

I'm here! said a dusky voice I did not know at all. This voice carried the awkward tones of an Alamedan tumbling over Proliux, like my own accent. This voice said, *What do you want?*

Seth whispered to me quickly, *Don't let him die instantly. Let him linger, so I can turn him into a golem.*

The crowd moved and spun. Kaleidoscopes turning away from the middle mirror. Like human gravity against a stained glass window. Does that make sense? No, Esumi. I don't make sense. I can't. Gorgeous colors, they had. And I had not the eyes for it. I focused through them all, and saw them only at the fringes of my eyes. I didn't care who watched as long as the deed was finally done.

I wanted to see him because I wanted evil to have a face. I wanted him to see my face with my mother and my father reborn in my skin. The killer had to face the teeth of Alastair-of-the-Wolf. I faced the direction of the voice. I tensed hard, and then forced my body to relax. I took a deep breath. Seth rubbed his neck. He pulled out a vial. His hands shook. He pulled out a match. He lit the match and held it under the vial.

I hope this works, he muttered, *Goddess willing this will work.*

Esumi, I don't feel guilty. I don't think this dutiful deed killed Ilhota, or Tsuin, or anywhere because of our slower speed over the mountains. I think that if he were alive he would have led us astray. I am sure of it. He would not work to save a nation from the sword when he worked so hard to destroy it all.

I think the crowd wanted to see him die because he was a hunter who had lived alone for centuries above the tree line and had no sense for nations, or dragonslayers. After he had revealed the mountain passes they were done with him, looking for an excuse.

He had no sense of anything but hatred and milkweed demons.

In the village called Bear where there are never bears just before we left, Partridge took Adel's hand. She tried to let go, but he held on. She sighed and said, *For now, at least.*

Adel and I returned to the rest of them with the dead wolf across my shoulders. Partridge followed behind Adel in her grip like a short leash. He stared at her arm peeking out from her coat. He saw the tip of the tattooed sword there. He reached out a hand to lift the sleeve and see the rest. Adel slapped his hand away.

We moved into the hut quietly. I saw Seth there, sleeping in Korinyes's arms. Seth Immur, a liar and a killer. I lifted my spear. Adel grabbed it. *Don't,* she said. *Not yet, at least. Wait until I tell you it's okay.*

Fest sat up. *I heard the wolves attacking something. I didn't know it was you. Who's your new friend?*

I threw the dead animal on Seth. He jumped up with a shout. The cold, thickening blood spilled over his blanket. *Wake up,* I said.

Zhan, muttered Adel. *Zhan, be quiet. We'll bring this up later.*

Korinyes grimaced at the dead animal. Six ants crawled across the corpse's head, black specks of dust against the white fur. *Ugh . . . Zhan, what was that for?*

You have poor taste in men, I said.

Partridge smiled and waved. *I know you! Seth! Hi, Seth! You went away. Everybody goes away but me. I'm the lord of the village.*

Partridge? said Seth, astonished. *What is he doing here?*

We found him, said Adel, *they left him here to die.*

No, said Seth. His jaw dropped open.

Look around you, I said, *can't you figure it out for yourself? They left him here to die. The village died, and they left him here to die with it. And you did this. You did this to them. It's all your fault. All of it. Baba would have kept them alive through the winter. She would've done something. She would've known what to do!*

Zhan! said Adel, *Zhan, sit down. Skin the animal and get the meat cooked fast. Burn it if you have to, as long as we have something to eat on the road. We won't be able to make a real fire out in that weather.*

I can, said Seth, *we have milkweed left, and there are other ways I have, too. I made something.*

Just be quiet! I said. *Be quiet and don't ever speak to us again about anything, or I'll gut you like a beast!*

Seth cocked his head. Grandfather's golem stepped in behind us. He staggered over to the dying fire. He sat down slowly, arduously. No one spoke while the golem moved. His green skin stank of death. His deadly wound was black with mold. His eyes were sick yellow cataracts. He couldn't bend his knees correctly. He sat down so slowly. He tried to force his knees to bend. Bone popped and crackled as though it was breaking.

The golem looked up at Seth, and neither spoke. They looked at each other.

Father and son.

He came from the crowd and he died before the light of recognition could fall across his face. This man, this evil man. He was Seth's father, nominally my grandfather, but older. He had pinkish gray hair, like burnt flowers. His head had fallen closer to his chest. His face had pulled closer around his shrinking nose. This black hole of hatred inside of him—him, who had spent years alone in mountains with an unfaithful wife at home with so many children—had sucked him into his skull by the nose. He moved well enough, I think, for a man like him. His steps were sure, if distorted in the freeze and rock and breaks of his past life.

And all these things I saw in the blink of a moment. The hair's breadth of anticipation. A face appears from the crowd. One face moves forward a millimeter into my vision. One face that emerges as if from parting waves.

His neck.

My spear.

Before his eyes could fall upon us, his hands wrapped around the shaft of my weapon. He gurgled a little. A mouthful of blood spilled out from him. He fell to one knee.

Seth watched in shock.

Seth! I shouted. *Seth, what are you going to do?*

Seth blinked. He jumped forward, holding the vial in his finger with white knuckles. He popped open the lid. He grabbed at the spear with his trembling hands. Blood spilled everywhere.

Goddess, Da, he said, *hold still.*

He tugged at the weapon twice. It moved out with sickening sucking sounds. The ball of hate inside of the man's skull reached out for the weapon, and pulled it in. Seth pulled it away. And away. And then, the spear was gone, and only blood remained.

Red blood poured out in rivers and oceans and eternities from the wound. Grandfather's clothes, that I hadn't even looked at, were only blood now. I don't know what he was wearing until he wore his own blood.

And Seth poured the vial upon the wound. I could smell it from where I stood. Rotting fish, and rotting corpses, and the disgusting contrast of perfume and fresh flowers. The cinnamon pouring from the perfumed faces all aghast at this hideous sight. And the blood clotted up around the wound. The man died in an instant, but he did not die. His face took on the flat look of death, but he did not fall back limp. Instead, the black ball of hate in his brain unsealed and tumbled out from his ear. The ball of black hate rolled out into the stunned crowd. They parted for the ball. They let the ball roll and roll all the way out the door until the ball knocked past the open doors and leaped into the air like a carrion bird, drifting up to heaven to face the judgment of the dead.

There wasn't really a ball of hate, but the skalds insist upon it, and I think there was in places we couldn't see.

And the golem was born on this floor. The face of death still animate. The gaze cold. The words colder.

This being like the animation of the ice in my lungs, Esumi. He sat up slowly. The crowd gasped in horror. He said—for my spear had missed his larynx—*Hello, Seth. My son.*

The deed was done.

Justice, and a golem.

And later on, with the charred remains of a wolf in our packs against the cold, we turned to the golem. We did not need him over the mountains anymore. We had no time to spare against the cold. The corpse had decayed so much.

I do not know what happens to a golem that is only bones. Do the bones themselves maintain the spark of life, even if the soul is gone, and the organs don't pump, and the senses don't sense? Do those bones buried beneath the snow hang on to life? The slow erosion into dust and rock fed into the grass of early spring—containing that spark? The golem spark may have given birth to the flowers, or the crickets. A murderer's extended existence spread out down to tiny specks of animate life.

And now the universe is revealed to us, Esumi. All life from grandfather's golem eroding away in eternal Alameda, animating the tiniest flecks of dust that gather in the blood.

When we stood we said nothing to him. He sat next to the fading fire. I would've killed him again happily, if it would have mattered. It didn't matter. The dead don't mind a thing you do to them. Chop off their head or clip their fingernails or kiss them on the lips and none of it matters to the dead. No, the dead are gone from us forever. Sometimes they get a little angry, but it is only the shadow of the living pressed into the body, like a soul but much smaller. They obey you when you tell them to do something until time has passed and they forget the command.

The golem sat next to the fire in the house in the village, Bear. His body did not tremble against the rising cold around the embers. He said nothing. We said nothing.

And this is goodbye to the dead: silence.

We left him there. Fest didn't want to do it, but Adel insisted that the golem moved too slow.

Outside it was snowing again. The wind was strong against our bare faces. I turned my back on the wind long enough to see the hut. Through a crack in one of the windows a little smoke poured out. Then a little more.

The golem fell against the window, I don't know if he was forward or backward. The glass shattered. He leaned out, and his arms did not move from his sides.

The fire was all over him. He had caught himself on fire and maybe he watched us leave, burning slowly. Flames lapped at his head like spectral hounds. The smell of smoldering, decayed flesh was a whisper in our wind, because it blew the wrong way. But it was a strong whisper—strong enough to find our noses upwind. Maybe that was some holy miracle of burning golems.

Korinyes had turned, too. She shivered and turned away. *These things I have seen in my life,* she said. *Someday a gentle god will grant me ignorance.*

Do you worship gods? I said, still watching the golem burn.

Not lately, said Korinyes.

Rustle. Adel's gentle whistling in slumber. A morning nearly arrived in full glory and birdsong. I couldn't sleep because the birds were singing so strong now. The lovers spoke louder to hear themselves above the kil-de-beers and the sparrows.

My mother lived her whole life in one place, said Seth.

She was trapped, said Korinyes.

No she wasn't, he said. *We can all always just get up and walk away whenever we want.*

No we can't, she said.

Why not? What obligation do you have to anyone? Just get up and leave, said Seth. Rustle. Kiss. *You're free. Introduce yourself as someone new, and start a new life. Adel did it.*

She kept her name, said Korinyes. *I did it, and I kept my name. You almost did it, and only one person knew your name.*

I know, he said. *I couldn't.*

You were trapped by the hunters of your past. We could leave right now, she said. *They're all asleep. Zhan and Adel will take your father to your lord, and warn your people of the war.*

I can't, he said. *I have to go back.*

Why?

No reason, he said. *Lots of reasons.*

A long pause. Silence. Then, she spoke. *Okay. I understand.*

You don't have to come, he said. *You can go back to the city. I'll find you again when this is all over.*

Do you want me to leave?

No.

Then I won't leave. I don't want you to leave me either, she said. *Will you stay with me?*

Yes, he said.

Forever? she asked.

Yes, said Seth, *forever, my beloved.*

Kiss. Rustle....

Love, I think. The husks turn in the wind, with empty sockets. When empty sockets gaze upon each other, they see nothing. The web binds them together. They cannot break the grip of hands wrapped in memories in the web.

My hand holds another wrapped in gossamer.

Fest, Fest, when I was a child I didn't know how to look. His ghost is a part of me. Your eyes are a part of me, too, Esumi, but would I have loved you without Fest?

In the mountains, we walked behind a golem. He moved slowly. His legs were stiff. Sometimes we carried him and he was so heavy. We couldn't move fast enough, Esumi. Goddess, we tried. We tried so hard. We spent two nights in our village because we needed to rest in shelter before we tried to run through the falling snow. We were so tired. Those two days didn't make a difference in the war, but they made a difference to us.

There is no quiet like an abandoned village in the first breaks of snowfall. I never saw anyone I knew from that village again. It was Seth's fault. I believe in my heart that he killed the whole village when he did whatever he did, whether it was what he told me, or what I thought at the time. Small villages depend on their shamans. Baba would have known what to do.

And Seth.

Seth.

Ineeded to learn Proliux, and he needed to learn Alamedan. We both needed to talk with someone, when most talked at us.

He was older than I could have even guessed, and I was as young as he knew so well. We spoke between the two languages. Our tongues changed color just as the snowflakes change with every drop. And we got to know each other, and that is all it ever was. He was older than I am now, and me a whip of a girl, and both of us had been so lonely for so long.

I told him everything you know, and everything you don't know. Things I can't remember telling, I told to him. He told me other things.

There was a man, said Fest, *who raised me when I was little.*

Your father? I asked him.

No, said Fest, *Korinyes and I have the same kind of father, I think. There was just this man who raised me with my mother.*

Tell me about him, I said. My hand lingered on his face, *The man who raised you. I want to understand the mercenaries better. I want to know more about you.*

He was accustomed to stories. That is what people do when they cannot read or plot wars or drink themselves into bored oblivion, because they keep watch over a dangerous horizon, or they keep a farm in a land of long sands. They tell stories. And he told me stories, and I told him stories.

Fest stared up into the twilight sky past the barren branches of autumn trees. Somewhere a horse whinnied—mine, I think.

He told me everything he remembered. He stared up into the stained-glass purple sky of barren branch against twilight, and his voice eased me down into sleep. These ghosts have no divide between what I dreamed and what he said.

This was all before he saved me. After he saved me, a pause came in his voice, a blush diminished his gaze. He looked away from me.

He would not snatch my knife from the air with a smile. He would not talk to me anymore at all. And at night, I rolled my blankets out closer to Adel than him. Adel was poor company in the mountains, so lost in the milkweed memories.

And I was too embarrassed to reach for him, and change the shame between us of my life debt. And I have been embarrassed to speak of it before now because I wish it hadn't happened. I wish I could wave my stylus over this page and cut the event away from my web. I want to so bad. I can't. I was almost raped by a mercenary and it's my own fault.

And Fest spoke, and his words and my dreams wrapped around each other for a little while in the early nocturnes. And I think I am him, some nights. My eyes close and I see his world of desert and orchard and monsoon rains and an old man and a mother, and even the sufferings of a lowly *mang*.

(Fai'zen stood up.)

I stood up.

(Fai'zen's mother grabbed his hand.)

My mother grabbed my hand.

I reached out to her shoulder. She smiled. *My little warrior is almost ready for battle. First, he must eat his soup. No warrior can go into battle without eating his soup.*

I shook my head. *Not hungry,* I said. I shoved my finger in my mouth and sucked on it.

My mother picked me up. She spun me around in the air. We laughed. I reached out a hand and placed it on her slim neck. She placed me back down on the cushion.

Not hungry for my soup? she said. *What is this? You will finish your soup, little warrior, or I will send you out into the world all alone, and you will never get any soup from anyone.*

I sat back down on my cushion. The soup was in a wooden bowl. I picked up the bowl and sipped at it. The soup was yellow and tasted like yams and onions. I slurped it in one breath.

See, you were hungry enough for soup, she said. *Now eat some more.*

No, I said. *Not hungry.*

I don't believe you. You said you weren't hungry before, and then you ate it all up. I'm going to give you more.

The old man rolled his eyes. *If the boy isn't hungry, don't make him eat,* he said. *If he ain't hungry, he should go to the stream.* The old man had a high voice, nearly a woman's, and he had a scar on his throat, too, that he scratched at a lot. *I want him to go to the stream and kick some fish out of the water before it gets dark. You hear me, boy? Go kick some fish out of the mud. Take two buckets with you.*

I stood up. My mother frowned.

The old man put his own soup bowl down. *Too much onion,* he said. *Tomorrow don't put so much onion in it.*

My mother took the soup bucket from the center of the rug. She sat down and slurped at it. She said, *There's too much left. I won't be able to finish it.*

Give what you don't want to the pigs, but be sure to add lots of water and hay to it. The onion'll make the pigs sick, he said. *Don't put so much onion in it tomorrow. Boy, you still here?* His fat, white eyebrows growled at me. *I told you take two buckets and get all the fish you can kick out of the streambed. Make sure you scoop up mud in the buckets. Don't bring home any dead fish, you hear? They ain't no good to smoke if they been dead too long.*

Okay, I said.

If you move quick, you can get two or three loads before sunset, he said. *Wait, boy. I thought of a name for you.*

I turned back.

I'm gonna name you after my first boy who died. Fest. My mother had always called me something else. She had called me *Fai'zen* which means beloved boy. *You look like a fine boy to me, Fest, and you seem quiet and obedient and I like that. I'm glad to call you my own. Next time we go to town, we'll run your blood dry and fill you up with mine, and you can be my own son. Now go on, get.*

Mid-afternoon sun on a full stomach was like carrying an oven inside of me. I walked through the shea orchards. The wind scurried through the leaves, and the green fruits fell all around my feet. I patted the wide leaves of the yam plants while I passed. They wrapped around the trunks of the shea trees, and their leaves danced when I touched them, like in a wind, and the whole trunk came alive with dancing yam leaves. I wiped sweat from my brow.

I carried two buckets with me, in one hand, dragging on the ground and clattering. I walked to the edge of the old man's land, at a place where a large stream ran nearly dry. The buckets clanked and clattered.

The dry season was upon us. The rain hadn't fallen for months. The land was brown and the earth was cracked up like dead skin. In spots, where ponds used to be, the mud dried and curled into round chips. I remembered before my mother and I were on the farm, and we walked all the time. We dug into those old, dried mud-holes. We found little lungfish and frogs encased in slime and mud. We ate them raw because then we could preserve all of the foul juice inside of our parched throats.

The stream had carved a small ravine into the ground, the length of my body four times over. Even when it rained and rained, the stream wouldn't reach the top of the ravine. I sat at the edge of the small cliff, and ran my hand across the sandstone. I dangled my feet and watched the poor, wriggling fish. Birds picked at the dead ones, cackling and grackling at each other. Even the most beautiful songbird, with reddest beak and the whitest wings, had become a vulgar vulture in the dry heat.

I clanked my pails loudly. A few of the birds scattered. Most remained, too absorbed in their feast, too hungry to care.

By tomorrow the stream would be completely dry, and all the rest of the fish would be full of juicy maggots. The man would send me to the stream again with another bucket to gather maggots, and he would call me Fest.

But that's tomorrow. Today, I wiped sweat from my forehead.

I stood up.

I looked down on the man who took the key and turned the lock. The chains dropped away from me. I had been purchased for three cows and a thick-ankled woman.

For weeks we had walked through the mud of monsoon grasses. My chains rusted. My skin held the burnt orange taint of the rusting chains for days after the chains were gone. I lifted my wrist and rubbed it. The rust rubbed like powder and spread across my skin.

I looked at the rest of the long line of people, hardly dressed, and starving. We limped under the weight of mud-soaked chains. Even the cattle lowed longingly and staggered beneath their chains. All our eyes were sunken like muddy footprints on our faces.

I was pushed. I fell over.

Get up, you. Don't look so beat, said the slaver. *If you don't look good enough they won't take you, and we'll kill you if it's your fault. If they don't take you we'll throw you in the pot.* He kicked me. *Get up!*

I rose slowly. I looked down the rows of women and cattle and I couldn't find her. I don't know if she was still alive. When anyone died they were unhooked at the end of the day, and thrown into the soup that fed the living. At first this turned my stomach. But hunger only cares of emptiness, and never cares for souls. I ate because I was hungry and because it was all I could eat.

My dizzy eyes refocused on the path where I was pushed. Six men, with nut brown skin and slanted eyes fanned themselves and stood next to a dark man with no hair and the exact same robe as the lighter men.

I tried to straighten my back. I tried to walk. I did this because I was told to do this.

I walked. My feet were caked in mud and grass and it hid my bleeding.

The men who had purchased me talked as I came closer. I heard them talking and it sounded like frogs and mangs making popping noises with their throats. I was too tired to be scared. I was so tired.

My mother's blood welled up in the mud prints behind me. The dark man wrapped a rope loop around my throat. The rope loop was at the end of a long metal tube, and he pulled the rope tight, nearly choking me at the end of his metal pole. The man tied a firm knot.

It's too tight, I said. Tears welled up in my eyes.

The clouds in my wake filled to bursting with their heavenly liquids, and like an explosion the rain came. But it wasn't rain at all. It was ocean water, salty and laced with flailing fish like wet hail. The ocean was over my head. Cannons fired above us, and with each splash of the metal balls, the fish died and fell around us, the droplets fell around us, and all of my tears.

The nut-brown men spoke gibberish, and lifted their robes over their heads to protect themselves from the whip of the anchovies, and the hard, wet thuds of the red snappers.

I had walked a long time in thick, rain-drenched grass. I had eaten the flesh of my step-father's tribe because I was hungry and didn't want to die and be eaten.

And we had come to a point near an ocean enough to smell the salt in the air. Over the next ridge, the village did not want the stinking chain of flesh to come within sight.

And foreigners purchased me and I was removed from my chain.

And this was what I remembered, and the image stayed with me for the rest of my life, the feel of it in my bones, my hands creaking with the old weight of rust, and my back wailing sharp pangs of too much weight for too long. I was bought. I looked down on the man who took the key and turned the lock and the chains dropped away from me.

Did you see that earlier? Korinyes squeezed my hand earlier today, and I squeezed hers gently and let go. *I wonder what a man like you does here, so far from the desert,* she said.

I looked down at my hand. A bracelet was missing. I raised an eyebrow. *Give it back, gypsy.*

She held my silver bracelet up. She tossed it into the milkweed fire. *Why am I the scorned gypsy and you the honored mercenary? Why do your brethren walk the streets with no fear, and roam the halls of the capital? Why you? Your blood flows through my veins, and I am an outcast.*

You remind them that my brethren are the same race as theirs. And we are, in many ways, less honored than you. There is a pride in scorn that slaves envy.

Seth frowned. *Korinyes, what are you doing?*

I don't know, she said. Her eyes rolled and she looked up at the sky.

Korinyes, I warned you about the smoke! shouted Seth, *Lay down, and get out of the smoke!*

Korinyes squeezed my hand, and I squeezed hers gently and let go. My bracelet was back on my wrist, and as cold as her skin.

Zhan squeezed my hand, and I squeezed hers gently and let go. *Are you awake still?* she said.

You woke me.

Good, she said, *I'd hate to be the only one awake. Were you dreaming?*

No, I said.

That's so sad, said Zhan, *Dreams are messages from the grave, where mortals visit the spirit world while we sleep. Dreams are important.* Her hand on my cheek. It felt like limp bark.

Death and dreams are nothing alike, I said.

If you say so, she said. *What do you think dreams are?*

I think they are the only time a slave is free to kill his master. And I think when a slave is awake, he feels guilty about the dream.

Slave? she said. *What's 'slave'?*

You don't know?

No. I don't recognize the word at all.

That's the Proliuxian word for them. In Rhianna they are called 'Ohp'. And in my land, we call them 'Mang'. Mang is also the word for the animals that look like men and live in trees.

Are they an animal?

They are men who obey like animals, who have no life of their own but duty for their master.

Like you?

No, I said. I shook my head, *Not anymore.*

Adel squeezed my hand, and I squeezed hers gently and let go. *Here we are, prisoners,* she said. *We who have killed three.* Her eyes looked around us at the long shadows of cobwebs and insects and the rot of dungeons. *Here we are,* she said, *the two wicked strangers from dangerous places.*

I said nothing to her. I looked around the room. Korinyes and Zhan huddled against each other for warmth, fast asleep. Partridge ate insects in a corner. The prince lay down in the filth, but I could not see if he was asleep or not.

There is a man I must kill if I have the chance, said Adel, *If I can't, I want you to kill him.*

Who? I asked.

I'll tell you if it starts to look bad for me, she replied, *Right now, I think it looks worse for you.*

I knew why I came, I said. *And them? Do they know?*

Korinyes knows. Zhan doesn't. Partridge doesn't. And the prince is untouchable. You know that. Korinyes and the prince are both untouchable.

And Korinyes is Seth's lover, and she knows it.

Be kind to Zhan, Fest. Take her with you to Garzakhan. Be kind to Partridge, too. They are in your care after the decision is finally made.

Zhan doesn't need to know, I said.

Adel squeezed my hand, and I squeezed hers gently and let go.

A woman touched my shoulder. Her face was worn wrong, twisted up forever under swords and smoke. Part of her ear was missing. We stood together in the cool morning beside a bakery. A small girl crouched up against the bakery, standing on tiptoes to see inside.

The woman and I walked together, past the girl. The woman said something.

What? I said.

Are you looking for work, big man?

Maybe.

You've worked for a friend of mine, and he spoke highly of you, she said. Her eyes glared at me, an alchemy of colors in her eyes. A bad omen. *Have you ever worked for a dragon?*

No, I said. *Aren't they all dead?*

Not all dragons are dead, yet. Some of them are men, these days.

Do dragons pay well?

Better than you are used to.

Who do I answer to? I said. *You, or the dragon?*

She smirked. *An astute question, big man. You answer to me when I tell you something different from him,* she said. *He is a foreigner. His skin is white as milk.*

White? I said. I looked around. I had seen a girl with white skin before. I had stared at her. I had smiled because I thought she was deformed and I felt guilty for looking.

White, said the woman.

What will I be doing?

Making money, and leaving this city on a noble quest for glory.

I'm too old to change my ways.

You are old enough to know this city will never embrace your people. You do this job, and you make enough money to buy your own city. She gestured to an alley, where we could talk alone.

I followed her. *I can make fifteen copas guarding a fruit-stand, and for five copas I can sleep in a bed tonight. Then, ten copas can be spent on food and drink and I am happy.* I lowered my voice when we got down the alley. *I am not greedy, just a man of my profession.*

She smiled. *Everyone is greedy,* she said. *Even people who have all the money and power in the universe want more to protect what they already have.*

All I want is a bed tonight, I said. *Will I have that at least?*

She shook her head. *Not tonight. We will find a new land,* she said, *and defeat our enemies in this land.*

I have no enemies, I said, *that are left alive, anyway.*

Her worn face looked at me with the weight of centuries. She said in my true language from the desert, *You should be a general by now, or on your way to Garzakhan with the other dark heroes, to find your mardar. Instead, you guard fruit stands just to get through one day. If you led a noble, glorious life with me, we could find you some enemies. And until you have your own, you can borrow mine. You know why I am hiring you, old one. It will pay better than you ever dreamed of because you know why I am hiring you.*

I do, I said. I responded in Rhiannan, *The mardar lead us where they will.*

She lifted a large bag of coins. *Will you work for me, or not?*

What will I do? I asked.

For now, you will follow me. You will stay out of sight of the girl I am with. And when we find the dragon, you will do what he says unless I tell you otherwise.

What's your name?

Adel. I have seen you around, mercenary. I have heard of you before.

I took the money. *Do you even know my name?* I bowed. *My name is Fest Fasen, and I will die for you, Adel.*

The dungeon had six distinctly different kinds of spiders. The smallest spider had two white stripes down its back. It's smaller than half my fingernail. When I first discovered it, I was half-asleep. Two white lines crept over my hand. I jerked awake. Partridge was leaning on me. I pushed him away. He woke up and moaned. I said, *Quiet.*

I pulled my hand closer to my face to see in the torchlight. A spider. I watched for them afterwards. I saw more spiders smaller than my fingernail hiding in the corners of the rocks.

The largest spider didn't pay any attention to us, and we didn't pay any attention to it. In the corner of the dungeon the huge black spider hid behind the shadows of the fly and ant mummies. I watched the huge creature ducking in and out of its own silk dungeon, guarding husks, sinking teeth into them and gazing out at us, stuck to its own web.

I point to it. *Adel,* I say in Rhianna so no one else will understand, *See that spider? It's in a dungeon inside of a dungeon.*

She said nothing.

Adel, did you hear me?

Yes, she said, *very interesting.*

How long have we been here, with Seth away? That was a question I didn't ask. How long have you sat quiet? How long have we waited for the decision that never seems to be made?

Later on, I knew that the decision took exactly as long as it should have. The blade came down, my throat burned. I made the sound of fish on a boat floor when I hit the dungeon floor. A wet slap. A futile gasp. Then nothing.

Another kind of spider had huge fangs. The fangs were bigger than his little body. I held him on my palm and smiled at him

Put that down! shrieked Korinyes. *It might be poisonous!*

Maybe, I said, *I used to be poisonous. Back when I first got my teeth I was poisonous. Now I'm not anymore. Maybe I'm not a serpent anymore. Maybe I'm a spider. I live in a dungeon within a dungeon.*

Has it already bitten you? You sound delirious.

No.

I put the spider back down onto the ground. It crawled away into the dungeon. Maybe it escaped.

I had friends in the city. I drank with them during the day. I worked all night. I drank with them during the night. I worked all day. Usually I worked in the day.

We came in from the street sporadically.

We were in the sun, because we were too old to look good inside of the homes, and too old to fight our own children for the favor of the lighter-skinned in the courts. We kept our hair shaved off because no one hired white hair. When we did not work, we drank and talked of things we had seen. Places we had been. We made jokes about our penises.

I was a young man, and I just ran away from my home after my mother was taken.

I slithered in the tall grass like a lion near the edge of the zebra tribe's camps. I heard the men talking about the cannons and arquebuses they had encountered while working for the Proliuxian merchants near the southern cape. I heard a joke about penises. They roasted a pig over a spit, and poked at it with their spears. They drank mead from ox-horns.

What is it like to kill a man at sea?

It is like waiting to die. The cannon may explode. The sounds are very loud. And you cannot even see the face of the men you kill. You see a red flag, and you make loud noises. You see a green flag and you stop. And you wait for a cannonball to land in your lap and knock your happiness off for good. What are the arquebuses like?

I only had one once, for one job. A near-sighted merchant thought I was half my age and put me on his convoy. He gave me an arquebus and I got to stand with the younger warriors. Some of them had the same nut-colored skin as the employer. I can only tell most of those young bucks apart by the size of their penises. I know they have our blood in them because they have giant penises.

I don't care about the penises. Tell me about the arquebuses. I've always wanted to shoot one.

Give me a drink, and I will tell you anything you would like to know . . .

Zhan asked me about my teeth. I wanted to tell her everything, but I couldn't. I was tired. She was tired. We lay in the dark, and every whisper was heard by the golem glowering on the other side of the low fire.

I told her that I was thirteen monsoons old. I told her I went into town with my step-father. All the women were gone on women's business. Only men were in the town. It was a small town. We ate meat and drank blood and practiced with our weapons. It was old farmers, too long gone from wars, and their young boys. We weren't ferocious, really.

And at night, the oldest man started a massive fire. The men grabbed the boys, and held our mouths open. The old man ripped out our teeth, and burned in new ones.

It hurt. Everybody cried and screamed. We tried hard not to, but it hurt so much.

When the women returned, the girls had them, too. For days we all lay in our hammocks, our mouths hanging open. Even my step-father let me rest, and heal. And when we were healed we were given poisons for our teeth. We had to develop a tolerance for the poisons first, which wasn't so bad. It just took a long time.

Zhan said that she couldn't imagine going through that. I told her it wasn't so bad after a while. I told her that it wasn't too long after the teeth that my mother was taken by the zebra tribe. They were passing through, and raiding every home they found. They took women, mostly, and cattle and pigs. My step-father didn't seem to care. A day passed, and we didn't go after her. He had me making his soup. He had me sweeping. I asked him if we were going to go after her. He told me we wouldn't. He told me she was already dead, with new blood in her body from the zebra men. I didn't care. I left.

Did you find her?

No. I found the zebra tribe, but I never found her. I looked for a while, but she was gone.

When did you stop looking?

I was hungry. I was in the desert, and I was hungry. Some slavers found me eating poisonous fruits. They made me throw them all up, and then they took me away. I think my mother was in their chain. I might have recognized one of the slavers from the men who took my mother. She's probably dead now.

She might not be.

She's dead to me.

Maybe. Do you have any other family?

Not really.

What does that mean?

It means that I don't really have a family. The desert languages do not have that word.

What word does it have?

It has *Ka*. That means tribe.

What is that?

Men and whatever women they've taken. Will you be asking me questions all night or will you get some sleep?

I had hoped you'd be boring. I wanted to fall asleep.

I'm sorry I'm so interesting. Maybe you should just close your eyes and let me tell you a story, and it will bore you to sleep better than questions.

Right.

Close your eyes. Here, I'll rub your feet while I tell you the story, and you will fall asleep. Move your blanket.

Mm.

In the desert, only fools and foreigners travel during the day. My mother left in the morning. She never spoke to any of us about why. She just left. The old man said nothing about it. He finished making us our morning meal out of mashed yams and yucca root. He said, *Your mother left this morning.*

How long will she be gone, I asked.

She didn't tell me. Mayhap her mardar took her. I hope she dies well. The old man said this calmly and pleasantly. The mardar were wind demons, who rode the dust and stole things in the night. We keep wind chimes in every doorway to listen for them. We talked about them over breakfast as the things disappeared. Sometimes the things were taken by people, and sometimes just misplaced. Anyway, the mardar were a casual monster, and children sang songs to taunt them. The old man was not worried.

No army had been through. I was old enough now to know what happened on this small farm. An army came through, and my mother traded to keep our yams. Without her, our yams would be taken.

And an army came through, and she was suddenly gone.

A mardar crept slowly past the wind chimes in our back door. It moved slowly in the deadest of night, and it did not disturb the chimes. It found the most valuable thing in the house: the woman who provided for us all. It clutched at her. She opened her mouth to bargain, but no, the mardar wouldn't hear it. The mardar dragged her from the house while the old man snored, and while I had nightmares of my death in the tundras of a foreign land.

For a few days I looked for mardar tracks near the oasis. The greedy mardar had to take her to the oasis to keep her alive. If she were dead, she'd be worthless on her way to Garzakhan. The village was out of the question. Too many people watched that well. A mile away a single oasis lived on into the dry season. Elephants slept there, disguising themselves as mountains with all that mud.

Are those animals?

Yes. All I could ever find were lion tracks, and a few suspicious looking meerkats.

Closer to the house I noticed some things missing. A broomstick.

Dried food for the dry season. Some small coins. A kitchen knife. Clothes. I went to the village and found her there, with an army of men that had stuck to the towns on the coastline to find plenty of food and salt.

She danced beautifully. That's how she convinced the men to bargain with her. She danced for them and they would do anything for her. She was so beautiful. That was the last I saw of her. She was just dancing and dancing. The army left, and she was gone. This army took her with them because she danced too well.

I'm sorry.

Don't be sorry. I made it up. Some of it happened to me, and some to a friend who died when we were still young, and some of it is from an old children's story about mardars. I don't like the children's story because it ends with a moral.

What's the moral?

Go to sleep.

That can't be the moral.

Right. The moral is sometimes bad things happen for no reason, and all we can do is move on.

You should tell the whole thing to Seth. He knows many stories with morals. He always likes to hear a new one.

I'm tired of telling stories. I'm tired. How do your feet feel?

Mm. Good. Keep rubbing them.

Tomorrow night you will have to rub mine.

We'll see.

10

The old man whistled while he walked. I don't know if he realized that he was doing it.

I was gathering the shea fruit from all around the trees. The other boys and girls from nearby farms helped out. The absence would be felt on their own farms, and punished. They came because this old man taught us things, and while he whistled, sticks rattled on top of his bent back.

He called out in his high voice, *Good work, kids. We still got some daylight left. You want to let the mardars take their share and learn a thing or two about being a warrior?*

The others and I dropped our bags of shea fruits wherever they fell, forgotten. The old man tossed the sticks on the ground. We dove for them. There weren't enough. I didn't get one.

Ain't enough sticks for you kids, he said, *but there ain't ever enough weapons anyway. Use your hand, but don't use your fist. You'll just break your knuckles on somebody's skull.* He lifted up his open hand, thumb tucked in, and fingers pulled together tight. He pushed it against a yam vine lightly. *Use your open palm like this. It's stronger than a fist for sure, and it's easy to grab an ear this way. Try to get the stick from 'em if you can. You kids be careful, now, and take it slow.*

We got into a large circle. The old man walked around the outside of us. The ones with sticks clutched and fidgeted. Everybody else stood tense.

The old man hobbled up behind me. He thumped me on the skull. *Get in there, Fest.*

I jumped into the circle, empty-handed.

Remember, everybody, take it slow!

In the kitchen, my mother was crushing shea fruits and herbs with a mortar and pestle. The stone hammered up and down, and she turned it hard to grind the fruit into a pasty pulp. She did this silently. Sweat beaded up on her thick shoulders. I was behind her. I watched from a tree outside an open window. I looked in, and I looked down and she was there. Her heavy breasts swayed like udders underneath a staggering cow. Her tightly bound hair bobbed in a bun. The old man whistled from somewhere next to the window. He appeared without his shirt. His old body was wrapped tight with bent, knotted muscles like a tree.

The old man came up behind her and touched her arm. She didn't flinch. She kept pounding away on the shea fruits.

I climbed down from the tree. I ran to the river, and I threw rocks. The old man had told me to take the cows out for pasture before he went into the house.

Instead, I climbed a tree.

When he would come out, he would see the cows. Then, he would thump me on the skull, and I would take the cows out to pasture.

He would say that I do not get to eat dinner tonight for my laziness. My mother would put me at the table. He would say that I should not get to eat. She would say that I worked to put food on the table, and it wasn't his right to take that away. He would grumble about how I wasn't working this afternoon. She would say that he wasn't either.

But now I threw rocks into the river, and tried to hit the fish. The rains came every few days, and the water flew hard and fast.

A bird warbled in one of the trees. Cicadas hummed. I stood up from the riverside. I turned to the gray-speckled yellow bird who so callously sang to me. I threw a rock. The bird was too high in the tree. I listened for cicadas and I threw rocks at them. Nothing happened. I ran out of rocks at my feet. I ran up and down the river gathering the rounded stones from the riverbed. I hurled them at the clouds. I hurled them at the trees. I hurled them everywhere.

Nothing seemed to care.

The old man thumped a girl on the head. She flinched and jumped into the circle. She was holding a stick. She was taller than me by at least two hands, and older. She spun the stick lazily around her fingers and swayed side-to-side.

Remember Fest, you got to get that weapon from her, shouts the old man. *One hit with a spear and you're dead. Ten hits from your hand and she might fall over. Get that stick out of her hands,* he said. He clapped his hands and gestured at the girl. *And you, girl, don't get cocky. If he's alive, he can fight back.*

The other kids clapped and shouted. The old man continued to walk around the circle. The kids heard him come closer and the kids leaned forward, ready to run in and fight.

She lifted the stick. I stepped to the side. We moved slowly, like fighting under water. If we moved too fast the old man would yell at us and send us home. Some of the older kids got to move fast, but not me. Her stick came down again. I stepped in the other direction.

The old man taught me all that with pigs: how to hit a man, and how to move away from a man.

Korinyes plopped down next to me. *I'm cold,* she said, *and Seth and Adel are busy talking.*

We sat in the forest, on the northern side of the mountains. We looked down to a hillside. A village used to be there. The houses were all empty. The fields were grown over already in small grasses and young saplings. Small bushes stuck up between the gravel of empty furrows. I was trying to trace the lost marks of pasture by surveying the tottering fences through the fields of grass. Korinyes pressed into my body and wrapped her arms around my waist. *Did you hear me?*

Start a fire, I said.

They won't let me, she said. *It's cold, and you're warm. I can feel the desert in your body.*

I'm from an orchard, I said. *Why does everyone call it a desert? I grew up surrounded by trees, next to a river. People who call it a desert just can't navigate the ocean during the monsoons. None of you people see the brown hills alive with green and the golden flowers. You are from a desert. Rhianna is more of a desert than my home ever was.*

I am from the city, she said. *I sprouted full-grown from ribbons tossed into a fire. I'm a fiery miracle child from Proliux. And I'm losing my heat. Don't talk too much. Just keep me warm. Seth wants to talk to Adel alone. Why does he want to talk to Adel alone?*

I don't know, I said. The sharp wind bit into my skull. When Zhan came back from hunting, I would take the skins of any animals she found and dry them as best I could. I would fashion them into some kind of hat. I did it with goatskins in the mountains, but that hat fell apart for good a few days ago. I ran a hand over my bare skull to warm it. My hair grew back slowly, and only around my ears and the very back of my skull. It grew back white. I saw myself reflected in pools of collected water, and I was tired and old. Zhan liked to sneak up behind me and pull my hair. Zhan hadn't returned, yet.

Korinyes ran a hand over my belly.

Of course you don't know, said Korinyes. *That's why I ask you. Because you are always duty bound to never know anything. Tell me why, Fest. Please?*

Korinyes peeled away from me. *Can't you hear the suspicious sound of whispers among friends.*

I stood up. Korinyes placed her finger on her mouth and looked up at me through her eyelashes. She shook her head gently. She spoke words from a thousand years ago, and in an orchard. I had never heard Korinyes speak the desert languages before. She had a thick accent, and probably knew little of the language. *Tell me, Fai'zen,* she said.

I placed my swirling head down into a small puddle of spilled drinks at my table in the tavern. My head hurt from the cheap gin. I felt hands in my belt, but I knew they wouldn't find anything. I had spent it all. I gave the rest away. I kept nothing. I was a sea warrior, and I could be dead tomorrow.

I could smell the one doing it. She smelled like flowers and sea breeze. She patted me on the head. *Fai'zen,* she said, *how sad to see you sleeping here without a single coin. The tavern owner will throw you out on the street, and my brothers will kill you for having empty pockets.* Her hand appeared on my leg.

I tried everything I could to hold her gaze. I was too drunk.

Fai'zen, she said, *we could be dead tomorrow.*

My stomach curdled and turned over. The tavern keeper shouted something. Men picked me up. My head rolled back. The stars moved too fast, and spun madly. My stomach curdled again.

The men who had grabbed me shouted at me.

I smiled. I could feel the stomach acid on my teeth, eating away at my steel fangs.

The men dropped me on the street. Carts moved inches from my head. Horse hooves. Wheels.

Fai'zen, said the gypsy, again. The gypsy girl grabbed my shoulders and pulled.

I was on my back now. Her smiling face before the stars. Dark golden skin the color of the moon. Dreadlocked hair like a lion tribe daughter. The Rhiannan city moved with the speed of the defeated. At night, the dark-skinned guards opened the gates for the fleeing faces. Somewhere in the night, patrols carried arquebuses and waited for these men and women who had slanted eyes full of fear.

The people who fled knew what to expect. This was an honorable death for them: fleeing a captured city and dying in the night. Maybe some slipped through and disappeared. Just as long as they didn't live a moment in bondage longer than they must have. The dragon would die the same way, soon. The paladins fought hard, but their dragon knew what would happen when the armies arrived at his gates. The dragon embraced his death.

Fai'zen, said the gypsy. She tried to kiss me. I pulled back. My eyes rolled.

I watched the carriages flee. The houses along the promenade all still had lights on. Inside, enslaved sailors slept in empty rooms. They stared at white plaster ceilings or they embraced a gypsy girl.

Come with me, Fai'zen, she said. *Can you stand up?*

I groaned and my head rolled back. I saw a carriage pass. Children looked at me with wide eyes. A mother grabbed for them. The carriage was past me.

Mother, I said

Oh, Fai'zen, said the girl, *You're too drunk.*

She let go. I fell down again. The smell of flowers lost beneath the smell of my own stink. That faded, too, under the weight of kerosene smoke. So many lamps burning in the city. Everyone wanted to be seen fleeing.

Then my eyes closed. When they opened again I could smell the sunshine, like gunpowder, it was so strong upon my skin—so hot. It burned into my eyes. The crackle and pop of it reached my nose. The sun burned the city, and the sun burned my headache, too.

I crawled to the docks, with the gypsy women in my mind.

A moment's peace for a slave at war. And soon the cannons blew holes into my brain with their sound. My blood rushed louder in my ears. The wax that protected my hearing leaked in the heat. I could hear death everywhere. Sometimes it fell from above. Sometimes the men around me froze and stared a moment and I looked away and covered my ears.

War.

The old man taught me how to hit a person by teaching me how to hit a pig. He brought a pig with him into the orchard. I was on top of a tree, howling like one of the mangs. He shouted at me to come down and to take my friend with me. I didn't have any friends, yet. I just made lots of noise.

The old man had a sick pig like a sack of yams in his arms. It gurgled and its eyes rolled. Its gurgles sounded like the old man's rough, high voice, and the pig had the same scar on its neck.

This here runt is sick again. We can't eat a sick pig. We can't let him stay with the others. I'm going to teach you how to hit with this pig.

It's still alive.

If you hit it good, you can put it out of its misery faster, he said. *I'm gonna put this sucker down and show you how, Fest. Hit it good, and I'll take you to the village and you can show the young men there how good you can hit. They might like it, and give you a good spear to practice with.*

No, was that what happened, Esumi? I don't remember. Wait. I remember a dream. I was Fest. I was with Fest's old man, and he looked like Sensei and my father and Adel wrapped into one being, with dark skin. We were sleeping in our hammocks, each of us in our own hammock. White hammocks, threaded like cobwebs.

A pig crept into the room, bellowing smoke. I saw it first. I jumped up and I punched it right in the smoking nose. It squealed. The old man woke up. His colorful eyes burned in the midnight and smelled like cinnamon and sweat. He jumped from the hammock and grabbed the pig by the throat.

Tomorrow you will have to kill this pig. It's swallowed fire. We will have to kill it tomorrow. Today, we will take it out of the house and lock it up. It will start a fire if it runs around the house.

And in the morning, we took the pig from its cage and poked it. It was already dead. *Either you hit too hard, or the pig burns too quick. Either way, we can't eat it. Take it to the river and throw it in. Let the fish have it.*

(Or was it something else entirely? I can't remember this dream exactly, Esumi. I will try another that sounds correct.)

I think I punched him in the nose. I was snooping around at

night. He caught me. He grabbed me by my hair. His hands felt like talons in the darkness. My mardar had come for me, but it was the old man. He had sent me to bed without dinner. I was hungry. I had been skimming rocks at night across the tree trunks. I was eating raw fruits harvested too soon. He threw me into the house.

She saw me and him in the other room, and she rolled over and closed her eyes.

The old man grimaced at me. He opened his mouth to speak.

I punched him in the face.

He flinched. He closed his mouth. *Is that how it's going to be then, Fest? I give you everything, even my blood, and you hit me in the face?*

I shouted something. It doesn't matter what. It was defiant. It was loud. I wanted my mother to wake up and roll back over and tell him to leave me alone. Tell him that I can go out at night if I want because the mardars will take me when they please whether I am in or out.

She started snoring.

I yelled louder.

The old man said nothing. He rubbed his old hand over his jaw. He said, *Right.*

Right, what? I said.

Right, you are going to learn how to hit a man in the face to knock him down. You want to hit me, too? I'll give you that, you little runt. See my hand?

He held his hand out. It was a lumpy hand, sinewed, and calloused and shaped like an anchor when he balled up his fist.

You're going to have to use my hand, Fest. Yours just ain't enough. He frowned at tiny little pellets balled up in his face. *I've seen your hands already. They just won't do it,* he said. *I'll loan you mine for a while until you get older.*

I don't want your hand, I said. *I already have a hand.*

You should take mine, boy. His fist extended out to me. It was right in my face. *You want to grow up and be a man don't you?*

No.

Don't lie. You do. Take my hand. Here, I'll help.

He pulled a dagger from his belt. He pressed it into his skin. His hand detached like a tree limb. He would graft it onto my stump.

Right, he said, *now you take the knife and give me your hand, and you can have this one for a while. You want to learn how to knock a man over with one hit, you need a man's hand.*

I looked down at his stump. I reached out with an open palm. He cut into my wrist. It stung, but I didn't flinch.

I grafted his heavy weights upon my stumps. He took my small, nimble, and soft fingers for his own. My palm was bigger than my head. His palm was as small as his wrist.

I tried hitting him again. I pulled back and swung as hard as I could. He didn't flinch this time.

I punched him in the jaw. His whole head spun and twisted six times around.

He landed without a sound because we didn't want to wake my mother up from her heavy snores.

Esumi, I remember my own mother snoring, and sleeping as heavy as death. I remember pressing into Fest at night for the warmth. Running my hand down his black back. He was older than I am now, but his body was the old man's body. It was balled up with odd-shaped muscles like the knots of a tree.

His voice rumbled up and down his chest when he whispered to me in the night. My ear pressed into his old chest like a pillow for the dreams of the desert. His small white hairs scratched like dead grass against my cheek.

He rested a hand on my head. *Shh...* he said. He smelled like an ocean and a desert, all salt and sand. He smelled like drink. He smelled terrible.

You're tired, aren't you, Fest? Or you have a headache. And you do not want to hunt in the darkness with me.

I am tired. Zhan, you do not know why I am here.

Why are you here?

To die, and save one of you with my life, and go to Garzakhan in shame.

What?

Take Seth. Take Korinyes. Do not take me. I am too old. And I am tired.

I don't understand. Why? How will you die?

You'll see.

Where's Garzakhan?

It is the place we desert men go after we die. The mardar comes for us and leads us away. And the men who were generals, and the men who were brave warriors and died in battle all enter through the main gate, and the large, steel door. And all those who were not glorious, and led weak lives of slavery and the men who are captured in battle . . . We must climb in through a window.

What is inside?

Who can say? I have not known a man to come back.

When I die, I will go to the glory of Alastair-of-the-Wheat, and fall into her arms. And she will take me to her warm center and my soul will shine down in the springtime. If I am wicked, and die a murderer, or a monster, then I will freeze for all eternity under the blind eye that never opens. I will go on for eternity without the heat or the light, and only the aurora borealis will flicker in the distance, and that is the flickering of souls who regret. Good men and young girls are reborn again, but not women, and not heroes, and not the wicked. You will be reborn, Fest.

Are you still going to go hunting?

Yes.

You're too stubborn. One of these days it's going to really hurt you. I'm too hungry to fight you over it.

We were in a village, Esumi, drinking again. Attempting to ride past the army. Always ahead of it, we were, and then, at night, we heard the mercenaries roll into town. The roaring drunkenness after nightfall, and the women disappearing into hiding places.

And us six? We talked. We gambled. We drank together. We kept the dead one from acquiring too much attention. And then, the army arrived like howling wolves. They were right there, reminding us.

I was in a public house, drinking and thinking of which city those dark men would invade.

I paid one money to tell me a secret about his war. He told me that they would fight in an imaginary land for imaginary things. I told him I wanted a bigger secret. He smiled. He had Fest's steel fangs. I told him I wanted to know the name of the imaginary nation. He told me to meet him around back.

And in the alley, he pushed me against a wall. He tasted like alcohol. I pushed him back. I kicked him. He laughed. I pulled a knife. His was already out. I told him that I wanted to know the name of the nation he was invading. He asked me for my name. I didn't tell him. He asked me again. He said I was going to be the only invaded nation tonight.

His hands did not explore me right away. He saw my eyes had fire in them. He smiled again with his serpent teeth. He had scruffy black hair like a neglected hedgerow. He reached out his hand and his dagger at the same time. He told me not to worry. He wouldn't take too long.

I grabbed his dagger hand and kicked him in the groin. He grunted. I stripped the dagger from his hand fast, right over the top of his fist like a sword. I tried to stab him. He blocked that, and grabbed me by my throat.

That wasn't very nice, he said.

I choked under his heavy hand. I struck him in the nose with the butt of the dagger. It bled. I should have killed him, but my angle was bad for a deathblow, with his big arm in the way.

He bit my hand when I tried to pull back for a kill. His silver teeth locked into me. The dagger fell. I tried to scream. I couldn't breathe.

He tore at my shirt. I felt the air across my body, so cold against the fire in my lungs. A whole continent in my body. The cold north of my white skin. The burning desert from his black hand.

I didn't know Fest was there. I should have told someone. I should have told him what I was doing with the mercenary. I don't know how long Fest watched. It felt like forever when I was dying.

Fest was giving me a chance to fight back because he knew I was a killer. But I am a killer with a weapon in my hands. I am a killer when the man cannot hold my breath. This one had me. He had me dead in any way he wanted. I was dying there, with his hand on my body, and his hand on my throat. I was dying with only the feel of his teeth left to me, the numb sting of pain, punctured skin and touched bones inside my hand.

You have seen my scars, Esumi. You have kissed them.

And I think Fest was watching this, waiting for me to turn the tides of war against this dark enemy.

And my head fell back into the night sky. The stars dissipated like dying embers.

And I heard a sound. A voice. From a thousand miles away, I heard his sound. His rumbling voice, Fest Fai'zen called to me.

I opened my eyes, and I was on the ground. My shirt was still torn open, but that was all that was open. The dark man of the serpent tribe was dead. His mangled head was at my feet. His body leaned against a wall. Both bled buckets.

I blinked. *What did you say?* I said.

I said, are you okay? Fest wrapped his cloak around me. I shivered underneath. I fell into Fest.

No, I said. *No.*

What were you doing here? he said.

I wanted to . . . I drifted off into the fear of this moment. I let the world wash over me. I grabbed Fest by the neck and I pulled him close. *Oh, Goddess . . .* I said.

Shh . . . he said. His hand touched my hair. His hand moved down my head to the curve in my back. *Shh . . .*

And I was crying, Esumi. I wish I hadn't cried.

I wish I had died instead of crying in front of him.

And next? What next between us. At night I turned to him, and wanted to speak, but I had no words. He looked at me. He said, *Good night.* His eyebrows furrowed and because he was bald, thin furrows spread up his whole forehead like plowed rows.

I opened my mouth to speak. Nothing came out. He didn't even open his mouth.

In their tribes, in the desert, everyone with serpent teeth is the same flesh, the same people. All who do not have that flesh are not the same type of being. They are edible. They are inhuman beasts of burden for slavery: *mang.* They are enemies. The ones who are of your people are worth dying for, and rape is not a crime in a nation of rapists.

And long ago he left the desert. And that night he killed his brother without thought to stop something from happening to me.

And he never spoke to me again like he did before. His whole history locked away in his mind, I wish I could grab his husk and wrap his bones around these pages for you, Esumi. But he killed a serpent without a moment's pause merely to save some stray foreigner's life. That would be like killing a person to save a cow, I think. I sink my teeth into his ghost no more. The bones deny me. We are broken, he and I.

And when we were in the dungeon, he talked of spiders as if they were brothers. And I never learned how or why he got his silver teeth, but for one small conversation in the dark.

I knew when he gave them up.

First, we scorched the wolf meat as best we could. Nobody talked when we did this. Partridge fell asleep by the fire. He had been long without fires.

Then, we dragged Partridge up from his rest. We turned our backs on the golem's burning body in the window—empty yellow eyes, and plodding, passionless decay—and we moved fast to the fork in the road. One wagon road to Tsuin. One footpath off this road to Ilhota.

Partridge, Korinyes, and Fest stayed with Seth, and on the road. Adel and I took off alone on the footpath through the forests, where heavy rocks lined the sides at intervals across the tundra so we could see the path even in the early snows.

Seth's road to Tsuin cut through the piney woods, and then turned up to follow a river into the city. Tsuin was a castle upon a giant salt lake, and a city grew inside of the outer walls like bosoms spilling from a harlot's dress. On the northern lip of the lake, a thin glacier crumbles into the waters, and slowly the salt waters rise. What used to be a castle at the edge of a river became a castle at the edge of a lake. Someday this castle will slowly sink beneath the waters.

I look out my window now and see them building dikes to hold the lake at bay a little longer. They are small dikes, just outside the city walls, and no water touches them now. Nor will water touch the dikes within my lifetime, or the next emperor's lifetime, or the next. But someday, the water will seep into the sewers. Someday those small dikes will hold back a summer flood.

And Seth led Korinyes, Fest, and Partridge up on the trail through the woods and up a freshwater river of melted snow.

Later on, Adel, Prince Tsui, and I would find them in the woods, with some puny lean-tos to shelter against the snow. Seth's eyes would be hollow and cold. His fire would be small. It would barely give off a single breath of heat. He would be conserving his fuel for a long winter in the woods. His filthy hair would be frozen into red icicles.

Korinyes would cling to him for warmth. Fest would cling to his ragged cloak. Partridge would cling to his belly and beg us for food, anything that might be food. His mouth would be full of cold dirt. He would have been swallowing it to fill his stomach.

But that's later on.

Before that, Seth watched Adel and I walking fast with milk-weed torches in our hands, away from the village, and out onto a footpath through the pungent pine forests that smelled like brisk winter breeze and rotting vegetation. Adel and I walked long and fast. We slept little. We ate little.

We ate the horrible wolf meat until we ran out. Then we went hunting, and found a small, white bear, too young to fight us hard. I had never seen a bear before. Adel told me what it was. I laughed.

What? she said. *I'm not joking. It's a bear.*

I can't really explain, I said. *I just never saw one before, and now it's dead.*

We have killed it, she said. *That makes us bears.*

I do not understand your people's idea. We are who we have always been, no matter the dead in our wake.

Adel smiled. *Whether you understand or not, I don't really care. I think it is just a thing we say when we have killed something to encourage people not to kill the odious things.* Adel's eyes drifted off. Her breath stilled. She shivered and turned away from me.

Wait, I said.

Adel turned.

Your demons are not your own anymore, I said, *because you aren't alone.*

No, she replied. She turned to the road ahead of us. She turned back, and cut into the bear's belly. We ate the heart and liver raw.

Start a fire, she said.

And I killed the men in their throats. And now my throat scrapes the air down into my lungs like I am a fish and cannot breathe it.

In my bed now, the blood runs thick from my mouth. The shamans come and brush my white hair. They touch my face with sacred things and reach into my lungs to help me breathe a little longer. They extend this life longer and longer at the cost of their own.

Because I am an empress, and because skalds sing songs about me, I deserve a longer life.

My whole chest burns, Esumi. I can't feel my feet most days. I see them down there, lumps beneath the blankets. I move them a little. Sometimes I can feel them. I can't speak without a stylus in my hand to carve these words to you. My voice is dead.

I'm dying, my love. I am dying, and I will not resurrect with you. Women die the moment they are women. Their bodies taint the earth where they walk. And this body stains me with agony. I want to die, I think. I wish I could speak and tell the ones who die for me. Instead, I can only gasp for air and burn with every breath and write these words to you, my love. I will hand the shamans my letters and they will know what they must know from reading them.

Stop saving me.

I will bring my love for you to our child, Esumi.

We scorched as much of the flesh as we could carry, and ate that bear slowly along the road. I tore off some of the beast's furry skin, and wrapped the stinking flap around my shoulders. The skin stank, but it stopped the wind a little better than before. I didn't care about the bloodstains on my filthy cloak, or in my hair. I only cared about being a little warmer.

It's too cold and dark to walk in silence. Adel, you must talk to me.

What? Why?

It's too cold and dark to walk in silence. Any moment we could fall over and get lost in the snow and the other won't even know. We must speak to each other. We must stay together and speak to each other.

I don't have anything to say to you right now.

Think of something. I want to know about dragons.

I've told you about dragons.

Then don't tell me about the dragons. Tell me about the one dragon you knew. Tell me about the one who died.

Him?

Yes. Tell me about him.

Right. He was gigantic. He was far larger than the largest buildings in Proliux. He was green, too, with yellow spots on his scales. He had teeth like giant sabres. His voice was deep and slow, like Fest's but deeper, and slower. Every word was heavy with his enunciation, and he never said anything stupid.

And he was old?

Dragons watch the centuries, Zhan. They live in the ground until they're too big to stay in their lair, and then they fly away somewhere. I heard that they fly up into the sky until they reach the shining center of the universe. Then they just keep flying in until the light consumes them.

It was snowing and snowing so long. Adel stopped us along the inner wall. Nobody was above us. We could barely see the top of the stones at all. And the sun would set behind the ruptured outer wall soon.

We had already passed through the outer wall. It had been cut with one powerful burst from the bottom. I didn't quite understand that, yet. The black powder of the arquebuses was piled up together in one place. The mercenaries poured through the hole, and lathered the town's outer houses with the fire.

The snow was high enough to cover most of the dead.

We have to get inside. It's getting dark, she said. *Where's the gate?*

It's closer to the road, I think. Follow me.

I dashed the other direction around the wall until I saw the large boulders that marked the path back to the main road and the footpath back to the village, back over grandfather's trail and back over the mountains and rivers and boats and buildings to an alley, and all alone.

Adel, I said. I waited for her to answer me. She didn't. *Adel.*

What? she said.

I turned around to her. I pointed at the horizon behind us.

Adel slapped her hands together to feel them again. She breathed warmth across the cloth over her fingers. *What?!* she shouted.

I took two steps away from her and away from the wall.

Do you miss the city? I said.

Now isn't the time to speak so we can walk safely in the night, Zhan. We have to get inside, and see if the two of us can conquer an army, she said. She coughed, hard, *And I'm freezing. I don't care if the army's in there. I'm freezing and I'm hungry. We have to get inside.*

I laughed. *Winter is barely here. The snow melts some in the afternoon. The ground hasn't even iced over yet, and you complain of the cold. This is nothing. And the army doesn't know about us, so we can pause a moment.*

Zhan, please stop talking to me. I'm sick of it. I don't care about anything but finding a fire. I'm so cold! Teach me a curse so I can tell you how cold I am!

My Goddess, it's cold, I said.

My Goddess, I'm cold! she shouted. Maybe someone heard her inside the wall.

We stood in the shadow of the inner wall. The weak sunlight was a mile away past the snowdrifts and ruined houses.

Adel coughed.

I don't think we'll overthrow the army today, Adel, I said, *We're too tired, too weak, and too everything but ready to take on an army by ourselves. And people are dying in there, too. And if we go in there so will we. And I want to know if you miss the city we came from, because right now I miss it because it never snowed, and I hated it there most of the time.*

I have a plan, and I'm too cold to talk about cities right now. She tried to walk around me to move to the gate by the road.

I stepped in front of her path. *It won't work,* I said. *No matter how you look at it, there's only two of us and we've pushed ourselves too hard to fight on nearly empty bellies through nearly empty land. There's hundreds of them, and they've been resting for days.* I grabbed her shoulder hard. I shook it. *Tell me how you feel about Proliux before we go to die! I want to know why you fight Proliux so hard your whole life,* my voice a plaintive cry and my heart confused. *You know you don't belong here, and you didn't really belong in Rhianna, either. Why did you come here at all? Before I die, I'd like to know.*

My plan will work because I don't belong here at all, she said. She rubbed her temples through her hood. She closed her eyes and smiled. She said, slowly, *I . . . have . . . a plan.*

Great, I said, *what can possibly be your plan, paladin?*

Look at me, said Adel. I looked in her face and I didn't understand. Her eyes opened and caught a stray beam of light from somewhere. The kaleidescopic colors flashed blue in the particular angle of her face. She smirked, and jutted her jaw out. Her dark brow, checkered in old wounds, creased hard above. Scar tissue crinkled. Her slender eyes growled at me, like joking.

What am I supposed to be seeing? I said. *Because I don't see anything of consequence.*

You did a moment ago. I don't belong here, said Adel. *What business do I have knocking on Ilhota's gate?*

I took a deep breath. I held it. Then I laughed hard. *We won't talk about the city until after we've stormed the castle, then. What do you have in mind once we're inside? Total war? You figure we get the gate open and kill them right away, or wait until we've eaten something and they're asleep? Poison perhaps?*

Poison is too risky for the general population, always. Mercenaries are hired hands, she said. She took up step along the wall. *I've told you this before. When we kill the pocket that pays them, many will lose their loyalty fast. I . . . may be able to hire some of them, but they will not be the very loyal ones and we will not be able to count on them. Regardless, the mercenaries unleashed will hire each other and fight amongst themselves, and we will secure the people still alive as best we can. It isn't the best plan but it will do, I think.*

I laughed more. I was so tired from all this journeying. I was so hungry, too. All of my joints ached in cold. And all of a sudden, hope. *And in the spring,* I said, *we will go to Tsuin and find Fest sitting happily at a banquet table, and then we can bring justice to Uncle Seth, and hopefully Fest won't interfere with us. I don't know what Korinyes will do, but she won't like justice very much after, or us. Then you and I will be heroes for a little while.* I sighed. *And we can put all this behind us and rest our weary bones.*

Yes, said Adel, *I guess that is also a good enough plan for the spring. What, you had a different plan?*

Mm, she said. Just like Seth she said it. Neither yes nor no. She turned to the west and the falling sun. The sun was a white ghost behind thick layers of gray cloud. It fell upon the flat tundra hard and fast. Adel's eyes squinted into it. Then her concentration broke.

She turned back to me. *Yes, I did,* she said. *But I like yours better. It will do just fine, I think.*

Did you ever see him fly?

No. No, he was so old. His wings were cobwebbed with war wounds, and I don't think he could fly anymore. He was so old. He had fought so long against the mercenary armies. He left his lair to fight them sometimes, before the arquebuses. When they only had arrows and spears, he left his lair and tore through them with his fires. When the arquebuses arrived and the dragonslayers' armies, we paladins took him to the palace. We fortified ourselves against them. We would have died for him. Every single one of us would have died for him.

I heard about that once. Who said that?

Proconsul Argarax mentioned it, I think. I'm surprised you remember, or even understood. Yes, he did, actually. Now I remember.

Why would you die for him?

Love, I guess. Maybe respect. Dragons live a long time because when they eat a person they acquire the life of the person. They become what they kill, Zhan. They live longer. They never eat evil, or feebleminded things. The paladins who are wounded too bad to fight anymore volunteer. We give ourselves willingly to his teeth. We smile from his jaws.

When the riders are too old to fight anymore they train the young, and attempt to die in battle. When they are too old for that, they ride into the winter with only a cloak, a spear, and a bow on the oldest bison. No arrows. They don't return. Very few make it that far at all. What did the dragon do to deserve respect besides his age?

The dragon was our . . . what is the word? Maybe it is proconsul. Maybe it is lord. Do you have a word for *emperor*?

What? I don't know what that is.

Well, it's like a proconsul but there's only one of them. That's what a dragon is in Rhianna. Zhan, are you still there? I can barely see you. Say something. Tell me about something.

Oh . . . The sun is rising soon. I can't wait for it to rise. It won't be night forever.

12

D o you even remember what it's like to see your homeland, Esumi? Do you see it in your mind, from the top of Korhal Hill in autumn? The whole world alive in fire red and orange. The purple grasses and the tussocks like the explosion of a rainbow at your feet. Do you remember the braided rivers through the trees, like my wet hair across the grass? The ptarmigans stuttering at each other in the valley while the long cries of the kil-de-beer soar like three different birds from the treetops.

This place is inside of me. I hate the snow. I hate the white world, and the gray world. I hate the dark granite rocks beneath the glaciers, like the bones of heaven tossed to a dead, white sea. I hate that. Adel's bones—say the skalds—turned into granite boulders beneath the weight of snow. They sing about how long she waited to kill her husband. She waits until the dagger fall is clear. Then she will come for us.

The shamans and the skalds have turned her into winter.

But I think of autumn and I don't think of Adel. I see it in my mind, our autumns near Korhal Hill, and my wet hair across the purple tussocks. I think of the frozen breeze that nibbles my skin to bright white. I think of the warmth of two bodies pressed together against that cold: yours and mine.

Against that breeze all we have is each other to keep warm, Esumi. All we had was each other. And then we had a daughter. And you couldn't watch her grow because she had your hair, and my husband knew it. Our baby girl had your hair, and he didn't want people to see you and her standing next to each other. He sent you away from me.

Goddess, I hate him.

The gate was heavy gray ironwood, knotted with metal bindings that hid it in the granite. All of it gray and rough, a slight rust like the moss in the mortaring.

Adel turned to me. *You are my guide,* said Adel, *You work for me in here. Don't speak unless spoken to, and defer all answers to me.*

I shrugged. I kicked on the door. I shouted in Proliuxian. *Let us in! We're cold and hungry!*

Did you not hear me? said Adel.

I winked. *I did. You were taking too long.*

Adel kicked on the door. She shouted in Proliuxian, *I come bearing news! Open the door and so may I give it to you!*

From behind the door voices shouted at each other. Above us, high above us, black faces peered over the wall and down into the snow. They shouted something down on us.

Adel stepped back. She tore off her hood. She shouted something back at them. I don't understand what they said to each other.

The gate creaked open slowly. I smiled at the arquebuses behind the door. I had never seen them so close before. The long steel bell with the fluted end was as close as a frozen lover with lips too big to kiss. The men held them like horns. One end pressed under the shoulder, and the other aimed at me.

(Say the skalds: the future empress for whom they play—the stranger at the gate that day.)

And past those men, in pens with the animals burning dung and small bits of coal, people stared at the activity at the gate with hollow eyes. Hunger and defeat.

Mercenaries captured Ilhota, not cannibals. And Adel jabbered in a stranger tongue than I had heard before. All of them seemed to speak it. I listened to her words and wished I could understand them. I had only just begun to grasp the Proliux when we left the nation for the mountains. And this language was new to me and like nothing I'd heard before.

The sun was so low on the horizon now. Inside the city were only people huddled under the shadows and dark men like shadows with dangerous weapons.

The men led Adel into the city. I followed. I was stopped. Adel shook her head. *No, she's with me*, she said in Proliuxian, *let her go*.

I said in Alamedan, *What did you just say to them?*

Lots of things, said Adel.

Inside the city, the sun dipped beneath the wall for good, like a premature sunset. I looked at the people here, huddled among the beasts. They looked back. One of them smirked. He was fat and proud, and I am tired of telling you about him.

But others. A little boy with brown hair and dead white skin. An old woman like all the old women I had ever seen in my life. A mother from somewhere, crammed in with the caribou and the sheep, waiting for death. Women and children and foolish men filthy and cold and empty as husks.

Except Prince Tsui, who had a thought in his head right then about me, standing among the sheep and the prisoners.

Adel and I walked past all of the bodies bound here like golems waiting to burn.

Inside of Ilhota, I saw him for the first time. He leaned against a wall, and had his hand resting across his stomach. He watched us enter with a smirk. He hadn't seen anyone else entering. Later on he said that he saw me with a stranger and thought he had figured out the whole war. A filthy woman, covered in the grit of winter tundra. Hollow eyes of too much sun in her face, with chapped lips and long brown hair that hadn't been combed in a century, grinding out from beneath her rotting bearskin hood. This child of the dirt must have been an entity of the very hills. The nymph of the long grasses here with her servants to take shelter against this longest of winters.

I think he was trying to seduce me when he told me that. His fat jowls curdled into a smile. He rested his head on his arm, and ran a hand down the space next to him on his blanket.

They are broken, aren't they? I said to Adel, in Alamedan.
Be quiet, said Adel, in Proliuxian.

How can the day be so short here? How can it be so short?

If it is the will of the Goddess, all things become true.

That isn't a very logical approach to the universe. The dragon frowned upon religions. He did not discourage them, but he did not support them either. He told us that our souls were our business, as long as we didn't hurt anybody.

In our land, shamans bend the ears of lords. The holy books are law, and the lords uphold that law. And Alastair's law is not logical. It can't be. Only men are logical.

Why can't it be logical?

Because the Goddess allows for thousands of logics. Each person contains a new one, each bird and tree. All will and all nature are illogical, and we are the Will of the Goddess. Her Will grants for empty places where souls are born. What did the dragon teach you about love?

Nothing. It was our own business to love, like religion. I could tell you so many things, Zhan. I could tell you so many things. I had a daughter. Did you know that?

Maybe, but you didn't say anything about her. Is she still alive?

No.

I'm sorry.

Her father isn't alive anymore, either. He was a baker in Rhianna. He made me cookies with little flowers on them all the time. They tasted terrible but they were very pretty. He was a terrible baker. You never knew what you were going to bite into.

How could he keep baking?

He worked in a rough part of town. Nobody else had the courage to open shop there. He didn't have talent, but he had courage. I wish I could have saved them.

I'm sorry.

Yeah. You tell me something.

There will come a day when the sun doesn't rise at all. It peeks up from the horizon, but it drops away so fast that it doesn't really matter, and then we know that winter has the world now, but summer will also have a day like that and we will know that summer has the world then. And in between we live our lives as best we can. And this is the will of the goddess, Alastair-of-the-Wheat.

Did you just quote a holy hymn or parable or something?

Almost. I can't remember it exactly. I learned it when I was a child, and I have since had time to forget.

I don't forget my daughter or my horrible baker for even a moment. Every morning's another day where I wake up and they're dead.

I know.

Mm.

(A long silence was here, Esumi. Only the wind talked to us, then. It was cold and gnawed upon our bodies with tiny icicle teeth. Our feet crunched the slowly melting snow beneath us. Then Adel sighed deep. She spoke again.)

Talk about something else. Please, let's talk about something else entirely. Tell me about your food so I will not be surprised.

Inside the wind wasn't so bad, with the wall up. It was cold, but the wind was broken at the wall. The wall was breached, though. A gaping hole let the wind howl into the broken village around the tower.

The granite buildings with thick, unbroken windows were full of dark bodies, huddled against a fire and cursing the day they left the desert for a coin and some glory.

And we walked down the main thoroughfare of the city to the next wall. This one separated holy Ilhota proper from the outer homes and businesses. This wall wasn't really very large. It was made from many wooden planks carved into the dirt only an arm's length over our heads. The gate was torn open. Past this was the holy tower of Alastair, and the councilmen's homes. The united lords held council in Ilhota, sending their ministers to meet and negotiate, and all the laws of the land and the heart of Alastair's faithful were here.

In our throne room, before the birth of the empire at the death of the lords, we had no throne behind the men to tempt them to be kings. We had a holy officer of the shamans, praying for justice, and burning incense and spilling tears in the name of Alastair-of-the-Berries, who gives herself up for the hungers of the peaceful. I am a shaman. When Lord Tsui forced my hand in marriage, he took the shaman's seat.

These days, our shaman sits in a new seat beside Emperor Tsui who sits in the shaman's old chair. This new shaman is an elderly fool who drinks too much tartberry wine. He occasionally falls asleep, and snores to wake the dead. When he is awoken by the volume of his own snoring, he usually vomits. My husband keeps a little fat boy to clean the vomit. We call the boy the shaman's young apprentice for politeness, though the boy is just a servant who cleans up puke.

And through the gates of the inner city Adel and I followed the mercenary.

I reached out a hand and touched the dark gray stone of granite and mortar as we passed through the wall, and it was so cold.

He stays in this house over here. A noble used to live here. I think it was that one, said the mercenary who guided us. He picked his nose with one gloved hand, and pointed with the other at one of the tall pikes. At the top, ravens fluttered around human bodies. The bodies were gray and the bones showed through the skin like granite boulders from beneath dirty snow. Days dead, at least. Down the poles blood had hardened into brown paint. The mercenary shrugged. *I don't know which one for sure, though. We took some things from this house to make room for the commander, and that one's woman cried at seeing that.*

Where did you put the women? said Adel, *I didn't see too many women with the sheep.*

We keep some there, and we keep some of the nicer ones inside.

Mm, said Adel.

Yes, Lady Jardan? said the mercenary. He was not familiar with Seth's expression.

Go back to your post, she said. *You may not come in with us.*

A moment's pause. *Yes, Lady Jardan,* said the mercenary. He bowed slightly, with cold eyes.

And give your cloak to this girl. She needs a new cloak, and yours will do nicely. Adel's voice was colder than the wind. *Your gloves, too. She needs gloves like yours to protect her from the cold. She has had not the benefit of a warm fire or a full belly or a warm bed of late. You have. She fights the same war that you fight, but she has fought with poor equipment.*

The mercenary's eyebrows creased deeper. He tugged off his gloves. He pulled off his cloak. He handed them to me hesitantly. I wrapped the cloak around my body, and tugged on the heavy gloves. They were both too big, but I didn't care.

The cloak smelled terrible, like old blood and dusky sweat. It smelled better than I did. It was still warm from him. It dragged on the ground behind my feet. Later on, I'd fold the top over and over and up to keep my neck warmer and keep the bottom of the cloak out of the mud.

The gloves were heavy leather, and well worn in to his gigantic hands. I had to hold them on, and stuff my rags between my fingers from within to get the gloves to stay in place, even a little. Adel looked down at them on my hands.

Hm, she said, *perhaps you can just hold on to them while we go inside. Tie them to your belt.* She pulled my spear from my back. *Here, hold this. Let me tie the gloves right there so they will be out of your way.*

I nodded. Together we quickly strapped the huge gloves to my spear loops.

Now my spear was in my hands. The wood was mostly rotten, but it worked well enough for now. I knew that in the days to come, I had to cut the blade free, re-fashion the spear into a dagger. I held the spear and tested the wood to make sure it wouldn't crack on me today. I had to be careful with it.

The mercenary didn't seem to care much that I, an Alamedan, was armed and walking in to see his general. He stared at my gloves in my pack. He blew warm breath over his fingers.

We stepped into the building where a fire crackled in a fireplace behind the main desk and filled the room with heat.

The now cloak-less, gloveless mercenary set his jaw against the cold. He rubbed his hands together. He closed the door behind us.

The sun was up, I think. Adel, the prince, and I had the city behind us. We stopped to hand each other raw mutton to gnaw upon. We didn't have fuel enough to cook our food in the daytime, and it was day now for a little while.

Adel chewed quietly. She sat on one of the giant stones placed to mark the road against the snowy tundra.

I swallowed the raw flesh fast. It reminded me of my training. I stayed on my feet while I ate.

Adel stretched out like a snow nymph. *I don't think I've ever heard you pray to your goddess, Zhan. Is that something you do?*

Yes, I said. It was a lie.

Would you tell me one of your prayers? Call it a curiosity. Seth told me some of his, but he says different kinds of people have different prayers.

I swallowed the rest of the raw meat whole in one gulp. I took a deep breath and thought a moment. Then I spoke.

Prince Tsui watched. He choked down bad meat with empty eyes. He squatted down and rubbed his knees. He was unaccustomed to walking so long and fast.

He listened to me.

I begin this song with the white cloak of death
that pulls the sheep into one long dream
that terrible Alastair who culls her herd
who, with her icicle teeth, infects this song
turn from me, Goddess,
let me see instead your bright eye
the arrow I throw in the fear of fire
the axe I hold in your name; I pray
and scream the work of wars,
the men and women who seek you:
the army, when it comes
and when it also goes.
With you I begin,
And having begun with you,
I turn to another song.

Korinyes had soft skin, and her hair was always cleaner than it should be with all of our traveling. Her eyes were dark green. I think they were dark green. I can't really remember what they were. Maybe brown? They were beautiful eyes, and two of them, like anyone else in the world. They looked at you like they loved you when she wanted something from you. When she was mad at you, you saw it in her eyes right away. Her honesty was charming. She braided ribbons in my hair, and I did the same to her, but my hair was so dirty, and hers was so clean.

She talked about nothing at all important, and it was wonderful. I believe she loved Seth. I do.

And I heard her scream when she died. It was like icicles. Icicle teeth chewed my spine.

Adel cocked her head when she first saw who sat behind the heavy stone desk.

On the stripped walls of the room, I could see the discoloration of the plaster where furniture once blocked the light, and had made dusting difficult. A long table. Shields and spears hung up on the walls, or perhaps poles and mounts for tapestries. Above my head heavy oak rafters held the ceiling in place against the weight of snow.

The man behind the desk wasn't who Adel expected to see. The man was an old mercenary. He was bald, like Fest, but he had a white beard growing between a pattern of facial scars like animal stripes. A zebra, I would learn. He had beady eyes, and a fat belly. He was much older than Fest, too. He had such a wrinkled face.

Adel glanced over her shoulder. Two guards stood behind us, with arquebuses in their arms. They listened in, of course, but they did not appear engaged. Adel looked back at the old man in charge.

You aren't a commander, said Adel. *You are only an employee.*

The man behind the desk leaned back in his chair. He scratched his wrinkled old nose and nodded. His chapped lips parted slowly. He took a deep breath. *I have been left in charge of this town. Employee or no, I am in command. You are a strange sight indeed. Who sent you here?* He had a small voice, like raspy wind through pipe smoke.

I come from Proconsul Argarax, said Adel. Her voice was stronger now. Her voice did not sound like we were starving with stiff joints after a long and cold trek all the way from the city of Proliux. Adel cocked her head, again. *Who sent you here?* she said.

I also come from Proconsul Argarax, said the man.

Where is the general? said Adel. Her hand rested on her dagger's hilt. She had slung it into her belt and put it on display before we came into the city. A paladin's weapon in Proliuxian hands would have some meaning to them, though they wouldn't necessarily know the truth because her arms were sealed in ragged layers of leather and linen.

I presume that our general is in that other city near the pass, said the old mercenary, *After taking this one so easily, he divided his forces and went for the other.* The old man wrinkled his nose again. He scratched at it lightly, and snorted. *These folk here were no great challenge at all. Why take one city, when we could divide the food stores up among two?*

One of the mercenaries at the door shuffled his feet lightly. I turned and got a better look at him. He had the steel talons of a hawk. His eyes drifted around the room, lazily. I would kill him second, if it came down to it. He wasn't paying attention.

Their armies have not yet arrived, said Adel, surprised at the folly of these men. *The Alamedan armies winter in the southeast, I believe. They fight some monstrous beings that we have never encountered that devour all the fallen. They don't fight men. Not men like us, at least.*

Alamedan, you say? So this whole place has a name. The general shoved a finger up his round nose. He dug into it casually. *I thought it was only the cities that had names.*

I flinched.

The language has many subtle inflections, and you said something else entirely, said Adel, *However, yes, these nations have a name for themselves.*

I had heard about those creatures you mentioned, said the old man. He leaned back. He put his feet up on the desk. Cocky. *Still, the few warriors here didn't even know what an arquebus was. A disappointing capture this place was. Too easy. I have suspected all this time that something was in the works. I took care of their leaders to be safe. But it was nothing. They are captured sheep.*

You are arrogant to assume sheep are not dangerous, said Adel. *Stampedes of sheep have killed greater men than you.*

Well these sheep won't do it, he snarled. *They're beat. They're scared and they're beat. I wish I knew what they were saying so I could learn what they're really thinking.*

They think you're going to eat them, I said. *They think you're the cannibals from the northern shores.*

The what? You speak our language? Who are you?

This is my guide, said Adel. She smiled at me, whistfully. *My guide who was instructed not to speak unless spoken to.*

Where did she learn Proliuxian? said the mercenary.

From me, in Proliux. Please, tell me if the general succeeded in Tsuin.

Tsuin? Oh, the other city. He pulled his feet slowly off the desk. He placed them down on the ground. He scratched his neck at the place it joins with his skull.

Yes, I mean the other city. It's name is Tsuin. Was it taken or not?

Frankly, I don't know, said the old man. *I don't expect to hear word until spring. That weather is worse than an army. Only a fool would go out there.* He glanced down at her arms. She had covered the tattoos with her warmest clothes, but the mercenary knew they were there. *Or you, paladin. Don't think I don't recognize you, Lady Jardan. Why did you come here, traitor?* He gestured at the soldiers.

Behind us the arquebuses lowered toward our backs. I felt the fluted bell of one against my spine. I clenched upon my spear.

Your men ... are they loyal? said Adel.

They are now, said the old man. *We have good men here.*

Of course. What do you think would happen if one of the ... Adel smiled. She squinted her eyes and spoke slowly, and softly. *...the sheep managed to assassinate you?*

I think they would be killed, said the old man. He stood up from his chair. *You come a long way to ask such odd questions. Did you not have a message for my general all the way from Argarax himself?* His voice slowed, too. His voice softened and slowed and his hands moved slowly. They reached beneath the desk. *You could try to reach Tsuin, but the weather does not improve with time.* A curved sword emerged from beneath the desk, in the old mercenary's left hand. He casually stuck the point of it in his mouth and picked at a tooth. He spoke past it, still clear of voice, despite the blade in his teeth. *Nor does your reputation improve with time, Lady Jardan. Give me your message, that I may know if you tell the truth or not.*

Adel nodded. She looked to me. A stray eyebrow gestured slightly at the guards behind us, with their arquebuses on our backs.

I understood.

First the guards. Then the old mercenary.

Adel had more in mind, but she could not convey her full plan to me with one eyebrow.

In a fight with an arquebus there are two things you must remember.
Adel poked the small fire with her boot. She left her boot near it,
soaking up the warmth.

I huddled in my cloak and watched the snow fall across Adel's
body. Her cold, gray skin and filthy, ragged clothing looked just like
the granite boulders that marked the road. She and the rocks were
covered in that snow as if emerging from worn white lace.

Her words came from nowhere. We had been sitting and
attempting to rest without sleeping too deeply, not speaking to
each other.

Too tired, Esumi. Far too tired.

We would sleep deeply against our will and wake with the sun in
our faces and wet hair from the place we fell in the snow. Our fire,
made from small amounts of milkweed, would burn all night and
into morning.

(Milkweed is a mixed blessing of the Goddess. In Pascanus they
have taken up raising it on rocky soil. It has replaced coal as a fuel
in places where people will not be near it. The demons are ferocious,
but the fire is long and warm.)

And Adel told me how to fight against arquebuses. *They fire a bullet
faster than any arrow you've ever seen. You will never outrun that bullet.
You must remember that,* said her voice, as if disembodied and float-
ing in the air like a fading banshee. Thirsty, and tired, and cracking
was her voice. *However, you can outrun hands and fingers sometimes,
and you can keep them from loading another bullet if you are close to them.
And this is what you must remember,* she stopped to breathe a moment
under the snow. It wasn't so bad underneath the snow because it
helped against the wind. We had to sleep with our faces down, and
we awoke in mud, but the snow broke the wind. And the wind was
so cold.

Adel's head bobbed. Her voice wavered. Her will kicked in. She
came back and spoke more. *To fight against arquebuses, you must get
within arm's reach, Zhan. And you must be sure that when they fire you
have already outrun the hands that direct the bullet through the chamber
to you. Are you listening to me, Zhan?*

I am, I said. My eyes had already drooped shut.

You have not fought against an arquebus, have you?

No, I said, *I've seen a few of them. I don't quite understand how they work.*

Just remember that if someone points one at you, you must be sure to get out of the way. Her voice was weakening. It barely reached me over the winds. My head lolled. I snapped it upright again. *And you must remember to fight as close to the guns as possible.* My head drooped again, but I did not fight it. I let it droop. I hurt my neck, but I couldn't move my head anymore. Adel's voice continued on, like snowing. *Ultimately, arquebuses are excellent weapons for open fields with hundreds of soldiers in lines, or oceans with no cover in sight. However, in swamps and forests and cities, as well as in single combat, the usefulness fades. Are you listening Zhan?*

And my head had fallen into the crook of my arms.

Zhan?

I had heard her voice, but I did not respond. It was in a cold place, far away from me. I was inside of my skull—in the empty center of my being, where all my senses point. I was between sleep and wake.

And it was a black place, and I was very hungry there.

I could taste the slight grease in the air of our milkweed fire. The sour taste of demon dreams slowly crept into my hunger, and dark dreams walked toward me in the darkening world.

And after nights like these I woke up so stiff that I could barely move my legs. My head ached. My throat was parched and my lips cracked and bled. I licked at the blood and swallowed as much as I could. I pulled up slowly to sitting. And I felt like a golem there, in the early snows of late autumn.

And we moved ahead to Ilhota, and a room where two well-rested mercenaries pressed arquebuses into our backs, and a third prodded at his teeth with a saber.

I would remember, too.

Dodge the man before the bullet.

I dropped to the floor. I whipped my spear up my back and fell fast into the ground.

I heard the explosion. I felt the wind across my back. I smelled burning hair when the hair whipped into my face from the fall. I spun up and my spear found belly.

Adel hadn't even let hers pull the trigger.

I looked and the body was on the floor. The arquebus was in her hand. The old man had his sabre raised up in the air. Adel aimed the arquebus into his face, point blank. The steel smothered the mercenary's face.

I felt a small line of blood, and a light burning down my back. I touched my hand there, but it was only a grazing. It barely broke the skin. It burned more than it bled. It had ruined my new, warm cloak, but I would wear the cloak anyway and merely curse the bracing wind that slipped into my shoulder blades.

Outside our door, we heard people shouting and running. An arquebus had gone off. A crowd would gather outside to see what it was about. I flipped the bolt to lock the door.

The old mercenary smiled. *I will see you in Garzakhan and seek my revenge, Paladin. Know that I killed many of your kind in Rhianna.*

Whoever said I was going to kill you? said Adel. *You aren't the general. I don't know what to do with you.*

What? said the man. He smiled. *Ah, I am valuable to you, then? Excellent. Two dead you have made. That will be two dead in return.*

Do you have another magnificent plan, Paladin? I said.

Mm, she said. *Maybe. Do you have a magnificent plan, Rider?*

Someone banged on the door.

I say we kill him fast, and we go out there and tell them whatever it takes to survive this day.

Good plan, said Adel.

The old mercenary grimaced. He forced his eyes open. He was determined to see his own death. He raised his saber and keened high and proud.

The hammer fell. The arquebus unleashed the thunder into the old mercenary's face. Blood splashed out from the collapsing bone.

The body fell back into the chair.

The door crashed open behind a large man's boot. The mercenaries had more arquebuses aimed at us than we could possibly defeat. They shouted at us. I don't know what they shouted.

Adel put her weapon down slowly. I followed her fine example.

Adel shook her head. She shouted, *I come from Proconsul Argarax with news that the family's commander did not like. He had decided to disobey the family and betray our trust and to take our employees off for his own purposes here.*

Do you have proof? said the nearest mercenary, with weapon closest to Adel's belly.

What proof do you need but that a Proliuxian in the service of Proconsul Argarax came here today this far north of the mountains and executed the criminal.

The nearest mercenary shook his head. *This is not good enough proof,* he said.

Adel smiled. *I have coin as well, if this will serve as proof enough.*

The mercenary lowered his weapon. *How much?* he said.

Adel lifted a purse from her belt. She tossed it at him. *Two coins for each man who obeys Proconsul Argarax, and six more on top of that later. This is, of course, supplementary to your current income.*

The coins disappeared into the crowd of dark men.

What are Proconsul Argarax's orders? said the nearest mercenary.

Gather all the men together in the center square below the tower, said Adel. *I will address them all there.*

Right away, he said. The mercenaries ran out to spread the word and the coin. I heard the gathering men, with deep voices and heavy boots running and calling out new orders.

13

Prince Tsui and I were more than just two people from the snow. I was Adel's company before her apotheosis. Prince Tsui was the last of the noble council. Certainly, there existed other nobles, and many of them were quite competent. Unfortunately, none of them were there, in Ilhota, and surviving alongside the people. None of them led the revolt to take back Tsuin.

Empires are not forged in the back rooms with political ministers. Empires are forged on the streets, where people talk and work and love. And the people collectively gossip in the same words after a time, and a man is worthy to hold their yoke, or not.

Hundreds of the survivors of Ilhota watched as the dark soldiers with the most powerful weapons left the outer city in long trails into the inner city. These frightening beasts moved of a single mind on this one day when a strange woman accompanied by an Alamedan—me—arrived at the gates.

I looked over my shoulder at the Ilhotans. From the windows of the houses, women and some young men peered. My heart choked for them in the houses. My eyes lingered on a dark-haired woman, with bruises for eyes. The woman leaned against an elbow beside a leather flap. The glass had been destroyed, and only that leather flap kept out the cold to her room.

Adel didn't seem to pay attention to my people. She glowered at the herd of dark men. Her jaw was strong, and so was her back. The paladin returned to the body of the wanderer, who, this very morning, had to rub her blue calves hard six times before she could attempt standing up.

The slant of the fading sunlight, and the lingering flecks of snow and her strength looked like a saint, even to me.

Korinyes leaned against my arm. She nibbled slowly on the meat I had given her. Only Partridge was foolish enough to devour it whole in one swoop. Korinyes was no fool. She chewed slowly, and with much noise. I think the sound of food in her mouth gave her as much satisfaction as the warmth in her belly when the hunger pangs subsided. Also, the slow eating kept the food down.

She took a piece of the meat, a very small piece, and placed it at her hairline.

A small black ant peeked out from the black grassland of hair and snatched the meat. The ant disappeared back into the black. Prince Tsui must have seen it, but he said nothing. He didn't know about the Rhiannan gypsies.

I had seen ants thousands of times. Infested in the rafter of an old man's house, tearing through the thin threads of pine, and tumbling down upon his dinner with wooden splinters like shrapnel. I helped my father cut the damaged wood away to reach the queen. I laced honey in a line away from the nest to lure the angry ants into an enraged confusion. My father hacked with a stone pick. The ants spewed out of that small corner of rafter.

Father found the queen deep inside the thick rafter. He dragged the queen's fat body out from the wood with tongs. The queen's legs had too much dignity to dangle. Her jaws did not quiver in fear. She pulled her legs in shame against her nakedness. She closed her mouth with stiff lips of rage.

That night I dreamed of retribution and did not sleep well. The slightest prick of hair or blanket brushing me woke me with a start. Once I screamed, and my sister hit me hard.

Go to sleep, already!

Korinyes screamed when she died. I know she was not a queen ant.

I know it.

Korinyes has gone with little mention in these letters, Esumi. Had I the knowledge to don the mask I would. I do not. She was always mysterious to me because her version of love was mysterious to me. But she was less mysterious than Adel, I think. Her eyes were plain, and one color only, whether green or brown I can't recall. Blue? No. Not blue.

And her hand guided me to the base of her skull one night, when I followed her from our little camp. She nodded sadly. *Don't tell Seth.* My hand climbed up until I found all the tiny pores held open. The gaps in skin, and bumps like livid leprosy. Ants.

Seth never knew, I think.

Adel spoke the desert languages, too, in the fading light before the army. She spoke every word in existence. Necessity is the mother of all knowledge, I imagine. I am glad I never gained her kind of knowledge.

We stood with our backs to the Ilhotans, right up against the inner wall. All of the mercenaries stood below Ilhota's tall tower. Some crawled up the buttresses for a better view.

She was a sight, to be sure. Her voice was so strong that none strained to hear.

Afterward, Prince Tsui asked her what she had said. I was too tired to care. She was leaning on his shoulders to climb over a hill. Her breath was fast, and her legs weakened by the winter. Her knees popped all the time. At this moment Prince Tsui asked her. *What did you say to them?*

I saw her in my mind smiling wanly from a tavern at a similar question. But today she did not even look him in the face. *I told them many things,* she said, *if you knew what was good for you, you wouldn't truly believe anything I say without proof.*

Prince Tsui raised his voice against a cold wind that whipped through his hair. *What will you tell me that you said to them?* he said. *I need to know because I will be fighting them. I need to know how they think.* He pushed his hair from his eyes. A strand came loose in his fingers. He watched it a moment in his hand, pulled by the wind. Then he opened his finger and the hair was gone.

The snow grew thicker and thicker all around us. The cold wind whipped across our squinting eyes. I felt the cold all through my eyeballs, and back into my very skull.

Your general has made an unwise decision, which Proconsul Argarax explicitly commanded him not to do. For this reason I had reminded your commander the will of Proconsul Argarax. He refused my wisdom. For his disloyalty, he was killed. Pray the same fate does not befall you.

The shuffling of the bodies. Adel's words were strong. She stared at them with fire and they saw the strength in her. I did not know what she said. I saw only strength.

Prince Tsui and I listened to this strength while we watched her hunched against the cold, rubbing her purple joints beneath ragged clothes.

I saw Korinyes in the moonlight with black ants across her skin.

I had followed her because it was my watch, and I was awake. She had rolled over, poked the fire with a convenient stick, and winked at me. *Be right back,* she had mouthed.

We were in the mountains. We had been surviving on goats and the memory of cinnamon tea.

And I followed her quietly through the rocks and the cold. I expected her to find one of the low, crumpled trees of the mountainside and answer her body. It was my watch, and I watched her to be sure she did not find a ledge too narrow, or a footing in the dark too loose.

In the daylight we tied ourselves together by a rope. This far along, the rope was too worn to save us, but we did it anyway. At least Korinyes felt safer.

And I watched her because it made me feel safer. She found a low, crumpled tree, and placed her hand upon it. I watched her hand and it was gray in the full glow of Alastair's blind eye. And then her hand was black, and flickering like blind fire.

I ran closer. And I squinted. Korinyes did not notice me at all.

And I saw them pouring from her hand. Ants.

As soldiers all of you know the fundamental rule broken here. Your general divided his army. This is the foundation of defeat. You think this land so easy to conquer, but the armies have not arrived yet. We do not know the strength of their armies until we face them as a whole.

Adel touched her forehead and rubbed it gently. *I can only guess what would be wise. I could send you to the general, if the fool even managed to take that city, or I could remain here as your commander. Both of these options have benefits. One would reunite the army. The other would at least maintain Argarax's hand in this place, despite the coming of the enemy armies in spring.*

She paused and delved into deep thought. Her forehead wrinkled. Her lips pressed together smaller and smaller. She seemed to grow taller when she thought. She paced with wide, easy steps, but only a moment.

We watched her in the snow, Prince Tsui and I, delving deeper into thought. Her forehead wrinkled. Her lips pressed together smaller and smaller. She seemed to sink into her knees.

Ants. I smacked at them. She gasped and shouted, *No! Don't! Her eyes like plaster plates. Don't hurt them! Please! Please don't hurt them!*

The ants disappeared into the tree, and up Korinyes's sleeve.

Please, don't hurt them. They don't hurt any of us. They are only little ants, and they don't mean harm to anyone. They eat little bugs and dead things, and they don't mean harm to anyone.

I cocked my head. Nothing I had ever seen prepared me for this sight. I decided not to be afraid. Instead I remembered the milkweed and decided it was dark, and I should get out of the fire when I returned.

Korinyes grabbed my sleeve. *Don't tell Seth. Don't tell Adel. Don't tell anyone. Please?*

A cracking voice called out, rumbling deep, like Fest's. *Have you nothing else to say but possibilities? It's cold out here! I want to go inside and get some sleep before I have to guard the sheep tonight.*

Adel looked up at the direction of the voice. She had been waiting for this moment. *Are you so impertinent, hireling? Are you so bold because the weather is cold?*

The voice was silent. No one looked back from Adel. All eyes on the mud.

Her voice was wicked now, oozing with rancor. Her eyes twisted up. Her mouth sneered. *Perhaps this war is unsalvageable after all because our brave soldiers quiver in the face of uncomfortable weather. If you are so impertinent because of a little snow, I think you should return your weapons to Argarax at once and request freedom.*

Adel took a deep breath. She smiled wanly, and gazed above us all. She gazed past Prince Tsui and past me and over the heads of the soldiers into the gray sky beyond the walls. The tone of her voice changed from anger to confidence. *Thank you, soldier. I have changed my mind. You all look at me with such defeated faces.*

Were they? I don't recall. I looked at the wave of black faces wrapped in rags and saw only eyes and noses. I saw those features repeated. I don't know if there exists a difference in a human face when it is placed among the herd. Like bison, only the traits that are the same are seen. Black faces, with white eyes. That's what I saw. That's all I saw, empty of true expression.

Well, I will report to Argarax myself, and I am certain he will support my decision on the matter. You are cut loose. I have no way of receiving your weapons, so I must leave them in your hands. Keep them, and return them when a new army—a worthier army, with a worthier general—comes for these sheep next season. I offer you use of the weapons for this time in return for safe passage for myself and my guide. Your hostages are not yours. They are the property and responsibility of Argarax. Send them into the outer city, and the weather will hold them hostage better than you ever could, incompetent cowards.

Bodies moving now. A stirring sea of dark faces spinning and chattering. Motion sickness, I felt.

Adel turned to me, and spoke Alamedan. *Zhan, I have given my orders. That is all we can do. If they are loyal, they will obey. If they are not* ... Her voice trailed off into the unthinkable realm of mardars and holy will. *We must leave this city now. We've done all we can for it.*

Where will we go now?

Tsuin, she said.

That is not a simple proposition, I replied.

Fest, Korinyes, Seth, and Partridge went there, she said. *I imagine they failed because they did not know what to do. Their fate concerns me. Also, the fate of your city concerns me.*

I will go with you, but this is no simple proposition, I said, *and I doubt the fate of my city concerns you because it certainly doesn't concern me very much at all right now.* I scratched my neck. *Fest, though* ... *And even you. You will go whether I go with you or not. We should take some of the sheep.*

We should take little. An unaccustomed army can strain a city's resources, she said. *Let us talk while we walk, and seal the doors behind us.*

The armies dissipated indoors. Passionate conversations erupted from the windows.

Shots fired in anger, and women wailing. I looked away from these things. I chose to ignore them, because Adel was right.

I watched Korinyes while she walked. The rope around her waist led straight to me. Before her was Adel. And before Adel, grandfather's golem, guiding us over the rocks with slow steps. Only he knew these mountain passes well enough to overtake an army, even with such slow steps.

Seth, the golem, and I thought this rope was a bad idea. If one falls, all fall. *If it is the will of the Goddess,* Seth and the golem and I had said.

Korinyes won't go a step without the rope. Her foot stayed planted hard on the ground, and her eyes glared at Seth in anger.

Most of the mountains aren't so bad: valleys and basins and rivers and smaller glaciers with goat-trails and lion trails.

Behind Korinyes, I watched her walk. I saw her and didn't know that inside of her mind were thousands of ants, sleeping underneath her skin. They thought with her. They shared minds. The gypsy choirs sing so beautifully because some of the members are infested with the ants, and the minds unite and the songs emerge from their voices. This was something Korinyes told me.

And I watched her walking. Her beautiful body moved over the rocks unsteadily at first. Then a month passed and she could walk as easily as she could dance.

In her wake thousands of tiny black ants like living hair spread over the mountainside.

I haven't told anyone until you. I knew she was my friend. What else was there to know?

I had so many questions, though. And in front of everyone else, I couldn't speak them. I didn't want to hear Adel's version of Korinyes's life. I didn't want Fest to raise his voice near a wall of loose rocks.

How to know what would happen if I told them? We walk as a chain of people, but one of us is also a sea of ants.

Adel and I walked quickly to the gates. We each tugged hard upon the heavy wood. It scraped against snow and mud. Past the gate the gravity of freedom descended upon the cold mercenaries. The herd broke quickly and scuttled into the houses for warmth. Behind us early arguments began already from old tribal rivalries left unchecked by duty and coin.

Adel turned to the sheep pens and the people locked up there, burning dried dung to stay warm. *Hello, my name is Adel, and I have just saved you,* she shouted as casually as discussing the weather. *Now please help me seal this door against the soldiers!*

A thousand eyes blinked.

Prince Tsui spoke. *Our people are in there, too. We will not seal this door until we are all free.*

Adel shook her head. *Your people here are as good as dead if this door is not sealed well. The ones inside may survive. They are what will be killed over. They are pretty.*

Arquebus shots rang out, and burst through the wood. Adel didn't flinch.

Please, if we seal this door, they will kill each other all winter, said Adel, *And in a few weeks, when more of them are dead, you can unseal it and free the rest.*

A man screamed past the door.

But now is the time to wait until they are dead, she said. *Let them kill each other for a while. I gave them freedom and coin to hire each other. Like ants without a queen, they will fight over nothing.*

The anonymous prince looked around him at his loyal subjects. They were too cold and beaten to be terrified. *What other choice do we have for now?* he said. *We will help you, stranger.*

Prince Tsui kicked the top plank of the fence. It shook the whole thing. He kicked it again, right next to the stake. The post cracked. He tugged it loose. Another man's hand grabbed the dragging end. Together the two carried the plank over to the door. The torch holes beside the door were designed for such a device as this, though the original piece was made of iron, not wood, so as not to rot in the snow. The wall was too low to make this arrangement permanent, but until organization developed inside of the wall, it would do. The fat man, Prince Tsui, remained. The other man walked back to the sheep pens. He helped people away from the animals and into the yard.

Prince Tsui spoke to Adel while staring at the barred door, *What is your stake in this, strange one?*

Adel tried to lead Prince Tsui away from the door. *My stake is justice, always. The last nation that fell before these armies is my concern.* She paused for a long string of sputtering coughs. They sounded like a rock bouncing in a hollow log. *We had the disadvantages of good weather in winter, and ports so close to the dark men's sea routes,* she said.

These cannibals are strange ones. Prince Tsui touched the door with his fingertips. His eyes squinted. *Hairless, organized, and well-armed with amazing weapons.*

They are probably not your cannibals. I would talk more with you, said Adel, *but let us get your people and their supplies outside the heavier walls.*

Prince Tsui frowned and turned from the door to Adel. *My people will have the longest winter. A few moments more here will not matter,* he said. *Besides, the longer we talk the less they will believe that you are dangerous, too.*

Past this barred gate sporadic explosions of arquebuses and powder and people screaming. Someone ran into the gate and punched it with a heavy fist. Adel and Prince Tsui continued their conversation without a breath.

Do you know your people well? she said.

Are you our leader? What makes you our leader? I said. I was growling at him. *I saw the pikes, and I did not see you upon them.*

He smiled. *I am Prince Tsui of Tsuin, and I was hidden among the population. My uncle is the lord of Tsuin, and I am his representative and heir.*

How noble of you, to hide while your people are dying.

He flinched.

I spoke on. *My name is Zhan Immur, and I am from one of Tsuin's villages. It's called Bear,* I said. *I mean, it was called Bear. Now it's empty.*

I've never heard of it, he replied.

You have so many villages, I said, *and Bear was so small, and it's no more.*

I'm sorry, he said. He shuffled his feet.

I clenched my fist. I pounded the door. *Of course you are,* I said. *You're sorry and hiding among the prisoners like a prince.*

His eyes creased. He sighed. *Look around you, girl. Don't you see? Duty or no, I can fight a lot better when I survive to fight again. I have served my people, and the council, but I have done it by surviving. Now that I have survived, we can win this winter.*

Adel raised her hand. *We're tired, Prince Tsui. We have traveled over oceans and rivers and forests and mountains and now this cold. And we must go to Tsuin.*

That's my home, he said, *why must you go there?*

Adel gazed past the broken barricades of Ilhota, past the people, and into the east. *The army divided and the general is in Tsuin. Our friends are there, too.*

I would come with you, said the prince.

And these people? Adel's hand gestured to the staring Ilhotans. They watched from a distance. Past the barred door were more explosions and sometimes screams. It was a low enough wall that smoke from the arquebuses, like fogging breath, dissipated before our very eyes.

Prince Tsui sighed. He looked at his people in the snow. *The shamans know better than me what they will need when they do not fight or barter. And these people would be better off without fighting or bartering for a while.* He walked away from the wall.

The population looked at him. Again, I saw only noses and eyes and the things that were similar. Bruises. White skin.

He shouted at the people. *Get everything you can carry and take it outside the next wall! Get all the food and all the sheep and grain and weapons you can, and take it outside the wall!*

They obeyed.

And Korinyes at night, lying in her blankets. Her hand upon Seth's chest. Her voice in his ear. *Beloved.*

And in her mind ants crawling and crawling. And Prince Tsui held onto me in the cold. I let him. His body was so warm next to mine. I wish I hadn't. I wish I had felt his hands upon my back and pushed him away, but they were such warm hands.

And the memory of his hands is like ants in my spine.

We moved again over the snow. Adel said little. I said less. Prince Tsui asked us questions. Sometimes we didn't speak. We just opened our mouths and breathed.

We carried two dead sheep between us, killed and scorched quick like the wolf meat. The snow had still not quite hardened into the ice of winter. It was only late autumn here. The snow was powdery and dry. It melted a little in the afternoon sun. The sun set quickly. The snow hardened.

Adel's knees didn't work right anymore in the cold. We had to carry her over the steeper hills. Her eyes drooped and we talked to her to keep her moving. Prince Tsui bore the brunt of her weight. I carried her voice in Proliuxian. We made cruel jokes about the fat prince who should have died.

My knees ached. My ankles ached. My back ached. My arms ached. My heart ached.

In the sky, a finger reached down and touched us, but did not kill these black ants upon the snow. We moved fast.

This tale is nearly over, Esumi.

We found the rest of our little group of saints in the snowy pine woods near the frozen river, though we were not looking for anyone. They had made no effort to hide too deep. The road was there, and they were just off of it, staring out onto the frozen river. They leaned against fallen trees with an emptiness. Hunger is a cruel death, and so slow.

They weren't speaking to each other. They were just hungry. Sometimes Partridge cried, but he wouldn't leak any tears.

Then we invaded Tsuin as best we could and three mercenaries died.

Prince Tsui touched her back. I tried to ignore them both. I tried to sleep with my head above the snowdrifts but beneath the wind. He did not ignore her. He touched her back.

What's wrong? he said. *I can rub your legs if they hurt. You don't want to get frostbite. You could die.*

Her demons are her own, I mumbled.

Adel looked up at me. I could barely see her over the puny speck of fire the prince and I had managed.

You will not die, said Prince Tsui. *Your legs aren't even that pale.*

Let her cry, fool, I said. *And don't talk nonsense. Get some rest even if you won't sleep.*

An old saying of the riders is that we never sleep. We simply lie down and watch the stars until morning. We lie real still.

I had told that to Korinyes once, and she had laughed at me. She told me that I liked to snore when I was not sleeping, then, and was doing it only to annoy her.

Ants don't have names. Korinyes's ants never had names. Korinyes's condition was only called *infested*.

When Fest said the word—*infested*—he spoke with a grimace. *People who aren't really people*, he said. *Who told you of these things?*

You did, I said. *You were telling me about the war.*

I don't remember telling you about that, he said, *The dragon was tolerant of many religions, even the truly disgusting ones that have no business being allowed to continue. The dragonslayers have stamped it out, and good riddance.*

Partridge was singing a song too loud and out of tune. Fest hit Partridge hard over the eye with a heavy fist. Partridge bled into the gravel. Tiny ants collected near his blood. Korinyes stroked Partridge's head and cooed at the small, quiet tears in the fool's eyes.

Why do you have to hit him so much? she said. *Why? He doesn't mean to bother you. He doesn't know any better.*

He should learn, said Fest.

Poor baby, said Korinyes. Her hand passed through the filthy, blood-stained hair at the top of the potato-shaped head. Partridge gurgled. *Partridge is not the only one with things to learn*, said Korinyes.

And conversation stopped for a time. Adel hadn't spoken for days. I poked her. She looked up at me.

Tell me about the food in Rhianna, I said desperately. *I'm so hungry I could eat a bug!*

She closed her eyes and rolled to face the wall.

There is no food in Rhianna anymore, said her back, *because we have spoken of it all before. We speak something out loud and then there is no more to say.*

And this is why I will no longer continue to speak of Korinyes. I turn my back to the wall. My shamans touch my shoulder. I push them all off.

One of them is singing. She's a woman, young enough to be my daughter, but she has the wrong color hair. She sings and I close my eyes and know that I have done the best I can to tell you all of these things, Esumi. I have done my best.

And still, you don't write to me.

14

The other three followed the main road to Tsuin. They walked up the side of a frozen river, and they moved far slower than Adel and me.

I don't know what they did on this journey. I know they ran out of food. When they reached the city, they were walking on empty stomachs.

I know Partridge got his nose broken by Fest. Seth had already straightened it in one painful crack before we met up again. The bruise was still there, on Partridge's face.

And Korinyes and the ants spread across the countryside, new ants everywhere.

And what else?

I don't know what they talked about while Adel and I were gone. Frankly, I don't think any of us had the stomach to truly grasp the politics involved, or the deaths. We were tired and hungry. Everything else was something separate from our little pockets of Alastair's empty center.

Adel's legs stopped working correctly somewhere between killing the mercenary commander and the big expanse of white broken only by large rocks. The prince and I helped her walk. We traded off all day and into the darkness until it was too cold and too black, and our makeshift torch from the femur of a sheep burned too low.

And all the war in the world would not have gotten me to take another step. I moved because I was tired and hungry. I moved fast because if we didn't move fast we would freeze.

And that is the birth of an empire, Esumi. Move, win, or die.

Fest grimaced at the broken wall. He shook his head at the signs of death. The bodies piled in heaps and covered in a thin layer of white snow. The wind blew the snow hard across the bodies. The wind drove the snow into our eyes. Fest sighed deep at the buildings torn open by explosions.

His black brethren paced the central walls with their arquebuses. They probably didn't see us, yet. We didn't really see them. All we saw was a black shadow against the wall of gray and white.

Goddess, what happened?

When we found them they were in a small lean-to, and burning pine nettles. They were eating wood and the leather that could have kept them warm.

They looked up and Prince Tsui introduced himself and they didn't care. Their stomachs were empty.

I handed them food.

Fest had aged a thousand years. His cheeks narrowed into his skull, and his ashen skin had the pallor of gangrene, but he wasn't sick. Just hungry. And Korinyes silently placed a piece of meat in her hair for the ants that lived beneath the follicles. Seth and Fest and Adel could have seen it. They didn't, but they could've. All the politics and secrets were forgotten. Her hands looked white like icicles. Her face was hollow, too.

Prince Tsui and I walked with Adel between us most days. Her knees locked up sometimes. Other times they simply let go. She couldn't carry anything. I could. This was my world, with the riders.

Prince Tsui and I talked to pass the time in the darkness, and she stayed between the two of us. Silent and cold.

And snow and snow and snow. Beneath my worn boots, some of the snow never melted. It clung to the frozen ground and more snow fell and melted and then clung to the frozen ground as ice.

We walked through snow as deep as our waist sometimes. We were wet from head to toe and this only made the wind worse. Prince Tsui told me about hunting seals.

I have spoken too much. Because I can only speak in these letters now. My voice is scraped away. My husband speaks for himself, and tells all of the love that grew as we walked. There was no love. There never was.

This letter will end now because I cannot think of anything else to add. And my shamans are here to close their eyes and soothe Alastair-of-the-Wolf and keep my soul away from her a little longer.

We didn't talk much when we met again in the woods near the fallen castle. Adel said, *We have to go to Tsuin.*

Seth nodded. *Giving ourselves up? I had thought of that.*

Prince Tsui shook his head. *And you are a shaman and you talk about giving up? No, my friend. We will not be giving ourselves up.*

Death, then? said Seth

Victory, said Prince Tsui.

Call it what you like, Seth replied, *the end is the same.*

Our throats were so parched, too.

Snow is so much cold air in your mouth, but you must swallow it all day long to drink a drop. It's grainy, too. The wind blew it and the dust and nettles drifted in and out. They hurt my throat, but I swallowed anyway.

When Seth spoke his voice cracked.

Adel sat down underneath the lean-to. She rubbed her legs and closed her eyes. *How close are we to the city?* she asked quietly.

Prince Tsui raised his eyes to his home. *We're close. We will be there before sunset.*

Adel rolled her hands over her knees. *We are almost finished, you and I,* she said to her knees. *Prince Tsui, when we get inside you are going to hide your identity again, aren't you?*

No, he said, *I won't have to. We'll kill the general and we will win.*

Adel squinted. *Mm,* she said. *I suggest that you are no longer Prince Tsui. I suggest that you are now a merchant we found on the road somewhere. I suggest that Seth is the prince.*

We won't need this deception, said the prince.

We need it, said Adel, *We need it all winter, whether we kill the general or not. Seth, you are our shaman, and therefore you are our leader. And if the worst happens, you will make the right choices, I think.*

What are you talking about? said the prince. *What does she mean?*

Fest raised his hand. He shook his head. *Adel is tired. She is speaking about things that tired people speak about. We're all too tired. I say one more day won't matter much, and we can use up all our fuel at once and have a good fire for one night. We eat all our food. Then, tomorrow we go.*

And you, said the prince. He touched his fat lips with his fat finger and had another idea, this one about Fest. *You are one of them, aren't you? I don't understand your loyalties.*

Of course you don't, said Fest. *Some days I don't. But I am always loyal.*

Seth had made a small liquid from the dried milkweed and various other barks and roots he had found back in the empty village. He had boiled it along with some melting snow. He had boiled it down and down until only a thick, grainy sludge remained on the bottom of the pan. This he had spooned up into vials and hid in his pockets. He had not given us any of it. He didn't tell us what it was for.

That night, he pulled out his vial and poured it all over the damp sticks we had gathered. When he lit it, there was an explosion of heat. Adel rubbed her knees in the heat. Fest rubbed her ankles. Korinyes slept hard on a half full belly. Partridge sang the same songs over and over again in his horrible singing voice. His eyes glazed over while he stared into the fire and then he fell asleep.

Seth and I spoke.

He watched from Baba's window while the old man did it all. He watched the bloody feet, and the bloody hands, and the bloody blade. The man moved from house to house so fast in the night. Seth saw it all, and saw the houses.

Tell me, I said, *about that night when this began.*

What night was that? he said.

When Baba was killed.

Seth was in an outhouse, and scratching himself. He lit matches casually with one hand, and dropped them to the dirt where he stepped on them. He heard footsteps and thought it was female. He mistook the heavy steps for a heavy girl with big hips for his wandering hands. He opened the door, and his father was there, eyes blazing and covered in blood.

Then the old man turned and ran.

That night everyone got . . .

Yes. Where were you?

I was asleep.

Really?

Yes.

You slept right through it all? Who woke you up?

Kyquil.

Seth was lying in bed. The old man entered the house. Of course he entered the house. His footsteps were bloody and in the house. He walked up to his son's door. He pushed it open. He poked his son with the dry butt of a spear. Seth woke up, terrified. The old man said, *Shhh . . .*

Do you think Kyquil made it to Tsuin?

I don't know.

I hope he did.

I hope he went on to Pascanus and missed all of this.

Seth heard the noises in the night. He heard the muffled moans of the dying. He grabbed a weapon, and crept from his room. He saw himself standing over Baba, but it was not him. It was an older him—a him with a slow limp and a grayish-pink mop of hair. But it was Seth, holding a spear over a body. Seth turned and saw himself, but younger, with a red mop of hair down to the floor. Both Seths nodded with blank faces. They pressed their finger against their lips. *Shh . . .* they said.

No one will miss anything anymore. There's another whole people that want to make war on us. Goddess, be merciful.

Don't use those words, Seth.

What words?

You don't have the right to speak about the Goddess anymore.

What? Why?

You'll know when you're dead.

What, because I have given up on her? Because I have taken a lover? You think I am the first shaman to take a lover? Baba had one once.

The old man opened his mouth. Nothing came out. His hands were clean because he had washed them. He peered in on his son slowly boiling water for Baba's morning tea. Baba was still asleep. The two locked eyes. They didn't speak.

Don't sully the dead until you are, yourself, dead.

I mean it. She did.

I can't believe a word you say.

Then why do you even talk to me?

I'm looking for something.

What?

Just something. I can't really tell you what.

You're not making sense.

I am, and I am finding what I seek with every word.

The snow picked up again. Korinyes watched it. I watched her. Seth touched her hair. He pressed his body into hers. She frowned, and watched the snow. Her body didn't move beneath his gentle hands.

Esumi, I can barely write. The shaman takes these letters and re-writes them for you. She adds her hand to mine. She's young. She's going to die because she has been reaching into my lungs with a long tube and pulling the bad blood from my chest.

And she doesn't know either. She shakes her head. She swallows her bitter teas. She conjures past this vision of the world and she goes down and up into the web where things come to you. And she doesn't know either.

Did he do it? Is he even capable of it?

Adel thinks so. I still think so.

But do I know? If I am wrong, I am a murderer.

Should I tell you what it was like the next day? Breaking into a castle again? Adel's loud shouts and foreign face? Fest held our ropes loosely. We were prisoners with thin bonds.

Adel smiled when they open the castle gates.

You know Tsuin better than I know Tsuin. What should I tell you about seeing them here? I can see them now, standing in corners. Their undead spirits tormented by the Goddess and lounging in the corners with their arquebuses flickering like the northern lights. They're picking their teeth with sharpened sheep bones. They wave this old spider away from them. They don't want to speak to the enemy empress. Their gigantic hands with stiff leather gloves are smeared with the gray ash of spent powder and vaguely brown stains of blood.

In the morning we woke with a little warmth in our bones. Just a little. The heat was strong and long. The dreams were ferocious. Worse than the milkweed, this terror was more than just an untouchable something deep inside of us coming out. This was real terror. Our last hope on our last chance to survive the winter. Live, or die. We had to get in. Or forever we would be in winter wilderness, wasting away.

We certainly didn't talk about it.

We boiled snow and fashioned something resembling a tea from the pine nettles and cones. I woke and sipped it and it tasted like oily wood, so wrapped in the oils of our fire. It tasted terrible. I threw up.

We ate all of our food quickly and raw.

Then we stood. We were in the forest. Adel had a plan, again. I didn't tease her this time. I listened. And I strapped my dagger to my upper arm. I took the lashes around my wrist, and practiced the tug that released them. We did it again. Then again. I nodded. I got it.

We would tie ourselves up when we got closer. First we walked through a snowstorm. Goddess, it was snowing and thundering and lightning and snowing.

Korinyes grabbed my shoulder. She asked me a question.

And then we were there, at the wall. Walking in.

I was so tired. I can't remember. I can't remember anything.

It went badly.

Adel touched my arm. She shoved me forward. *Prisoners. They were going to warn the armies out in Pascanus.*

A black hand on my face. *Pretty.*

Prince Tsui growled at that. He was behind me, but I heard him.

Adel said, *I serve Argarax, and I come with an important message for your general. These prisoners are part of the message. We must speak with him now. Do not worry about these here. They are tied up and we have walked too long for them to be dangerous.*

My feet were beaten down, nearly bloody from all their crackings. I stared at them poking out from the rags and wrappings that held my boots together. In front of mine, the gigantic black boots, muddy but with a shining buckle. We stood on wet stone, in the doorway of the castle. I stared at those boots. I could feel my heart in my throat. I was terrified, and the battle fury already came to my skull, like a white in the ears and a white at the edge of the eyes.

And then we shuffled inside. Past the yard where people slept in frigid heaps with their dead. Past the stomping boots and patient arquebuses in cold, bored arms.

Past the snow. And into the center stone building, where we would not see sun again for months.

And we saw him there, sitting in his chair.

Tycho Bosch Argarax.

He took one look at Adel and laughed. His laughter felt like icicles.

Should I tell you anything? You who does not write to me. You who do not speak to me. You whom I love. You, my love.

I can feel my body dissipating when I sleep. The tingling sensation of ants creeping up my legs and nibbling away the nerves.

When Korinyes died, I wanted to cry. Instead I waited for the next cry. Fest. Partridge. I only heard one. I only heard Partridge. Fest didn't cry out. I saw his body later, but until I did, I swore to myself that they didn't kill him.

I don't want to tell you what happened anymore. I can't. I just can't. It still hurts.

Korinyes dragged from her chains, her eyes alive with terror. Her ants crawling all over the walls and eaten by the spiders and fighting the spiders.

Fest lifted up bodily. He wouldn't move. He wouldn't scream. He was carried because he refused to walk. He smiled. He winked at me. His silver teeth came alive in that torch light while he was dragged and he was smiling.

And Partridge fought them a little. They hit him. His face had seen too many black fists and he fell and he was carried away from us with nothing in his eyes but early death.

And Adel sighed. It was a short sigh. It was too short, I think.

And I didn't even really know what was happening.

One. Two. Three.

Later on, their bodies were in the snow, piled among the dead people of Tsuin. I saw them. I watched Korinyes' ants scurrying across the whole mound.

Fest was as white as me on that pile, and he looked happy.

I remember when it was almost over. The empire forged in murders nearly done with the blood foundations poured.

Adel looked at me. *I thought it was going to be you,* she said. *Seth chose them all, you know. For the three we killed, three must die. Our leader had to choose. He lasted almost all winter. I'm surprised he lasted this long.*

The shaman shakes her head. She says I'm not telling you anything. How can I tell you what I did when you don't listen?

How can I tell you what it was like to sit in a dungeon for months on end, freezing cold and underfed watching spiders in the torchlight and studying the faces of the guards who brought us food and occasionally stood in the doorway, watching us. They changed the torches so we weren't given the comfort of darkness.

What is it like to defecate in plain view of Fest and Prince Tsui? What is it like to watch them?

When the piles were too high, and the smell too much even for the few guards who spent a little time there, they brought six buckets of melted snow and tossed them on the ground. Only six buckets, and never enough. They laughed about it.

Adel didn't get up to do anything. She shut down. She spoke little, just waiting.

We told stories. We talked about food. An iceberg, and the other stories Seth hated. Every story we knew, too, over and over.

Write to me. Tell me you want to know. Tell me you love me by telling me you want to know what this misery was to me.

Esumi, I tire of your silence.

Adel, the prince, and I were dragged into the yard with the other nearly dead. They saw him at last. They recognized him. It was the prince, at last! He was alive!

They led him to the body of his uncle, lying by itself in the snow with his closest advisor beside him, dead. Prince Tsui touched each of their hands. He touched both cold, green cheeks.

And Seth was there, too. He was next to them in the snow. His legs were in rough splints. One of his hands was just gone. A scorched stump. Black flesh and splintered, white bone like a long fingernail instead of a whole hand.

He breathed too heavily to be alive. His eyes were too white.

Adel smiled down on him. *You did well*, she said. *You chose well.*

Seth lifted his stump. He looked at it. He said nothing. His eyes screamed.

Korinyes would never see him like this.

We killed the three mercenaries too fast. The door hadn't even closed before Fest's dagger found a throat. Mine came next. My lashes flew from my wrists and my hands flew to the blade. My blade stopped a finger on a trigger. The arquebus jammed up under his throat, and I flicked my dagger and heard the boom.

Tycho lifted a heavy book, and Adel's dagger landed hard in it. The butt of the weapon left a dent in the leather. The blade found a mercenary's back.

Tycho laughed.

I felt the weapons on my back. I felt the hands everywhere.

Not so fast, stranger, said Tycho, *I've been expecting you. I expected someone to follow us up and undermine us so close to victory. Who do you work for? Which family?*

Adel works for me, said Seth, *I'm Prince Tsui of Tsuin, and this is my home you have invaded.* His voice was clear.

Tycho laughed and laughed. He let the lies stand.

Seth's hands were lifted up and retied tight. Black hands did this. White hands turned purple under the lashes. My hands were tied, too. I could do nothing.

Do you understand how fast this was? It was fast. It was so fast. We moved down a hallway. We didn't know where we were. Prince Tsui did, but he didn't speak. He didn't even get a chance to remove his bonds before the fight was through and three were dead and three more would die, and that is that.

And I would kill Seth when we get to the surface in the dead of winter when the ice was thick on the horizon and only the long cry of the ravenous wolves flying across the land in search of anything resembling food would remain of life in this great white expanse of wintry plain.

And Adel went to meet with her husband, Tycho, and Tycho was killed. And the mercenaries were unleashed. And I grabbed a weapon from the Earth and I drove it into Seth's heart. And I did it again and again.

I did it so many times.

And Prince Tsui abandoned the war for me.

She shakes her head. She's recopying what I say to you, because my hand is so unsteady now that I am so close to death. She speaks.

My empress, you have jumped so much in the end that I cannot think you are through.

I write down these lines, and you do not reply to me, Esumi. No one has until this shaman. Is it my duty to finish these letters to you, Esumi? Can I not abandon letters and fall to the rote mumblings of the chroniclers enunciating facts of human life with all the passion of the facts alone?

I have no passion anymore. None.

Do I die in vain, then, my empress? I came here because I believed you were writing important things. Your husband watches the letters leave the room, and he sends us in to help you with the last thing we can do to keep you here a little longer. And you just give up? How dare you. Finish your letters to him properly, or I have died in vain.

I did not ask you to die for me. You came here and you did not know what was in those letters.

I could have been writing anything. I could have been recalling the recipes for tea drinks and confusing them with herbal remedies and ultimately writing nothing but a mess, and sending it off in my delirium to a confused soul in some poor village that mixes my concoctions, drinks, and dies. No, girl. Do not blame your vain death on me. I will have none of that.

You die for something you didn't even read until my hand was too close to death.

If not for me, then for Adel. Will you tell me what happened to her? I want to know. If nobody else ever does, I do. Do I not deserve to know the right ending at least?

Fine. I am tired, though.

The shaman nods. She does not look very happy with me. My lines are too unstable. The stylus too impure in my shaking hands. Maybe she writes and I think it is my own work and I am too close to death to know.

She dies for me. You don't even write me back. What is your name, shaman, that I may know you and love you?

I am Adel Nahraf. I was named after her. I'm from Fearghus. My father fought in the war. My great-uncle survived the winter in Ilhota. He lost a leg to frostbite, though.

I'm so sorry for you, girl.

I'm so sorry.

I didn't want anyone else to die for my sake.

I never knew your name until just now. And your companion—the one who sits with me at night—what is his name? He's even younger than you.

15

We trudged through the snow, Adel. We woke up. We pulled our plan together. And Adel lashed our hands together so we could be her prisoners. We said nothing. It snowed so hard.

She and Fest shared a knowing gaze. I want to think they did. They didn't. But I wanted them to have had a plan better than this—underneath this. I wanted not to trust them because I wanted them to be smarter, better, and unable to let us die.

Korinyes snatched my hand from the air. We were outside of Tsuin. The dark gray walls of rock through the wall of snow was only visible in moments. A wind whipped the snowflakes like drapes out of our vision. And Tsuin appeared through the white fog.

It was so cold. I couldn't feel my nose or my feet. Korinyes wore her bedroll around her shoulders for the warmth. She was still shivering. When she spoke to me, her jaw barely uttered a sound around her shivers. When she grabbed my hand, I barely felt it, and-I think-neither could she.

What are we doing here? she said. *Why are we doing this?*

I bit my lip. It stung bad in all this cold. I wrapped my cloth-bound fingers around her arm. I rubbed it hard for the warmth and the blood inside of her to move again. I looked ahead at Prince Tsui. *We won't survive the winter outside the walls,* I said.

But they've taken the city, said Korinyes. *We'll die in there, whether we get their leader or not. The mercenaries won't stop killing just because they don't have someone in charge.*

I glanced at Adel's back. Her black hair against her cloak in the strong wind. Adel leaned against the winter and pressed hard forward, always forward.

Adel will lie to them, I said. *She is a Proliuxian noble in a land without them. That's what she told us she would do. It's what she did in Ilhota.*

Korinyes frowned. She whispered, *If I were you, I wouldn't trust her. She has betrayed before. She left her kin for the Rhiannan paladins. She told us as much. After the war she left the Rhiannan paladins for something in Proliux. Don't you remember? And now she leads us into the arms of the Argarax army.*

Seth touched Korinyes's arm wrapped in a torn bedroll. *We aren't important people in this world, Korinyes,* he said. *We are not valuable hostages. Maybe the prince is. But we're not.* He shook his head in consternation. He bit his lip. *Please, we don't have a choice right now. I'll keep an eye on Adel. I won't let her pull anything.*

Korinyes jerked away from him. *You wouldn't know what to do, if she did.*

The walls of the castle loomed ahead of us. Prince Tsui led us to the front gate. He and Adel walked side by side, their cloaks whipping around them.

Seth tugged his own cloak around himself hard. The wind grabbed at his growing hair.

This is the wind that steals children, he shouted, *This is the wind that carries the children into the mountains, where they are so smothered in cloud and snow that the boys become goats and the girls become wolves. This is the wind that has carried away Korinyes's heart. If love fails in this wind, so too shall we.*

Shut up, I shouted at him. *I don't want to hear it from you! I don't want to hear anything from you! I should kill you now! I should just break your legs and leave you here to freeze with the souls of the damned!* I pulled my spear from my pack and spun it toward Seth's legs.

Fest grabbed the spear. I don't know where he came from, but he was there, and he grabbed my spear. In his other hand he led Partridge. *In a war with mercenaries, every soldier counts,* he said. *Haven't I told you that already? I wish we still had the dead one with us.*

I pulled my spear from Fest's hands. I shoved it back into its lashes on my pack.

Come on, said Fest. *We're falling behind. We can't get separated in this mess. It's worse than a sandstorm. At least sand is a warm death.*

I didn't look at any of the guards, but I know them like the ones in Ilhota. Their ghosts send shivers through the web, always shivering. They were too cold to care about their duties at the gate, as long as they could close the gate against the wind. We approached the castle and the city. It looked like a monstrous wolf's frozen skull. Icicles clung to the rafters over the doorway like teeth. The hundred bright eyes of fire-warmed rooms inside of the castle gazed down upon us through the white clouds of snow. We walked into the skull of Alastair-of-the-Wolf. She devoured us whole.

And inside, I didn't look.

Korinyes saw her mother in white skin over and over again in the yard, curled up with the dead bodies, to stay warm. The ones who warmed them in life were better warmth than any monster's arms.

Partridge smiled and waved at the people with his hands bound. We had tied his lashes tight. He couldn't remove them if he tried. We tried to keep him alive by lashing his hands together. His hands waved over his head. *Hello!* he shouted. No one shouted back.

We pressed on. I stared at my feet. My heart pumped warm and hard. I was ready to die today. I stared at the floor because I knew my eyes of anger would reveal us all. I watched the mud and snow mashed together by thousands of black boots with polished, silver buckles.

We moved through the muck quick enough. My eyes kept down. I didn't want to see familiar faces, yet.

You haven't told me about Partridge hardly at all, Adel says to me. It's as if he isn't there at all most of the time. He's just somewhere with you, at the fringe, and you don't say anything about him.

Do you want me to finish or not? Besides, if anything has happened to me, it has all come from these moments, so it is always happening, I think. These memories return to me because I cannot make new ones and so instead I live again and again in these forgotten times. I cannot choose the life that comes to me. I cannot choose the husk that speaks. I cannot tell them apart anymore. All their faces are the same. Even yours has the nose of Tycho and the lips of Korinyes and the eyes of my reflection.

Besides, Partridge was Seth's worry, not mine. I would've left him to die, too. I would have left him and you and everyone to die because I'm tired of caring about it! He's at the fringe of my web. He was never important to me.

You promised me ...

Her eyes drop down to the parchment. She wipes her own blood from her lips with a rag. She strokes a long tube. Soon that tube will reach down my throat, and she will kiss me through this tube—kissing my wounded chest like a mother to make it better. Her heavy eyelids droop. She is tired, too. We are all tired. Her thick robes hang from her bones like starved skin.

She will smile when she reads my description of her. She will smile because it isn't flattering.

I did promise you. But, Partridge was Seth's. They share the same husk, in my skull.

We passed through a heavy oak door. Above my head more icicles threatened to fall down upon my skull, but they didn't scare me because I didn't look at them. Black hands lingered on my body as we passed. They only made me angrier. Fear, too, but more anger. I kept my head down.

The halls were long, and narrow. They stank of torchlight and too many bodies piled in against the cold.

Adel talked to them in their language, and I don't know what she said. They talked back. They laughed at each other. They pushed us. My own dagger pressed patiently into my ribs beneath my ragged sleeve. It felt like an icicle.

We turned a corner in the hall. It sounded like a flock of monstrous birds, with throats too deep to be beautiful in a room with too much echo. They were eating. I looked up long enough to see them doing that.

I kept my head down because Adel told us to act defeated. She had told us to pretend to be beaten down and defeated. Everyone but me didn't have to pretend very hard.

Down another hall, up a stairwell, through the laughter and the lingering hands. We stopped at a door. The mercenaries ran their hands over me, looking for weapons. They didn't look very hard, because they missed my dagger. My dagger used to be a long spear. I had cut it back long ago, when the wooden shaft rotted. It was small, sharp, and perfect for throwing.

My fingers touched the lashes of my bonds, ready to pull them loose. Adel had insisted on bringing all of us to the general, and her skin made it possible. She told them we were captured scouts with too much information to be left to the mercenaries.

I looked up at the door. I looked around me at my traveling companions. Fest was calm, unbound, and his hand was loose upon his sword. Seth had his eyes closed, and his hands trembled. Korinyes was breathing deeply, calming herself. Partridge stared at the torchlight and all the black men in the hall. Prince Tsui, like Fest, was calm, and ready for war.

Adel stood before all of us. She lifted her fist to the heavy oak. She pounded on the wood. It echoed.

A voice. *Come in.*

I tugged the lash to release the string. I was ready.

Tycho laughed. He didn't have his cane this time. He had a warm fur cloak and a golden brooch. He had a sabre on his hip, and an arquebus resting next to him. He stood in front of a desk, and he leaned into it. His arms were crossed as if he wasn't afraid.

Adel's face was dead calm. *My Lord,* she said, *I have been sent with news from the south.*

Fest's sword was too fast. He pulled his blade from the scabbard and found a throat. He reached for the arquebus. His face was a snarl like cannonballs landing in his lap.

I dropped to one knee to reach under my shirt, and when I came up again, my blade found a belly, and then I stabbed into the chest. An arquebus fired somewhere above me.

Adel's dagger flew. A book appeared from the desk, and took the blow on the cover. The book cracked like a bone. The dagger found another mercenary.

Or was he behind the desk? What did I say before? I can't remember if he was behind the desk or in front of the desk. He had a book. He blocked the dagger with a book.

Does it matter where he was?

Yes. Fest struck too soon. Behind the desk this makes no sense. In front of the desk, he had a reason. We were too close to him to let him go.

But behind the desk he would have the thick book to survive the blade.

Adel, this piece of the story is gone from my mind. I can't remember correctly at all. A little thing I forget that makes a difference, where he stood. But at one side of the desk, Fest is not the betrayer I think he might have been.

I wish for him to be loyal so much. I shake his bones and little flecks of skin fall from the web in my brain. Every time I come to him with this, I plead with him, and more pieces fall away from him. I don't know.

Three dead. Three black faces melted into the stones. The arquebus pressed into my back. Then I felt another. And it was over. Black bodies pressed into us all around. Our weapons melted from our frozen hands. The dark fingers clutched all of us, held us down, and bound us properly.

And Tycho didn't have the chance to stop laughing before we were through.

Why did the two of you talk like that? I asked her, nibbling bread and watching the ants crawl in a line across the floor around a dead spider.

Like what? said Adel. She didn't eat her bread this day. She rubbed her knees quietly. When Partridge would finish with his bread, she would hand him her own. She would say that he couldn't sing when eating.

Why did you not address each other as who you are? I asked.

Who? she said. *Oh, him. Such questions you ask of me, and I wonder why you will no longer die for your friend.*

Who are my friends? I said.

You're still alive, aren't you?

I asked you a question, I said.

Prince Tsui touched my arm. *Stop,* he said.

I punched him in the face. He flinched at my knuckles. I didn't punch him hard. I merely struck out at him. Then I remembered when my knuckles whispered against his grimy jowls. Prince Tsui of Tsuin, and my lord. No rider would strike their lord. I let my fist drop to my lap. I looked down at it.

He scowled at me. *And next will you hurt the fool?* he said. *Will you accuse him of treachery?*

Adel leaned back against the spiderwebs and dusty walls. Her eyes closed. *Let her believe whatever she wants. I don't care anymore about her stupid beliefs.*

Prince Tsui raised his eyebrow. *You, too? And what is left for me but your hatreds? I command you to give up your petty behavior. I command it.*

Adel did not move a muscle. I did. I laughed at him.

He laughed back at me. Partridge woke up and joined in.

Fest and Adel were silent and still. Korinyes ignored all of us for her tiny black army in the walls.

Do you wish to escape from here? said Staf Sru Korinyes.

And die in the winter? said Adel, *No, I think not. We will wait as long as we are allowed to wait.*

I see a crack in the top door hinge, said Korinyes, *We could exploit it. You could, or Fest.*

Fest shook his head. *Korinyes, look around here and tell me who will be left after such an endeavor. Will you?*

She smiled. *I will live forever, or hadn't you heard? I traded with my mardar and bought an eternity.*

With what? he said.

She smirked. *A lady never tells her secrets.*

Are you a lady after all? said Fest.

I say I am. Isn't that good enough for you?

Yes, he said. *I can think of no better reason.*

A spider captured an ant somewhere in the cracks. Fest smiled. Korinyes's eyes twitched above her own smile.

Dungeon. Eons underneath the ground, watching water from the snow melting down the warm rocks. Eons spent ignoring our own stinks. Drip drip drip drip. I see it in my bed, as my lungs drip out of my throat one cough at a time.

Spiders crawling in and out of their webs. Ants and flies and cockroaches everywhere. We grew accustomed to our foul smells. We grew accustomed to the feel of tiny feet across our skin.

We grew accustomed to ourselves, as well. We stopped talking so much. What was there to say anymore?

Nothing changed there. The spiders moved. Korinyes's ants moved. Partridge sang or not depending on Fest's mood. Adel stopped talking at all.

Seth was gone. Sometimes I could hear him screaming and I imagined that I didn't know who it was. I did want to kill him, but hearing his screams....

Fest died first. Then Korinyes. Then Partridge.

But Fest was silent. Maybe he died last? Maybe. His ghost tells me it was first. Seth tells me Fest died first. Adel says it, too. Korinyes says that she died first and it was the worst betrayal of her life.

But I think Fest was first. He closed his eyes while the dagger fell. It bit into his throat. Fest smiled at it.

He had said to me, *I live in a dungeon inside of a dungeon, just like a spider.*

In the yard with the mud and the snow, I found Seth. His hand was gone. A scorched stump with a splintered bone greened in the snow. People around him eyed him casually. His wounds were not the worst, and he was not the only one to watch his beloved die.

I saw it in his eyes. He had watched her die. Her scream had torn through him. His eyes seared shut when she died.

Her body fell to the floor and ants expelled from her skin like a splash. Millions of them poured from every orifice, and from her hair. Her skin melted into a puddle of blood and limp flesh. Her body piled among the dead in the yard looks human enough, but I watched it for the ants. I saw them in my mind everywhere I looked.

And Partridge didn't understand he was about to die. He tried to talk with Seth. He tried to say hello. He saw Seth's stump. It didn't register in Partridge's feeble mind. Seth's eyes glazed over, and Partridge sang a song.

The knife fell. Partridge cried out. I heard it.

Fest smiled when he died. He said two things, first. *About time you chose, my leader,* he said to Seth. Then he turned to the executioners, *I shall see you in Garzakhan, my brothers.*

Seth opened his mouth. Nothing came out. The black hole of his grief spoke all words silently.

And when the black hole would speak in sound, it would speak of the first golem and a night I have never left.

Their three bodies among so very many dead and dying bodies. The light too bright from off the snow. It took me a long time to find them. I didn't cry. I sat down. I looked at them. They were all white now. Even Fest was white now, like me.

Do you know what it's like to see your friends' dead bodies in the snow? Of course you do. Everyone does eventually.

I was numb. I was numb like a sleeping limb. I felt something vague rumbling underneath my skin. It was a harsh tingle like cold and death and bitter sex all at once. It left me in stillness. I held still and felt that emptiness echoing inside my own empty body. When hunger commanded me, I obeyed, but I did not want to, and I refused to enjoy it.

I longed for tears.

In the yard, I sat down next to Seth. Adel stood up. She could barely stand. She touched the back of a mercenary. She told him something I couldn't hear because her back was to me. Other people watched her. A mercenary took her away.

Prince Tsui touched his uncle's corpse, and the dead advisor beside the dead lord. Their jaws were all set firm. He is the lord of Tsuin, now. The noble ones died on pikes, and this fat bastard is the lord. I will always think of him as prince or emperor, and never as lord.

I ignored the easy grief of that silly husband of mine who did not understand grief. His uncle was old already, and on the brink. I ignored him. Instead, I lifted Seth's wounded arm. I touched the bone. It scratched me like a fingernail. He pulled his stump from me, down to the ground.

Tell me what happened, I said.

I had to . . . His voice cracked. He closed his eyes and opened them at the gray clouds above him. I can see through his eyes right now, because I have that same vision of the dying. Seth saw only the snow like ash drifting down from the gray all around him. My bed is like that, too, with the white curtains and the gray ceiling. White falling from gray. *Goddess, I had to . . .*

I know, I said. *I'll kill you as soon as I have the chance.*

Good, he whispered.

Did you kill Baba? I said.

No, he replied. His voice was still whispering, as if he could barely hear me at all.

You're lying, I said. *Who killed Baba?*

My father did. His eyes closed. The hand he had left clenched and unclenched.

He didn't, I said.

His voice ruptured from his throat. His remaining hand pounded the snow in a fist. *How do you know?!* he shouted, *That's a horrible thing to say!*

I know. We both know, I said. *Adel and me. You killed Baba.*

I . . . I killed Korinyes. I loved her. Why didn't I kill you? His voice was tired from so much dry-mouthed screaming. When he speaks, his voice cracks.

You will die when night falls because I will strangle you while everyone is asleep and too cold to care about another corpse. But I want you to tell me about Baba.

This silence was long. I touched his arm.

If she had died, I would have been stuck there forever. Don't you understand? His voice was venomous. *When she died, I was trapped.*

You killed her, didn't you? I said.

She was dying already, he said. *She was coughing and coughing. What else could I do? If she died, I was stuck there forever. I had to make her live.*

Did you really do that? I said.

His words came slowly. His voice cracked a little now and then, but he was calm, now. Torture does strange things to minds. *And then,* he said, *when I saw the chance—I mean, when my father . . . Why did I do it? Why? Why did I choose her?*

Staf Sru Korinyes. Baba is already gone to him. The moment she is spoken of—a rational act after all—she is gone. But his love? That will never leave him, no matter how long he freezes in the flickering of the northern lights. I snorted down at the murderer I had followed to the ends of the earth. I said, *If you don't know—you who did it—how do you expect me to know?*

I don't know, he replied. *You're just always so sure of yourself. You always know why you do everything.* His voice sunk into his chest. *I don't.*

Two flies buzzed across his scorched stump. They would lay maggots in the gangrene if they had the opportunity. I certainly didn't stop them.

I touched his shoulder, and pressed my fingers into it hard.

He gasped. He opened his mouth. His teeth were shattered like mossy clay shards.

I let go of his shoulder. I left him with the dead. I walked through the snow to the huddled living wrapped around the coal and wood that was simply not enough. Everyone was coughing and sick. Everyone was dying. I leaned back to back with a tired stranger. I pulled my legs into my body. I rested my head upon my cold knees. I wrapped my arms around my cold legs. I let the stranger's back warm me as best it could. *She would've known what to do,* I said under my breath.

Seth didn't even know I was gone. I saw him raise his gory stump to the sky. I heard his voice call out to me. *Please, don't wait too long,* he shouted to the clouds and the smoke. *It hurts so much I can't even feel my hand anymore!*

Your hand is gone, I whispered into my fist. I touched my wristbones. I shivered.

And the grandness of this moment before victory?

The prince was noticed by his people right away. He spoke with them in small groups, which spoke to other small groups. While I had been meeting with my shaman master, he and Adel had already found a new hope to spread.

Adel smirked at me. I left the stranger's back. I went to her. She was separated from the fires because no one trusted her. She was trying to stand up. I had her arm over my shoulder, and I was helping her walk. She could barely walk. She was heavy, too. I struggled to keep my own feet beneath her. She pointed at the hearty handshakes and politeness of the imprisoned.

He is their prince after all, said Adel.

You doubted him?

She shook her head. *No, not really. He moved like a prince. He acted like one. He spoke like one. I have met many princes. I compare your prince to my dragonslayers. He would not survive one day in our courts.*

Have you seen Seth? I asked.

No, she said. *He's probably with the dying, or the dead. Are you in a fighting mood, Zhan?*

No, I said, near tears, but refusing them. I squinted in the sunlight. My eyes hurt so much in that bright snow. Cold, and burning at the same moment. I cried because it hurt so wonderfully to see light. Those of you imprisoned know what that is like.

Too bad, said Adel. *You're going to have to fight, and soon.*

I heard them talking about it to him, their prince. They talked about how his uncle died. An advisor claimed to be the lord. The mercenaries killed him quickly. When the uncle cried over the dead body, he was killed, too.

Senseless, they called the death. They were wrong.

The prince told his people that the mighty paladin, Jardan Bosch Adel was going to kill the general and then the ranks of soldiers would fracture. All the people must rise up and push the army back into the main building. *Let them kill each other all winter long. We shall remain alive with the food stores in the outer buildings and the sheep,* he said.

The skalds make that speech last all evening.

And the paladin, Lady Jardan Bosch Adel? Ah, this is the moment the skalds truly adore. She waits so long and so long, until the dagger fall is clear.

I should've disobeyed the dragon, said Adel.

Tycho swallowed the beer whole. It left a foam mustache on his lip. He didn't wipe it away.

I know a killer when I see one, said Adel. *You've killed lovers and children before. Why shouldn't you shoulder the blame for mine? It was your armies that caused it all. You were the reason. Your greed. Your pride.*

That's quite a condemnation of a man, he said, laughing. *Don't be silly, Adel. No single person is to blame for your necessary betrayals. What of my father? Silly woman, you've come too far to give up now. No wonder your kind can't be proconsuls.*

I have, haven't I? she replied, *I've come too far to give up now. I obey you, always, by staying in my current role among the captured. I stay on their side, by your command.* She sat there. She held real still.

Too still.

Tycho looked at her. He tapped his finger on the table. He sighed. *Anything else?*

And she moved.

All of our hearts fall into a single gesture, and skip a beat. A saint is born this day.

Nations merge and drop away from each other and merge again. Stars swirl above us. Clouds sail past the barrier between the stars and us. Glaciers drop into the lake, and drop into the ocean. The icebergs crawl. They melt. They break. Wolves hunt every night and eat only every other. Caribou band together to keep themselves safe. Dust devils whip up in the castle yards, with the short lifespans of this or that gust. Lightning strikes, and the Goddess kills another pine. These were the homes of birds and bugs and sometimes children.

And while we walk in the empty center of this world, where all our senses point, the emptiness pushes us out into the land. We move like wolves hunting. We hunt berries. We herd sheep. We fight each other. We fall asleep.

And when we sleep we see inside ourselves at the web of memories. The smells, and the sights, and the tastes and textures. And after life, this is all we have. This is all I have left. I reach for the ghosts that melt together. I try to rattle the truth of my life. I wish I could have been there to hear them speak, if they spoke.

Adel and Tycho may not have even talked at all. Maybe the door closed and his death was faster than he could even imagine. Or, the door closed, and they talked for hours. Or, the door closed, and they said nothing at all. They played a game of chess to pass the time.

No, I don't think they did that.

I think they sat down. I think she played along long enough to make him comfortable. Then she turned her words into teeth. The words leaped over the table and snapped at his throat. Hers came true. His did not. He died.

He didn't even know why, in the end. She was too good at killing to wallow in her vengeance.

She was faster than he had ever seen. He hadn't fought a war. He had led a war. When the dragon stood before him he hesitated. She stripped his own dagger from his hands.

Adel knew all his tricks. The scuffle was very short, for Adel was too worn to win if it took too long.

And she won.

The dagger landed in Tycho's throat. It cut a path all the way through to his spine. The blade lifted out with the hideous sucking noises of cut flesh. It sought his heart hiding behind the thick chest bone. The dagger broke through. The heart ruptured. The man died.

The mercenary outside heard a scuffle. He opened the door. He looked in and saw her. She looked up, and she wore Tycho's blood on her body splashed over all of her scars. Tycho fell hard onto his desk. The mercenary lifted his arquebus and fired. Adel was beneath the desk, and the bullet. The bullet hit a glass window. The window broke a little. Adel heard it. She grabbed the chair. The mercenary grabbed a saber from his belt. He raised the blade. Adel raised the chair. The saber jammed into the wooden leg.

Adel kicked the mercenary in the groin. The blade handle fell from his hands and he doubled over. He backed out from the door and cried out.

Boots in the halls and the clicks and clacks of arquebuses.

Adel threw the chair through the window.

She was on the second floor of the castle. Before her eyes was the snow and the breached wall to the outer yards.

She jumped. Bullets followed her leap. Her bones cracked when she landed. Her ankles had snapped in two. She didn't seem to care. She staggered up to standing. She moved. She moved as fast as she could. No one followed.

Arquebuses found the window. They fired. They missed. They weren't accurate weapons when they weren't in long lines aimed at long lines.

Adel ran past the gap in the wall. She ran and ran into one giant white horizon. The sky was white. The ground was white. The dazzling white snowflakes blurred the lines into a soft white that never ended. And her ankles had broken completely. Her knees were miserable. She ran anyway, waist-deep in snow, and the cold numbed the pain.

Nowhere to go but forward. She ran.

We haven't found her body. Wolves perhaps dragged it around. Perhaps it eroded underneath so much snow and mud. Perhaps she made it all the way to Glacier Lake and fell onto the ice, and when it melted in spring her body dripped beneath the waves.

Maybe the skalds are right. The Goddess lowered her hands and took her bodily into the sun, where it is always warm. The paradise of heroes and saints.

They say I am destined for this place as well.

I know better who I am, I think.

16

The snow washed in pink iced blood. White clouds swam in smoke.

We prisoners in the yard of Tsuin watched the mercenaries turn their guns upon each other. We watched a beautiful girl dragged into the yard by two men. The men cut at each other with their sabers. The girl between caught a parry in her face. Her body dropped dead in the snow. The mercenaries kept fighting.

Prince Tsui screamed out his war cry. The skalds preen on about it, endlessly.

Tsuin screamed with him. Hidden weapons emerged, and new weapons were tugged from the dead. Old women and old men and young children took arms against the darkness in the snow.

I turned to Seth. He didn't scream. He didn't even sit up.

The battle was epic, of course. I shall avoid it entirely. I do not care for epic battles, Adel. I have seen far too many of them to think anything of them. They are battles like any other. I have seen more courage in lost battles than in victories.

Even during the battle for Tsuin, I didn't care about my people, or my survival, or anyone at all. I cared about my last duty. Duty owned my flesh, not glory. Never glory. Only duty.

This is what I did when the battle for Tsuin began. I took a straight spear from the body of a dead mercenary. Around me the lame and the cold did their bravest with what weapons they had against the fractured ranks of mercenaries. The mercenaries fought everyone, especially each other.

But me, I walked back into the empty yard where the dying lay in broken heaps—most of them dead by now. Seth was sitting there with his stump held in the air moaning Staf Sru Korinyes' name. He spoke her name like Partridge singing. My steps were harsh. My feet pushed up the snow. Some of this snow landed on his face when I got close to him. His voice stopped. His bruised face looked up at me. His stump looked up at me. He coughed up the dirty snow that had fallen into his mouth.

I drove the spear into his throat.

I pulled the spear out. I couldn't hear the sound of it coming out of his body. I could see his blood spilling. His throat overflowed with it fast.

His teeth stained red. The snow stained red. His eyes screamed red.

I did it again, right in his chest. His brittle bones cracked like kindling.

I pulled out the spear and did it again.

I did it over and over again.

I did it hard and fast.

Sometimes I missed. My rage knew no aim. I knew only stabbing and stabbing and stabbing.

Then it was all passed through me, into the heap I had created that used to be a man.

My knees trembled at his glassy eyes. Blood everywhere, so red.

I leaned against the spear. It still jammed through his body like a lonely fence post. I couldn't even see what his body looked like now, because my eyes were so full of tears.

I'm glad he couldn't see me crying over him.

Prince Tsui turned from the dead body of another mercenary. His stolen blade smothered in blood, and his men and women around him fighting for the yard, and he turned around because that is what one must do in a yard of so much killing. One must turn and look behind oneself to watch for coming death.

And he saw me crying over Seth's body.

He came to me.

The people saw him walking through the sea of violence and blood and red snow. He stepped over the bodies of his own dying people to come to me. And his living people watched from the corner of their eyes. What business does Prince Tsui have with this strange, useless young woman? Everyone witnessed even though they were busy fighting. Later on they'd hear about it, and they'd nod and say they saw it.

I pushed him back at first. The hand could have been a mercenary determined to kill me for all I knew, but I didn't even think of the battle going on around us. I thought the hand was exactly what it was. His hand in peace after so much pain. I didn't want it.

Women died on the ramparts, and men died at the doors. Arquebuses exploded and exploded. Metal hit metal. Metal hit bone.

My body spoke to that hand alone. *No*, I said.

He touched me again, and I pushed him again. The hand fell away.

Zhan . . . he cooed, *Oh, Zhan.* . . .

Then his arms found me. They grabbed me close. I couldn't fight them. I let them hold me.

The battle raged on in the yard. We would win someday. We would shut the mercenaries into the main halls, and let them kill each other all winter while we stayed out and kept the sheep, and ate all winter. But that is the story of our empire, and you know it well already, Adel.

First was the murder and the murder and the murder and this moment: I cried, and Prince Tsui's bloody, fat hand stroked my hair. He whispered in my ear, *Shh* . . .

Acknowledgements

First novels occur late at night, or early in the morning, as a public secret among close friends and relations. Everyone knows you're doing it, but no one dare talk about it, and it's probably no good. The many people around aspiring authors that indulge this odd habit deserve to be acknowledged as the enablers they are. If anyone's looking for someone to blame for my book, look no farther than this list.

First and foremost, I would like to thank my parents, Robert and Sandra McDermott, for their patience and support. Matthew, my brother, always seemed to have fresh bread and cheese at just the right moment. Ellen, my sister, is an inspiring woman to be around, in general. I'd also like to thank my grandparents.

Certainly all of my very large extended family merit a place here. However, the paper and ink required to list everyone individually along with everything they've done for me, would use up the world's supply of ink. I shall, instead, mention the individual family members that actively contributed to this book.

Visiting my aunt, Brenda Dazell and Uncle Ron, in North Dakota, in January, was the source of nearly all of my genuine snow experience. My aunt and legal counsel, Patty Nigro, helped me make sense of the contract stuff. Thank you, Aunt Patty. My aunt, Mary-Alice Mirhady, introduced me to her in-laws, Nader Mirhady and Christine Salton. They hired me to watch their house and dog one lovely summer in Vancouver.

I met lots of wonderful people that summer, who all contributed in some way. I'd like to thank especially my Uncle David, and my cousins Ephraim, Robert, and Renata. I'd like to thank Katherine Mirhady, Nader Mirhady, Christine Salton, Louis Actil, Susan Mirhady, Daniel Actil, and Elizabeth Mirhady.

All of my teachers through the years deserve mention, but I can't remember them all. Judith Jones, Dr. Chamberlain, Michael Moeller, Bruce Horn, and Brother Oscar Vasquez, all from Nolan Catholic High School, have my thanks. From the University of Houston, I'd like to thank Paul Guajardo, David Judkins, David Mikics, and Roberta Weldon.

I acquired much of my knowledge of medieval history and literature from Lorraine Stock. Thank you, Dr. Stock.

Thanks also, to my creative writing professors. I still quote the esteemed Daniel Stern regularly. Thanks to Pearl Abraham, Glenn Blake, Alan Gee, Christopher Bakken, and Roxanna Robinson for assaulting me with red ink.

Thank you, also, to the friends that had to deal with the writer in their midst: Stephen Tsui, Ben Fasenfest, Preston Partridge, Melanie Morth, Tene Kuo, Blake Egli, Brandi Egli, Jason T. Buckingham, Rob Billings, Andy Smart, Becky Williams, Seth McKinney, Isaac Sanders, Rance Costa, Cameron Payne, and Blake Brown.

I'd like to thank the Blue Knights Drum and Bugle Corps, for the summers of 1997, 1998, and 1999.

I'd like to thank Ivan Lewis, and everyone at the Japanese Karate Academy of Arlington, TX.

I'd also like to thank Elizabeth Granado, Sarah Johnson, Jackie Kessler, Jenna Glatzer, Victoria Strauss, A.C. Crispin, Dave Kuzminski, Peter Rubie, P.N. Elrod, and the entire Mod Squad and internet community at Absolute Write.

I'd also like to thank every editor who encountered my work in any slush pile, even though almost all of you rejected me. Rejection makes writers write better.

Speaking of editors, Phil Athans pulled my query and writing sample from his slush pile and saw the makings of an actual book. If anyone's to blame for this book, it's him. Thank you, Phil, for your guidance and support.

And last, but not least, I'd like to thank you, reader of my book. Without you, I am just a person with a hobby that's a shameful public secret. With you, I am an author with a job that I truly enjoy.

Thanks to all of you.

I hope I didn't forget anybody.

J.M. McDermott graduated from the University of Houston in 2002 with a BA in Creative Writing. He resides in Arlington, Texas with an assortment of empty coffee cups, overflowing bookshelves, and crazy schemes.